Governess to the Duke's Heir

DANGEROUS LORDS BOOK FOUR

BY
MAGGI ANDERSEN

BOOKS FROM DRAGONBLADE PUBLISHING

Dangerous Lords Series by Maggi Andersen
The Baron's Betrothal
Seducing the Earl
The Viscount's Widowed Lady
Governess to the Duke's Heir

Also from Maggi Andersen
The Marquess Meets His Match

Knights of Honor Series by Alexa Aston
Word of Honor
Marked by Honor
Code of Honor
Journey to Honor
Heart of Honor
Bold in Honor
Love and Honor
Gift of Honor
Path to Honor
Return to Honor

The King's Cousins Series by Alexa Aston
The Pawn

Beastly Lords Series by Sydney Jane Baily
Lord Despair
Lord Anguish

Legends of Love Series by Avril Borthiry
The Wishing Well
Isolated Hearts
Sentinel

The Wicked Governess
The Wicked Spy
The Wicked Gypsy
The Wicked Wife

Unmarriageable Series by Mary Lancaster
The Deserted Heart

Highland Loves Series by Melissa Limoges
My Reckless Love
My Steadfast Love
My Passionate Love

Clash of the Tartans Series by Anna Markland
Kilty Secrets
Kilted at the Altar
Kilty Pleasures

Queen of Thieves Series by Andy Peloquin
Child of the Night Guild
Thief of the Night Guild
Queen of the Night Guild

Dark Gardens Series by Meara Platt
Garden of Shadows
Garden of Light
Garden of Dragons
Garden of Destiny

Rulers of the Sky Series by Paula Quinn
Scorched
Ember
White Hot

Highlands Forever Series by Violetta Rand
Unbreakable
Undeniable

Chapter One

Castlebridge, Oxfordshire, Autumn 1821

T HE DUKE'S HOUSEHOLD was in uproar. His Grace and his guests were to arrive in three weeks' time. Every room was in the process of being cleaned, chandeliers taken down, walls scrubbed, carpets beaten, curtains washed, furniture polished. Not a cobweb was to be tolerated in any of the rooms, from the attics to the dungeon. Well, perhaps not the dungeon, or the attics. Jenny Harrismith, the governess, was confident that the schoolroom and nursery wing on the third floor where she and the children spent their days would also escape most of the fuss. His Grace, on his brief return to England some months ago, had not visited them there.

"Do you like the picture I've drawn of an Arab, Miss Harrismith?" Nine-year-old William raised his head from where he was hunched over a table with his pencils.

Jenny leaned over him to view it. She expected a sheik in flowing robes, but of course, the drawing was of a horse. William thought of little else.

"Well done, Lord William," she said a hand on his shoulder. "It's a magnificent horse." So tall, the horse's legs would be the envy of a giraffe.

"I shall be riding my father's hunters soon." William pushed out his chest, sounding like the duke he would become one day.

"You will," Jenny agreed. "When you are older."

William visited the stables every day and rode out with a groom, but she'd asked the stable staff to keep an eye on him for fear he'd take off on the duke's stallion. The boy was an excellent rider, having been on a horse since he could walk, but he'd have the animal over a high fence in the blink of an eye.

His Grace's children had been in her care for the past year, since the former governess, having succumbed to a footman's attentions, left after a hasty marriage to run an inn in Cornwall.

While relieved the duke was coming home, Jenny was determined he was made aware of his children's needs. But even as a lord's daughter, albeit an impoverished one from Yorkshire, it would prove difficult to seek a private audience with her employer, let alone make her concerns known to him.

Jenny had become quite familiar with Andrew George William Hale, Duke of Harrow, as William often dragged her to the portrait gallery. They would stand before paintings of his father at various stages of his life, from babyhood to lanky youth, and then the tall, imposing duke in his coronet and robes. Jenny was forced to admit that he did stir the imagination.

When His Grace had visited Castlebridge, she'd brought the two children down and waited in the corridor while a footman took them into the library to see their father. The next day, His Grace returned to the Continent, and William, a lonely little boy, had been unsettled at bedtime for the rest of the week requiring her to read to him until he fell asleep.

The one time Jenny had set eyes on the duke, was from three stories up in the nursery wing. The schoolroom window looked directly onto the gravel turning circle below. She had knelt on the window seat and looked down. It was the merest glimpse of him, leaving the luxurious coach and greeting his staff before disappearing indoors. Even from that distance, he looked very tall. Though tenderhearted about the awful tragedy that had befallen him, she remained annoyed with the duke. He was a busy man with an important position to uphold, but she disapproved of his neglect of his children.

The duke's dour-faced secretary, Mr. Bishop, kept the duke advised by letter of the children's development and health. Jenny had informed him of William's aptitude for arithmetic and how Barbara, who had just turned five, made steady progress at reading, in the hope those things at least would be mentioned.

The secretary showed little interest in how fast Barbara was outgrowing Nanny, who'd been with the family since the duke was a boy, and was becoming quite forgetful. Jenny feared the older woman would leave a candle burning and set the house on fire.

Mr. Bishop tut-tutted when she expressed a wish for the duke to be told how William had grown in the last few months—Jenny measured him against a doorframe in the schoolroom with a pencil mark. He dismissed as irrelevant that William learned from the gamekeeper how to fly fish for trout in the river, so the boy might surprise his father when he finally came home.

Jenny folded her arms, her annoyance pricked again by the secretary's obtuseness. But would it be any better when the duke arrived?

At the schoolroom table, William bowed his head over a new drawing of an equally tall horse, and Barbara, an imaginative child, made up delightful stories about grand balls. She was interested in fashion, drawing the latest gowns from the *La Belle Assemblée* magazine, her great aunt had sent her. The little girl loved her dolls, especially her new French fashion doll. She tucked them all into her bed at night. As Nanny dozed in the evenings, Jenny would slip in to remove them after the child fell asleep, and before she lay on them.

This morning at breakfast, Barbara's huge anxious violet eyes sought Jenny's. "Will Father come and visit my dolls?"

"He might if you ask him nicely, poppet," Jenny said. Surely he would. Who could resist such an adorable child as Barbara?

Well, he would soon be home, and she hoped it wouldn't be a brief visit before he left again for foreign climes.

Hanover, Germany, October 1821

BEYOND THE WINDOW, snow fell from a blackened sky and covered the grounds of the opulent mansion. In the overheated ballroom, Andrew, Duke of Harrow, ran a finger beneath his cravat as he stood beside his fair-haired Irish friend, Robert Stewart, Lord Castlereagh, now Marquess of Londonderry, the man who put Europe in order. They listened to the king and the Duke of Wellington reminisce about past glories.

Their voices faded as Andrew's thoughts returned to Castlebridge, his estate in Oxfordshire, where the leaves would be turning the rich colors of autumn. Four years ago, unable to bear his sadness after his beloved Catherine died, he'd left England to become a delegate to the Vienna Congress. Since then, his diplomatic posts had kept him from home, and his visits to Castlebridge had been brief. He'd been away too long. Soon his children would be grown up, and he'd have missed their childhood. He was determined that this would be his last diplomatic mission.

Along with Castlereagh, in charge of the British delegation, they'd attended many functions such as this. Andrew glanced around the room at the familiar faces, some enjoying the music and others deep in conversation. Prince Metternich appeared at the door. He crossed the floor toward them, acknowledging King George with a bow. The prince was the founder and driving force of the Congress which sought to bring a sense of balance to Europe after the devastation wrought by nearly twenty-five years of continuous war. It seemed to Andrew that the nations of Europe sometimes resembled badly behaved children, not satisfied with what they had, always wanting more. The Congress had imposed a degree of discipline on them all, but Andrew knew there was rising dissent everywhere. How long the status quo would hold was uncertain.

"You look concerned, Your Highness," Andrew said. "Is there anything troubling you apart from the usual difficulties?"

"I have heard some disturbing things which will be of concern to the British," the blond prince said, his handsome face lined with worry.

"We've received a report suggesting an attack of some kind on British soil. Unfortunately, we have no details."

"Where does this information come from?" Andrew inquired.

"We keep a watch on several dissident groups," the Prince said. "Our spies are attempting to ascertain more. I would advise your government to remain alert."

Andrew feared another distraction could alter his plans to return to his estate. He prayed it would come to nothing. As the musicians struck up and dancers moved over the floor in a perfumed kaleidoscope of color, Greta, Baroness Elsenberg came through the crush in search of him.

Chapter Two

M RS. POLLITT ENTERED the nursery where Jenny was assisting Nanny Evans with the children's clothes.

The housekeeper stood primly, hands held before her, a look of unfriendliness in her eyes. "You will have the children ready when His Grace arrives?" She directed the question to Jenny, rather than Nanny, who had just disappeared into her bedroom.

"They are ready, Mrs. Pollitt." Jenny looked up from where she bent over Barbara's shoes. She could never get used to the way the woman addressed her. Jenny was sure she had done nothing to deserve it.

"You are to join the rest of the staff in welcoming His Grace, then I shall introduce you." "It is not necessary for Nanny Evans to come down," she said in a louder voice.

"I understand." Jenny thought it entirely unnecessary to repeat all this when she'd been instructed several times over the past week.

Mrs. Pollitt smoothed down the skirts over her black bombazine gown with both hands, the keys at her waist jingling.

It was a nervous gesture.

Jenny suddenly realized that the housekeeper wasn't quite as con-fident as she appeared. "I'm sure it will all go well, Mrs. Pollitt. You have done a splendid job preparing for the duke's arrival," she said with a warm smile.

The lady's brown eyes hardened. "Please see to your own job, Miss Harrismith. I shall take care of mine. Bring the children down to the entry hall in..." she glanced at the watch pinned to her bosom. "One hour."

"Yes, Mrs. Pollitt," Jenny said meekly. A tactical error, she conceded. The woman didn't like her, or perhaps it was governesses in general. There was little she could do about it.

"Can I take my dolls?" Barbara asked Jenny.

"I do not think that wise, Lady Barbara," Mrs. Pollitt answered.

Barbara's face crumpled. Both children had been unsettled all morning, and Jenny had to find ways to ensure the coming event was a joyous meeting. In one sentence, Mrs. Pollitt had undone all her good work.

"Why don't you bring Annie," Jenny said. "I think she would like to meet your father, don't you think so, poppet?"

"Yes." With a gusty sigh, Barbara slipped off the bed and ran to find her favorite doll.

Mrs. Pollitt's lips thinned. "I shall leave His Grace to instruct you on how you are to go on," she said curtly.

"Miss Harrismith is doing splendidly," Nanny said, coming from her bedroom and kindly leaping to Jenny's defense.

"We shall have to see," Mrs. Pollitt said bafflingly and left the room.

THE COACH TRAVELED along the raked gravel carriage drive beside the beech-trees of the home wood, and the undulating freshly scythed lawns of the park with its magnificent trees in autumn foliage. They approached the sun-warmed stone walls of Castlebridge, Andrew's Tudor mansion, modified during the last century to become a more comfortable home, the tall chimneys and the tower reaching into the sky. He was eager to show it all to Greta. Much of the history remained: the long latticed windows, the lofty great hall, its paneling polished like silk, with the family motto carved on the stone shield above the Inglenook fireplace, the winding stair which led to the gallery where the family history was displayed in gilt-framed portraits, and the endless corridors and secret passages, that Andrew had loved as a child.

"How utterly charming," Greta, Baroness Elsenberg, murmured.

She sounded somewhat daunted. Andrew glanced at her. "I trust you and Ivo won't find the countryside too short of company. You are both so fond of Viennese society."

She touched his hand lightly with her lavender kid glove. "Of course not, I shall welcome a few days of peace." She narrowed her eyes at her brother. "As will you, Ivo."

Ivo turned from the window. "I gather there will be fox hunting?"

"I'm afraid not, unless the local hunt meets," Andrew said. "You might ask the squire. I've been absent so often that the hounds are not trained." The man was ungracious, and Andrew found him a total bore.

"What a pity."

"But a delicious dinner will follow after you gentlemen bag your birds," Greta said.

"In the meantime, you might try your hand at fishing for trout in the river, Ivo," Andrew said. "If you wish to ride, my stable is at your disposal. There are some excellent bridle paths."

"I imagine your cellar is more than tolerable, also, Your Grace," Ivo said.

"Of course it is," Greta said hastily gathering up her mink shawl. "We shall have a splendid time. And we have the shooting party to look forward to where I shall meet many of your friends, Your Grace."

Andrew absently patted her gloved hand, his attention drawn to the house where a line of servants awaited their arrival. The years had softened his grief over losing Catherine. Now with his time as a delegate at an end, he could contemplate marrying again, although he didn't anticipate falling deeply in love. Greta, a baron's widow, seemed a good choice. He found the beautiful, elegant blonde amusing company. They'd spent a pleasant month enjoying Viennese society. The baroness led Andrew to believe that should he propose she would be agreeable to marriage, but for some reason he'd held off. To force himself into a decision, he'd invited her home to Castlebridge to meet his children. He had not been pleased when she'd brought her brother, whose provocative manner got Andrew's back up. He would have preferred Greta to have chosen someone else to chaperone her, but Ivo was here now, and Andrew was determined to keep his temper.

The coach pulled up before the massive front entry where all the upper servants stood to receive him. Two liveried footmen rushed to attend them. When they stepped from the coach, Andrew, wishing his butler, Forrester, hadn't seen fit to make a fuss, walked along the row. He greeted each of them recognizing only the housekeeper, the butler and some of the grooms. His father's staff had slowly been replaced over the years.

He came to the end where his children stood waiting. He had not seen them for months and his heart lurched in his chest as William and Barbara were gently pushed forward by their governess, whom he was yet to meet. He'd forgotten the lady's name.

"Father." William bowed.

"You've grown like a sapling since I saw you last, William." Andrew wanted to hug him, but shook his son's proffered hand instead. "And who is this beautiful sprite?" Andrew fondly contemplated his daughter in her muslin dress, already a young miss, her blonde curls caught up with a blue ribbon. She was so like her mother that his heart ached at the sight of her.

"I am Barbara, have you forgotten?" She backed away and reached for the governess' hand.

"Well, of course I haven't. I was teasing. I have only one beautiful daughter," he said wanting to kiss her but fearing it would be unwelcome. He raised his eyes to the silent governess. Tall and willowy, she seemed very young and rather too pretty for the post. Now what was her name?

The housekeeper, Mrs. Pollitt rushed to fill in the awkward pause. "This is Miss Harrismith, Your Grace."

"Ah yes." He nodded at the governess who could only be in her early twenties. His gaze took in her large gray eyes, firm mouth and chin, her curly dark brown hair arranged in a top knot. Not fashionably dressed, but her appearance was as neat as a pin, in a modest high-necked green dress, a cameo brooch adorning the bodice. "Miss Harrismith. I trust you find your new situation agreeable?"

She curtsied gracefully, perfectly composed and obviously at ease in society. "I do, thank you, Your Grace. But I should like to speak to you about the children."

How efficient, Andrew thought. I am not yet through the door. "Very well. Please bring the children to me at two o'clock."

A wave of his hand encompassed Greta and Ivo. "Shall we go in?"

"Your son is so like you," Greta said as they entered the great hall.

"Do you think so?"

"But of course. The same black hair and blue eyes."

"And has quite the ducal manner," Ivo added with a chuckle.

"Good to see you, Forrester." Andrew addressed his earnest butler and introduced his guests. After arranging to meet them later in the yellow salon for a glass of wine before they dined, he left Forrester to see to their needs.

Andrew entered his library, which ran the length of the south wing where latticed windows overlooked the formal gardens. Nothing had changed. Nothing ever did. Bookshelves filled with gleaming red and gold bindings lined the walls, his carved oak desk polished to a high shine, and his favorite chair. He'd felt suffocated by it all after Catherine died, but now as the years passed and the pain ebbed away there was comfort to be found in the familiar. He welcomed the memories too, both sad and glorious. After reflecting briefly on the past he was determined to face the future, and not alone. He wanted his life back, and now felt ready, and keen to embrace it. Seated on the maroon leather chair, he leaned back, eyes closed and thought of his children. He opened his eyes and frowned. He'd made Barbara nervous. She'd sought safety with the governess. And William. The boy had stood ramrod straight trying to make himself appear taller. It reminded him of himself around that age. But Andrew was practically a stranger to them. Foolish to expect them to feel a deep affection for him. He must earn their love.

He closed his eyes again and instead of seeing Greta's beautiful visage, the young governess' gray eyes swam into view. His mouth twitched. The deuce! She'd been frowning at him.

Chapter Three

"**W**HERE HAVE YOU been, Lord William?" Jenny asked, as her young charge entered the schoolroom. "Your father will be waiting. I hope you weren't dirtying your clothes down at the stables."

"No, Miss Harrismith. I'm not dirty am I?"

He waited for her answer, his eyes wide and guileless. An expression she recognized. The, *I am innocent and unjustly accused,* look, with straw still clinging to his dark head.

"I'm not sure where this came from then," Jenny exclaimed, plucking it from his hair before the schoolroom mirror. "There." She gave his hair a quick brush. "We don't want to be late, do we?"

"No, Miss Harrismith," he said growing still.

She put down the brush and smoothed his collar. "I'm sure your father is looking forward to a nice long chat."

William merely nodded.

"Will Father like my dress?" Barbara picked up the skirts of the frilly pink spotted muslin frock Nanny had chosen and turned around exposing chubby knees.

"Yes, poppet, I am sure he will." Jenny bit her lip on a smile. "Shall we go downstairs?"

A liveried footman stood outside the library.

A hand on William's shoulder, she sensed how tense he was. She glanced at the grandfather clock in the corridor. It was precisely two o'clock. She nodded to the footman, and he tapped on the door with his gloved fist.

"Come."

The footman opened it and Jenny ushered the children into the library, a massive space with a high coffered ceiling. The room was warm and smelled of leather and old tomes. She would love to spend time there exploring the books in the bays around the walls.

The duke stood and came around the desk. "Good morning, Miss Harrismith. If you please." He gestured to the seating arranged beside the wide fireplace which was comfortably ablaze. Above the carved marble mantlepiece hung a painting of a beautiful blonde woman in a white gown, smiling serenely. The duke's deceased wife, Catherine. Barbara was the image of her.

The children sat beside Jenny on the leather chesterfield settee, their small bodies leaning against her, while the duke took the armchair opposite.

His Grace's portrait had not exaggerated. He was imposing: broad shouldered, with a narrow intelligent face, and faint lines at the corners of his blue eyes. He was thirty-one, but looked slightly older. It was not a physical thing, she decided, but more an attitude. As if the responsibilities of being a duke, and his work, whatever that entailed, lay heavily on his shoulders, and something else too. His tragic past perhaps.

In fact, he was so overwhelming, Jenny felt suddenly shy. She forced her mind to the matter at hand. What she needed to say.

When his gaze rested on his daughter, the shadows deepened in his eyes. "While we have our tea, you can tell me about yourselves, how you spend your days." He turned to look at Jenny. "And after-ward, Miss Harrismith can add anything else she deems to be relevant."

A painful silence followed when neither child spoke. Jenny turned to the silent boy beside her. "Tell your father about your fishing, Lord William."

William cleared his throat. "I'm learning to fly fish, Father," he said in a careful voice.

His father smiled approvingly. "Well done. A sport requiring some skill. You'll get the hang of it when you're older."

"The gamekeeper has been instructing him," Jenny said, unable to let the moment pass. "Lord William brought home a trout for Cook. It was made into a pie and served to the staff. They enjoyed it, didn't they, Lord William?" Jenny settled her features into a smile. She feared she'd been frowning.

His Grace raised his dark eyebrows, no doubt at her audacity. "A trout, eh! We must throw in a line together. But I fear you will put me to shame."

The boy ducked his head. "I would like that Father," he said politely, curling his fingers into his palms. It upset Jenny to see him attempt to hide the intensity of his feelings, his need for his father's approval.

Barbara had become bored with playing with a ruffle on her dress and began to wriggle. "Will you come and visit my dolls, Father?"

"I shall, my dear. Do you have many?"

"William counted them. He is very good at sums." She leaned forward to look at her brother. "How many dolls have I, William?"

"Eleven," William said promptly, looking pleased.

"That's a full cricket team," the duke said, laughter in his eyes. It made him look younger.

The boy chuckled.

Barbara huffed. "They are lady dolls, Father!"

"Oh yes, do forgive me, sweetheart. I don't believe ladies play cricket, do they, William?"

"No, Father." William grinned.

As William relaxed back in the chair Jenny grudgingly approved of the duke's strategy.

"I am told you are doing well at your studies," His Grace said, addressing William. "I shall engage a tutor for you this year who will prepare you for Eton. I have no doubt you will do well there."

His young heir straightened. "I am a good rider, aren't I, Miss Harrismith?"

"Lord William rides exceptionally well, Your Grace. The stable master told me he shows a natural aptitude."

"Good, good." His father accepted it without question. Jenny was sure all the males in this family would be incomparable riders.

A footman brought in a laden tea tray. The conversation halted while the children ate iced walnut cake and drank milk. Jenny poured cups of tea for herself and the duke.

"Thank you, Miss Harrismith." He took the gold-rimmed porcelain cup and saucer monogrammed with the ducal crest from her, and added a slice of lemon with the silver tongs.

Jenny's hand trembled. She carefully put down her cup and cleared her throat. "Your Grace, there are matters I should like to discuss with you if you have a moment. Alone."

He sat back and sipped his tea while his blue eyes gently mocked her. "Yes, I suspected there might be, Miss Harrismith."

He suspected? Now Jenny was as tense as William. She was relieved when the visit was over. "I shall see you here at eleven o'clock tomorrow, Miss Harrismith," the duke said, as she ushered the children out.

"Well that went well, didn't it?" Jenny said half to herself as they climbed the stairs to the schoolroom.

"I would like more walnut cake," Barbara announced.

"You always eat too much cake, and then you feel ill." William uttered a light-hearted laugh that Jenny was pleased to hear. "Do you think Father will come fishing with me, Miss Harrismith?"

"I believe he is a man of his word, Lord William."

If he forgot she would have to find a way to remind him.

ANDREW RETURNED TO the library where his man of business, Henry Thurgood, awaited him, having come down from London. Matters requiring Andrew's attention lay in files on the desk. When Andrew directed him to sit, he pulled reams of paper from his valise and placed them before Andrew. His secretary, Anthony Bishop hovered over him ready to assist.

Two hours later, with Thurgood gone, and the matters dealt with, Andrew was left to his thoughts. From his memory, the Castlebridge governess of his childhood had a small mustache and a rather fierce voice. She looked nothing like the new governess. He grimaced. His children were scared of him. And Miss Harrismith, well, she continued to frown. What concerns did she have that she couldn't express in front of the children? Wishing to see to his guests, he feared she would waste his time with her earnestness. But both his children were obviously fond of her. They'd almost hugged her while seated on the chesterfield.

Without appealing to Bishop, Andrew searched until he located her application for the position of governess, which the agency had sent for his perusal a year ago. At the time, he'd been away and barely glanced at the letter Bishop sent him. Miss Harrismith hailed from Yorkshire, a baron's daughter, which surprised him and made him uneasy. His secretary's cramped notes stated that her father had financial difficulties. A widower with a large family, he'd been forced to send his oldest daughter out to earn her living. A common, and sad tale, which made Andrew sympathize with her. How difficult it must have been to give up her privileged life for one of servitude. The list of her accomplishments was impressive. She had a sufficient knowledge of Latin to prepare William for school. A good grounding in music theory, and proficiency in the pianoforte. Her knowledge of drawing and watercolors would be excellent for Barbara. And it was obvious that Miss Harrismith had the poise and confidence to converse with him on equal terms.

Andrew picked up a pen and rolled the handle between thumb and forefinger as he paused in thought. He was inordinately pleased with the caliber of governess his children now had, the last one having been a disappointment, but by the same token, Miss Harrismith was a lady, and ladies were born with a certain knowledge of their place in the world. She would be prepared to speak her mind. And he was quite sure she would voice hers tomorrow. He expected if her father's finances improved she might be called home. It was to be hoped that she wasn't about to give notice, as he would be sorry to lose someone William and Barbara liked, but he doubted that was the reason. He looked forward with interest to what Miss Harrismith was eager to tell him.

He strolled to the fireplace and pulled the bell cord.

"Send the housekeeper to me," he instructed when the footman entered.

Minutes later, Mrs. Pollitt stood before him hands clasped tight against the skirts of her black gown. "Everything has been made ready for the shooting party, Your Grace. Is there anything more you require?"

"Thank you, no. This concerns Miss Harrismith. Is she fitting in well?"

"The children do seem to like her," Mrs. Pollitt said. "But a governess should keep a certain distance, in my view. It's my opinion that they have become a little too familiar."

"I imagine it would be difficult to stop them," he said mildly. "The children, I mean." *And perhaps Miss Harrismith also.* "I am not displeased with Miss Harrismith," he said. "I hadn't expected William to still be in the nursery."

Mrs. Pollitt's brow puckered. "According to Miss Harrismith, Lady Barbara begged Lord William to remain in the nursery with her." She shrugged. "I did suggest the governess not bow to your daughter's wishes, for Lady Barbara will become most dreadfully spoiled, but as you see, she has not chosen to remove Lord William from the nursery."

"I see." Andrew found himself much in agreement with Miss Harrismith on this issue, for it would happen naturally, when William wished it to, but he declined to say so. "Is Miss Harrismith's accommodation adequate? I should like to see her made comfortable."

Shocked, Mrs. Pollitt stared at him silently, as if he had suggested moving the young lady into his apartments.

"She has the attic room generally assigned to governesses, Your Grace. It is somewhat larger than those assigned to the maids."

The housekeeper's voice carried a hint of displeasure. Governesses were positioned somewhere between the servants and the family, which could prove difficult for them. "Perhaps a bedchamber on the same floor as the children's?"

"There is only Nanny Evan's bedchamber in the tower wing, Your Grace. Adjoining the nursery."

"Oh yes, Nanny." He rubbed his chin. "Thank you, Mrs. Pollitt. You may go."

The housekeeper curtsied and left the room, no doubt wondering what bee had got under his hat. He wondered at it himself.

With a regretful glance at the pile of correspondence which would require several hours spent with his secretary, Andrew made his way to his apartments to change, before he met Greta and her brother in the yellow salon. Although there was a mountain of things demanding his attention, he intended to be a good host and see to his guests' enjoyment.

Some hours later, as Andrew conversed with Greta and Ivo in the salon, the butler announced his cousin Raymond.

Raymond walked in with his cheerful grin. He shook Andrew's hand. "I heard you'd come home and as I was passing through Oxford, thought I'd call and see how you go on," he said in his easy manner.

"I'm glad you did, Ray." Andrew turned to his guests. "Allow me to introduce you. Greta, Baroness Elsenberg and Ivo, Herr Von Bremen, my cousin, the Honorable Raymond Forsythe."

"I see a family likeness, Mr. Forsythe," Greta said with her charming smile. "But I've never understood the English way of shortening names. Why do you call him Ray, Your Grace?"

"Because as a youth he was a ray of sunshine," Andrew said tongue-in-cheek. "Charmed all the ladies."

"Ah!" Raymond's blue eyes danced. "What rubbish! Don't believe him, Baroness. It's pure indolence on Andrew's part."

Andrew grinned. "We spent a lot of time together growing up. Sit, please, Ray. May I offer you a glass of claret?"

Raymond seated himself in an armchair and crossed his long legs.

"I would welcome a glass. Drove down from Caufield Park. That's in Yorkshire," he explained to Andrew's guests.

"How is your mother?"

"In excellent health. I was obeying the order to visit." He gave a rueful smile. "It's been a while, and she accuses me of neglect."

"Aunt Augusta is quite a formidable lady. She would shake Wellington to his boots," Andrew said. "She scared me as a youth after I broke a window pane with a cricket ball."

Raymond turned to Andrew's guests. "Are you enjoying your stay in England? I shall direct the question to you, Baroness. Ladies are more observant, I find."

Greta's gaze rested on Andrew. "I like it more and more."

"Not quite as civilized as Vienna," Ivo said. "But it holds promise." His laugh took the sting from his words.

"I haven't had the fortune to travel to Vienna, but I hear it is a beautiful city," Raymond said.

"Indeed it is." Ivo nodded. "The Austrian women are charming."

"I am sure that is so." Raymond smiled at Greta. "And very lovely."

"Greta and I are German," Ivo stated with a slight frown.

Raymond's gaze remained on Greta's face. "Then the German ladies are enchanting."

"You are still the same incorrigible flirt." Andrew laughed and shook his head.

The butler came in and poured more wine into their glasses and set a plate of sweet biscuits on the table. He bowed and retreated.

"Will you stay on for the shoot next week?" Andrew asked. "We should be delighted should you decide to. You will know many of the guests."

His cousin cast him a grateful glance as he picked up his glass. "Thank you. I should be delighted."

Andrew wondered if there was another reason for Raymond's visit. He supposed he'd learn of it soon enough.

That evening, Andrew joined his guests again at dinner. Across the table, Raymond looked what he was, a well-built gentleman in well-cut dinner clothes. His black hair was curled into a Brutus, his cravat exquisitely tied in the complex Neapolitan. But Andrew's earlier observation of his cousin seemed correct. Raymond's face was finely drawn, and he looked older than when he'd seen him last. Still in his twenties, he should rightly still have the fresh-faced youthfulness of a young man in his prime. Perhaps his mother had been right. Aunt Augusta feared the life Raymond led in London was self-indulgent, and perhaps even bordered on dissipation. His father had been a gambler, and early on in his life, Raymond showed signs of following in his footsteps. He gambled away money he could ill afford on curricle races, cock fights, boxing matches, and horseracing, and he was a friend of the reckless Baron Alvanley who was busily going through his fortune.

Andrew toyed with the idea of asking Raymond if he needed funds, but thought better of it. A man had pride. If Raymond was in bad straits, he would come to him, as he had before. Andrew supported Raymond's widowed mother, as he did all his relatives; it was his duty as head of the family. But he disliked throwing good money after bad.

Raymond was laughing at an amusing aside from Greta. The expression in his eyes caught Andrew's attention. He was looking at the baroness as if filled with a kind of painful longing. For some reason, Andrew found it disturbing. He turned to discover Ivo frowning at them both.

Chapter Four

WILLIAM USUALLY RODE immediately after breakfast. Jenny feared he would become impatient if none of the grooms were available to accompany him, and might ride off on his own. If only she could ride with him. The green wool riding habit hung from a hook in her cupboard. Why had she brought it here? Homesickness, and the struggle with her loss of independence stirred again, although it had begun to ease. There was little point in wishing for the moon. Her father, furious with her, had decreed it. This was her fate and she must accept it. She was well fed, with a roof over her head, which many could not claim, though she did wish for more company. Nanny was kind, if a little vague at times, while the children warmed her heart and gave her days a sense of purpose.

Yesterday, a letter arrived from her sister, Arabella, in York. News from home was always accompanied by a flutter of anticipation. Jenny pulled the crumpled paper from her pocket, smoothed it out and reread every word while she partook of her porridge, tea, and toast at the table in her room.

At seventeen, six years Jenny's junior, Bella kept her up to date with the latest happenings at home. It seemed that Papa still buried himself in his library engrossed in his Medieval studies and turned his back on the rundown estate. As with Jenny, there was no money for a London Season. Papa's hopes rested on Bella, the prettiest of the girls, who he was confident would attract a gentleman of means at the York or Harrogate Assembly dances, now that she'd turned seventeen.

Her sister wrote about how she longed to escape the miserable atmosphere at Wetherby Park. Jenny prayed Bella's union would be a love match. That she wasn't pushed into marriage with someone she disliked. Her sister would not be able to refuse an offer as Jenny had done.

Jarred, the eldest at twenty-four, was scholarly like their father, but he had to give up his dream of attending Oxford, and now worked as a clerk at the Inns of Court, hoping one day to become a barrister. Jarred sent money home whenever he could, but living in London took most of his wages. Colin at twenty was away in the navy. Jenny's other three siblings were too young to venture out into the world. Her gentle sister, Beth, was thirteen, then there was twelve-year-old Charlie, and Edmond, the youngest, who was eight. It remained a sorry state of affairs, which Jenny felt would not have come to pass had her mother lived. Mama had been practical and capable, and life had been much better then.

Papa did not expect you to accept his ultimatum to either marry Mr. Judd, or leave us, Bella wrote. He misses you, Jenny. I think he sorely regrets you leaving. You are the most like Mama, and Papa has not been himself since she died. I am still unsure what was said between you before you left us. I know you disliked Mr. Judd. I haven't warmed to him myself, although Papa thinks he's a capital fellow, they are often in the library pouring over old tomes and chuckling together. I wish you would come back. I miss you dreadfully. We all do.

Bella.

The letter cast Jenny into despair. Was Judd still visiting them? He would be, of course. It should have occurred to her. Walter Judd had fostered a shared interest in Medieval literature with her father. They spent hours reading poetry and discussing it, and she suspected her father had begun to regard Judd as a chivalrous knight. She should be there. If she'd accepted Judd's proposal, she might have been able to help her siblings. But after what she'd discovered about him, she just couldn't.

Her mind on her appointment with His Grace at eleven o'clock, she finished her breakfast, tidied her hair, and made her way to the stables to check on William.

The autumn mist still hovered high in the trees, the grass sparkling with dew as Jenny walked toward the stable yard.

Suddenly the duke rode out of the woods on his stallion, thundering down the driveway toward her, scattering gravel. For a moment, Jenny stood still and admired him. A glorious sight, he and the horse moved as one. If William was with him, it would delight the boy, but there was no sign of him riding behind his father.

The duke drew rein as he came up to her, close enough for her to read his expression. She gasped. His dark eyebrows were lowered in a heavy frown as he pulled his mount up, the magnificent chocolate brown horse's nostrils flaring. "Miss Harrismith, do you know which of the bridle paths my son might take?"

Jenny stepped back, although it was obvious the duke was in complete control of his mount. "Yes, Your Grace. Lord William prefers to ride to the river." With a feeling of foreboding, she pointed toward the bridle path which angled away through the beech trees and disappeared deep into the wood. "Is something wrong?"

The stallion threw up its head, pale mane flying. "William's riding Storm Cloud," the duke growled. "That horse is almost as big as Cicero and has a nasty temper."

She started. "Lord William knows he is not allowed to ride one of the big hunters!" she said, her uneasiness about the boy having proved right. "Isn't the stable master, Ben, or Jem with him?"

"Ben is laid up with an injured leg, and Jem has escorted the baroness and her brother over the estate," the duke threw back over his shoulder as he wheeled his horse away.

"Lord William would wish to impress you with his horsemanship, Your Grace," she called after him. He would not like to hear such a comment from a governess, and indeed he ignored her. He nudged his horse's flank, and urging the animal into a canter, disappeared into the trees.

William could not have saddled the horse himself. Did he ride bareback? She'd seen him ride one of the smaller horses without a saddle, but Storm Cloud? That was ridiculous. But she couldn't quell her fears as she hurried along praying it would come to nothing. William would manage the horse quite well as long as he didn't try to jump a high gate, or a fox or hare didn't startle the horse.

She hurried under the archway and entered the stable yard, a large cobbled area made up of the stables, coach house with the staff accommodation above, and storehouses. Inside the duke's immaculate stables, the stable boy was scouring out a stall with vinegar and baking soda, the same as they used at home in York. The air was tinged with the faint smell of urine, overlaid with oil and leather. Horses shuffled in the loose boxes, but several stood empty, swept and clean.

"Did you see Lord William ride off, Sam?"

"I did, Miss, but I was out forking straw bales off the cart and couldn't stop 'im. Not that his lordship would've listened to me."

"Storm Cloud was saddled?"

"One of the stable lads did it for 'im, Miss."

"Well there's that at least. I imagine His Grace will find him." But William would be in trouble, she thought gloomily. An unfortunate beginning when father and son were just getting to know each other. She left the stables to wait in the yard.

William was determined to show his father how accomplished a rider he was. She hoped the duke would keep a cool head, and not drive a wedge between them, although she feared he might, for he did look furious.

A lady trotted her horse into the stable yard with two gentlemen, a groom following behind them. Their mounts crossed the cobbles to the mounting block.

The tall dark-haired gentleman dismounted effortlessly, threw the reins to the groom, called goodbye and left, walking away toward the house. Jenny knew him to be the duke's cousin, Mr. Forsythe, come to visit, because the nursery maid, Mary, had told her so when she'd brought her breakfast.

The groom assisted the dainty lady to dismount. She was dressed in a scarlet-colored habit edged with black braid in the military style, and a jaunty black riding hat. A golden lock curled over her shoulder. Thanks to Mary's penchant for gossip, Jenny knew the guest was Baroness Elsenberg. Her brother, Herr Von Bremen, strolled over the cobbles toward Jenny, peeling off his leather gloves. He removed his hat, and smoothed his hair, the same color as his sister's, back from his brow.

The handsome man stood before her. Close up he was younger than she'd first thought, but still several years older than her. "How charming. And who are you, pretty lady?" he asked with a lift of his eyebrows.

Jenny bobbed. "Miss Harrismith, sir. The governess."

Bright blue eyes smiled into hers. "Do they allow you to ride, Miss Harrismith?"

"No, sir."

"You must be allowed some measure of freedom. Perhaps you might show me the rose garden."

"I'm afraid the roses are not at their best this time of year, sir," she replied.

"Ivo, come away. Let the domestic be," the baroness called in a cross voice. "Please accompany me to the breakfast room. I fear only English food awaits me, but I declare I'm famished."

With one last glance at Jenny, which took her in from head to foot, Herr Von Bremen nodded and went to take his sister's arm. "It is inelegant for a lady to mention her stomach," he rebuked her. "I hope you don't do it in the duke's company. Where did he ride off to, by the way?"

"He's gone in search of his son," the lady's voice drifted back as they left the stables. "I do hope the boy doesn't demand too much of his time."

Jenny stood stunned. Well, how rude, but the comment was not meant for anyone's ears. Anyone that mattered, at least. Was the lady about to marry the duke? She didn't seem the sort who would make the children a good mother. Surely the duke was too smart to be fooled by a beautiful face and elegant figure. But men, even clever ones, could so easily be taken in by sapphire blue eyes and a tiny waist. While ladies, she admitted, might be caught by Ivo's handsome smile.

ANDREW RODE OUT of the woods into a clearing. His son sat on the bank throwing pebbles into the river. Nearby, Storm Cloud cropped at the grass. William glanced anxiously up at him. As Andrew's rapid heartbeat eased, he buried his intention to chastise him.

William stood. "Have I made you angry, Father?"

Andrew dismounted, still patently aware of the governess's re-mark. There was condemnation in her tone, which irritated him, because he knew she was right. He reminded himself of his own youthful misdemeanors as he walked over to his son. "I was worried, William. That horse is called Storm Cloud for a good reason. A good hunter, but needs a strong hand. I'm relieved you're not hurt."

"I can ride him, Father," William said eyeing Andrew's stallion. "I can ride any horse, even Cicero."

"Perhaps you can," Andrew said mildly. "But I'd rather you didn't until you're older. Please don't do it again."

William glanced down at the smooth pebble in his hand. "Very well, Father."

It was pleasant here with a shaft of sunlight warming the ground, the familiar smells of mud and water and wet reeds stirring up memories from his past. For a moment, some of Andrew's concerns eased, as he focused on William. "Do you come here often?"

William turned and skimmed the pebble over the water. It bounced several times before it sank a fair way across the river. "I ride every day before lessons. Ben usually accompanies me, but he's hurt his leg."

Andrew hunched down and selected a perfectly smooth flat pebble. He stood and spun it over the water as he'd done as a boy. It bounced three times then sank just short of William's.

The boy's face lit up. "I say, I beat you, sir."

"Fair and square," Andrew said with a smile. "Time to return to the house. I'll give you a leg up."

William backed away, offended. "No need, Father." He untied the horse's lead from a branch and was up on the horse's back as fast as a jockey at Ascot. Storm Cloud turned his big head, his black eye fixed on William while he chewed on a mouthful of grass, but put up no objection when William walked him toward Andrew's horse.

Chuckling, Andrew mounted, and after William rode on ahead, turned Cicero's head for home. He would join Greta for breakfast and apologize for missing their ride.

Andrew found Greta and Ivo in the breakfast room dawdling over their coffee. While he ate his kidneys, eggs, and bacon, Ivo drawled on about the delights of Viennese society, which made Andrew wish the man would go back there. He drank down the last of his coffee, made his apologies and rose. After noting Greta's pout, he invited her to meet the children that afternoon, then returned to the library and his letters.

His temper flared again. This time it was directed at a letter which had just been delivered by a mounted messenger, recalling him to London to address a problem at Whitehall. He would be forced to leave his guests to their own devices for a day or so.

Someone knocked on the door.

"Come."

The governess entered, just as the mantel clock struck eleven. Well, she was nothing if not punctual.

"Ah, Miss Harrismith." Andrew put down his pen and nodded to her as she came to stand before his desk. He was reminded again of how she'd called after him as he'd ridden off to find William. While he approved of her defense of his son, he did not like the implication, however slight, that he needed advice. Presumptuous! His gaze roamed over her. He couldn't fault her tidy appearance, but the demure forest green gown was ill fitting. The bodice strained across her bosom, and as if aware of it, her fingers toyed with a brooch there. He averted his gaze. For some reason, he found Miss Harrismith unsettling.

Andrew did not invite her to sit. He needed to deal with any problems swiftly and be on the road within the hour. And there was one large problem. Greta would be most displeased, shut away here with little society for two days. He toyed with the idea of inviting her to come with him and sighed. No doubt she would expect him to squire her about Town, and then it would be a week before they returned to Oxfordshire. Still, he would welcome time to spend in her company. After all, it was a chance to get to know Greta better away from the distractions of society, and her brother.

"Now, what do you wish to speak to me about, Miss Harrismith?" he asked, aware he sounded impatient. "Is it imperative for us to discuss it now?"

She raised her eyebrows. "I consider it imperative. But you may not, Your Grace."

He sighed and ran a hand over his hair. "Semantics, Miss Harrismith. There is obviously something that you wish to advise me of, so please do so. I shall be leaving for London shortly."

"Oh. The children will be disappointed."

He was tempted to grind his teeth. She was frowning at him again. "I'm afraid not everything can revolve around my children, Miss Harrismith. That is why I have employed you."

She took a step closer to the desk. "I am concerned about Nanny Evans, Your Grace. She is becoming very tired. It is taxing caring for the children for someone of Nanny's years. Not Lord William, so much, but Lady Barbara can be quite determined."

He frowned. "Nanny Evans?" Nanny was almost as much a part of the fabric of Castlebridge as those whose portraits lined the picture gallery. Andrew recalled with fondness the woman who had cared for him when a youngster. He must make time to visit her. How old would she be now? Not in her dotage surely. "Nanny has always been most capable. I don't see why that would change." He sat back, folded his arms, and cocked an eyebrow. Miss Harrismith's gaze dropped to her hands clasped in front of her. As he'd suspected, the young woman overreacted. "Barbara is a most amenable child, I fail to see how she could cause anyone bother."

"Lady Barbara is delightful, but strong-minded. She is also quite creative. If you would care to visit the schoolroom…"

"I certainly plan to. When I return," he said shortly.

She gave a quick nod. "Of course, Your Grace."

Andrew found himself studying the charming shape of her upper lip. Dash it all, governesses shouldn't be so attractive. Wasn't that a stipulation made to employment agencies? Good-looking women got into trouble. Hence the last governess who was now in Cornwall with the footman.

"I shall look into it, rest assured, Miss Harrismith."

She curtsied. "When you return, Your Grace."

"Precisely," he said brusquely, suspecting she was laboring the point. He tapped a finger on his desk. "Now if there's nothing else?"

"No, Your Grace. Unless you wish to discuss the work I've set for the children?"

"No need for that now. William will soon have a tutor and we'll discuss Barbara's requirements at a later time." He paused, pointedly waiting for her to leave.

She made no move toward the door. "My main concern rests with Lord William. He wishes for his own horse, Your Grace, and dislikes riding the mare, Lavender," she said. "I fear he might be tempted to ride one of your hunters again. And while Ben is laid up there might not be a groom available to take him in hand."

"William won't. He gave me his promise."

Dammit, she looked unconvinced. Boys will be boys, he supposed. He pushed away the memory of some peccadillos from his youth that would make his hair stand on end, should William attempt them.

He'd been right, a lord's daughter was unsuitable to be a governess. Why hadn't her father married her off? She was certainly pretty enough. Perhaps it was her stubborn disposition.

Andrew rose from his chair and came around the desk aware that time was growing short. He needed to instruct his valet to pack a portmanteau and speak to Greta. If she decided to accompany him, there would be a further delay while she changed, and her maid packed her clothes.

"A groom will be sent down from London to assist the head groom until he is back on his feet. In the meantime, I could order Jem to ride with William." He gazed down at her as a thought suddenly occurred to him. "But he has to see to my guests. Do you ride by any chance, Miss Harrismith?"

Her straight dark eyebrows rose over surprised gray eyes. "Yes, I do, Your Grace."

"And you have brought riding clothes with you?"

She looked puzzled. "I have, Your Grace."

"Then please accompany William on his morning ride. I am confident your unfailing commonsense will keep the boy on the straight and narrow." He was rather pleased with the notion. It quite stopped Miss Harrismith in her tracks. Her face had become an attractive shade of pink, and she was no longer frowning.

"If you feel it best, Your Grace."

Andrew strode to the door. He pulled it open startling the footman in the corridor. "I do. Good day." He stood aside for the slender young woman to exit the room leaving the scent of lily of the valley in her wake.

Chapter Five

J ENNY'S MOUNT FOLLOWED after William's along the bridle path. They rode alone, because poor Ben's leg had not yet healed enough to allow him to ride, and Jem was out with the guests who'd wished to see more of the estate. It was simply glorious to be on horseback again. Her horse, an elegant bay mare called Rose, was well behaved, and the duke's woodland quite splendid. The dappled light filtered down through the canopy of leafy branches and cast patterns over the trunks of the trees.

The sense of freedom Jenny had never expected to experience again was bittersweet; she feared it would break her heart to give it up. But she didn't fool herself into believing this arrangement would last forever. She'd been astonished when the duke suggested she accompany William and terribly pleased that he'd come to trust her.

Really, she should not be so keen to impress the man. But when his blue eyes met hers, every nerve ending in her body seemed to stir. She must not forget that he could dismiss her with a snap of his fingers if she did something he disapproved of. Jenny feared she might because she intended to continue to stand up for the children.

She'd begun to suspect that her initial judgment of the duke had been unfair. He did not appear to be the aloof, indifferent man she'd painted him. He treated his servants well, greeting them kindly as they waited to receive him when he first arrived. They in turn were steadfastly loyal, for not a word had she heard said against him. Certainly, no one could find fault with the fact that he had served

England's interests, and indeed the world's. But his work left only a small corner of his life to spare for the children, and as she'd learned that his father was also politically inclined, His Grace probably suffered the same lonely childhood as William.

The mare picked her way around a ditch filled with rainwater as the familiar smells of cold wet earth, fungi, and the glorious autumn foliage, filled Jenny's senses.

Too impatient to walk his horse, William had suggested they race to the river, but Jenny sternly insisted he keep to a trot until they reached clearer ground. He'd reluctantly agreed, but still managed to move ahead out of sight.

The peaceful woodland sounds of twittering birds, chattering squirrels, and the breeze murmuring through the trees, was suddenly shattered by the crack of a gunshot, followed by William's cry. Startled, Jenny jumped and jarred her neck painfully as the mare bolted. Birds rocketed overhead. With a twist of fear, her years of riding came to the fore. Jenny settled the mare into a canter over ground strewn with piles of wet leaves, loose rocks, and treacherous hidden potholes. She vaulted the horse over a fallen log, as she yelled for William, somewhere ahead.

At last, she burst out into open space where the river meandered through a wide expanse of meadow. William sat hunched on the ground.

"William!" Jenny slithered awkwardly down and fell to her knees beside him.

He gazed up at her white faced. "I'm all right, Miss Harrismith."

She almost choked on a gasp of thankfulness. "You're not hurt?"

He shook his head.

"I heard a gunshot. It sounded awfully close," she said.

He pointed behind him. "The shot struck that tree over there."

Quickly on her feet, she ran over to the towering ash. A small section of bark was shredded. She gasped and put a hand over her pounding heart as she peered into the dense woodland listening for the approach of the shooter. No one emerged to apologize and inquire if they'd been hurt. She hurried back to him. "It must have passed very close to you."

William climbed shakily to his feet. "I'd just dismounted and bent to pick up a stone to toss into the water when it happened," he said, his voice wobbling. "I decided to keep low in case another shot was fired."

She wanted to hug him, but the boy was already terrified, so she fought to stay calm. "It must be someone hunting." But who would shoot so close to the bridle path?

As she spoke, another gunshot rent the air. Upriver, a bird fell from the sky. "I didn't know the gamekeeper was out with his gun. We should have been told. How dreadfully careless." She scowled as she turned to him. "If I'd known this would happen today, I would not have allowed you to ride. It's not safe here. We must go home."

William straightened up. "It was just an accident, Miss Harrismith. Sometimes shots can go wild. Perhaps whoever it was stumbled when they fired." He sounded surprisingly grown-up and quite an authority as he walked over to her horse. "I'll help you mount."

"Thank you, Lord William," she said, aware the boy attempted to hide his fear. What a fine duke he would be one day! With the aid of a nearby rock for her to stand on, William lent his arm to assist her onto the sidesaddle. She arranged her skirts, her eyes roaming the trees crowding around them.

William was up on his horse's saddle in a trice and they rode back to the stables. This time, she permitted a canter and followed hard behind him. Her heart still raced, and her gaze continued to rake the woods for any sign of activity, hushed now as if all manner of wildlife had retreated.

Who fired the shot? She'd never met Clovis, but the gamekeeper had been here for years and would know better than to risk the safety of the duke's family and guests.

When they reached the stables, Jenny asked the groom if he'd seen Clovis, or if any guests intended to hunt that morning.

"No, miss, haven't seen him around today," Jem said. "It's doubtful anyone's taken a gun out. Not with a shooting party planned."

Disquieted, Jenny returned to the schoolroom with William where Barbara waited with the maid.

"Where is Nanny Evans, Mary?"

"She said she needed to lie down, Miss Harrismith."

"Oh. Is she ill?"

"She didn't say."

"I shall go and see her directly. That will be all, thank you, Mary."

"Nanny is taking a nap," Barbara said, as she brushed her doll's hair. "Did you go riding, William?"

"Yes," William said shortly.

Jenny expected him to tell his sister about his lucky escape, but he said nothing more. Jenny sighed; they would not ride again until the duke returned. His Grace would have to be told, for an accident like this could not be ignored. It seemed unlikely his guests would take it upon themselves to go out with a gun. In any event, they would have been seen. As soon as she was free, she would go to the gamekeeper's cottage and inquire.

"Now," she said with a smile. "Shall we begin with a French lesson?"

"*Merci*," Barbara said with her perky smile.

William mumbled and shuffled in his seat.

At least here in the schoolroom things were back to normal.

Later, when Nanny woke, she seemed perfectly well. She took charge of the children, and Jenny left the house to cross the grounds to the woods. The gamekeeper's cottage was a good mile away. Leaving the formal gardens, she took the woodland path. As she studied the sky where rain clouds drifted overhead she failed to see the man coming toward her. She stopped so fast she almost stumbled.

His strong hands gripped her arms. "I've got you, Miss Harrismith."

The gentleman from the Continent, Herr Von Bremen, dropped his hands, gracing her with the full measure of his charming smile.

"I am sorry." Her cheeks warmed. "I was looking at those clouds.

It appears about to rain."

Blue eyes held her gaze. "I believe you're right."

"I regret not bringing an umbrella," she said somewhat inanely. Still uncomfortable, she rushed on. "Have you been to see the gamekeeper?"

He raised his fair eyebrows. "No. Should I have?"

"Of course not. Please excuse me, I won't keep you." She moved to sidestep him.

He held his ground, blocking her way on the path narrowed by encroaching shrubbery. "I hiked over to that hill." He pointed to a rocky outcrop in the distance. "From there you can see for miles."

"How delightful. Something for me to look forward to." She glanced again at the sky. "But not today, perhaps."

He didn't move. "Where are you off to alone?"

She opened her mouth to tell him, but his curiosity unsettled her. She wasn't sure why. "Just a short walk. I have some thinking to do."

"Ah." He nodded. "Then it is plain you don't wish for company." He moved aside.

With a polite nod, Jenny continued on her way. She didn't turn, but she sensed he watched her. Herr Von Bremen had been perfectly amiable. She had no reason to doubt him. He was a fair distance from the river and did not carry a gun. Surely she had nothing to fear from him, and yet she increased her pace hoping to find the gamekeeper at home. But when she reached his cottage, and knocked, there was no answer.

She hurried back along the path, her enjoyment of the woods somehow spoiled by an irrational fear that she might be accosted, and no one would hear her cry for help. It made her furious that she allowed herself to feel so vulnerable. Her imagination had taken flight, no doubt because of the episode earlier with William. By the time she reached the house, reason had returned, and those foolish fears had lost their power over her.

The episode with Herr Von Bremen forgotten, Jenny entered the nursery to see how Nanny fared. She'd become less confident than ever that Nanny was coping. Should she say something to the housekeeper? Jenny disliked the idea and decided it was better to wait. Perhaps the matter would be resolved without her interference. She had mentioned it to the duke and hoped he would take the matter in hand. It was clear that Nanny would welcome a rest for she spoke of it often.

ANDREW DEPOSITED GRETA at a hotel where one of her friends stayed, then traveled to Whitehall to meet Castlereagh. Four sober-faced men he knew well from Vienna greeted him.

"Some bad news, I'm afraid," Lord Fenton said. "Richard, Earl of Winslow has been murdered."

"Good God!" It hit him like a blow. Dazed, Andrew shook his head as he took a seat and accepted a glass of whiskey. Winslow was a good friend. "Where did this happen?"

"Here in London. Winslow intended to return to his estate the following day. Found shot near his club in Pall Mall in the early hours."

Andrew still couldn't believe it. "Were there witnesses?"

"Not one. He was alone," Fenton said.

"Robbed?"

"No. Still had his watch, fobs and his wallet." Viscount Bramsten took the seat next to Andrew. "The darndest thing. A white lily had been laid on his chest."

"A lily?" Andrew stared around at the worried faces. "What the devil does that mean?"

"We have no idea," said Bramsten, "But I have a feeling we are going to find out."

Andrew tossed back the whiskey welcoming the reviving burn in his throat. "You think this might have something to do with that dissident group the prince warned us about?"

"Too early to say," Fenton said. "Might be something personal.

Perhaps a misstep with a lady whose husband sought revenge."

Andrew shook his head determined to defend his friend. "Richard and his wife were close. Elizabeth will be devastated. She spent a good deal of time in Vienna with him over the years. I must pay my respects to her."

"You can never be sure about a man's secrets," Bramsten said. "But should it be some kind of message, I daresay it will be made known soon enough. While we shouldn't begin jumping at shadows, it is best to increase the guards around your London home. Until we find out more."

"And don't wander around London on your own at night, as Winslow did," Fenton added.

"Be armed at all times." Castlereagh pulled back his coat to reveal the pistols he always carried.

Andrew viewed his sensitive, melancholy friend with a measure of sadness. The burdens imposed on him as foreign secretary were taking their toll. He had been behaving out of character since the abortive Thistlewood plot to assassinate the Cabinet last year, and during the trial of Queen Caroline, when he took up residence in the Foreign Office for greater safety.

When Andrew finally departed for Mayfair, and Harrow Court, the distress of his friend's death made him weary to his bones. London skies were gray with low cloud. The air dense with smoke from the hundreds of fires lit to ward off the dank cold. He found himself eager to return to the clear skies of Castlebridge.

He now regretted a shoot had been planned even though it was long overdue, the frosts of the past month having delayed it. The proper upkeep of the woodlands was vital to its health and indeed, the future of the estate. He was only too aware of the important role he had in the care of his huge inheritance. Despite the enormous staff that served him, a number of responsibilities rested on his shoulders. There was an accumulation of important matters to attend to since he'd been away, and it would be wrong of him to evade his responsibilities.

Dusk had fallen when he descended from the carriage onto the sweep of white gravel before his London residence. Lights were being lit in the street. He wondered fleetingly how well Miss Harrismith was coping with his son. It pleased him that she'd developed a good rapport with both of his children. Clearly, William required a tutor, but it would take time for Andrew to select a good one able to gain his son's respect. He recognized himself in the boy, that firm chin and upright carriage, that stubborn streak. All the Harrows, himself included, were a determined lot.

In the salon, Greta ordered her maid from the room. "Did you have a pleasant day?"

"No, merely business." He decided not to mention Winslow's death, as he came to kiss her hand. "Did you enjoy your visit with friends, madam?"

She smiled. "Oh so much! We have been invited to see a play at Drury Lane tonight."

Not a keen theatregoer, Andrew disliked the idea. "Ah, that sounds…"

After a knock, the footman entered and handed Andrew a note from Castlebridge. Andrew tore it open and read it. "Good lord!"

Greta put down her glass of madeira. "What is it?"

"It's from my secretary. I must return to Castlebridge. My son's governess has informed Bishop that a shot was fired very close to William while they were out riding this morning."

She raised her eyebrows looking incredulous. "A governess' over-reaction to a hunter's stray shot would send you rushing home?"

He nodded, uneasy with Winslow's murder still fresh in his mind. "I can't dismiss it out of hand."

"What about the theatre? It's Edmund Kean as De Montfort."

Andrew frowned. "Surely, my son is of more importance than the theatre?"

"Of course he is, but you can hardly trust the word of a governess. They are more than capable of embroidering to increase their importance. My mother detested them."

"Nevertheless, I will leave shortly for Castlebridge, Greta. Please, stay another night or two. I should not like you to miss the society you so enjoy, or Kean's performance. I'll send the coach for you. Let me know when you wish to return."

Greta rose gracefully to her feet and cast him an uncertain smile. "I'm sure I shan't enjoy the play without you, Harrow."

"But you'll stay?"

She placed a hand on his shoulder and gazed up at him, imploringly. "It's only for one night. I hope you won't miss me too much."

"I shall. But I'll be comforted by the fact that you're enjoying yourself, when until the guests arrive for the shooting party, I fear you find the country rather dull."

In the coach on the way back to Castlebridge, Andrew tried not to give way to disappointment. He was perfectly happy for Greta to stay and enjoy the theatre, and she may well be right, the governess could be making a mountain out of a molehill. But still, he had expected Greta to understand, and at least offer to return with him. She seemed to prefer London, and he feared she might not wish to share the life he'd planned. He shrugged and pushed the troubling thought away, folding his arms. Instead, he thought of Winslow. A man he'd liked, and the horrible way in which he died.

His thoughts then turned inevitably to William. He wanted to reassure himself that the boy was all right. But it would be too late when he arrived home tonight. And he did not wish to disturb Nanny. It would have to wait until morning.

Chapter Six

I N THE SCHOOLROOM the next morning, Jenny was attempting to distract William who kept referring to the shot in the wood. What could she do to blot out the frightening experience from his mind? She took out a map of England and asked the children to find the major towns upon it.

The door opened, and His Grace entered. She had not expected him back so soon and wished she could have tidied herself. On her feet quickly, she smoothed the skirts of her gray gown and curtsied. "Your Grace."

"Miss Harrismith, children." He strolled over to the table. "William, I believe a hunter's shot came very close to you while you rode by the river yesterday?"

"Yes, Father," William said. "Someone shooting birds."

"Tell me what happened."

As William described how he'd dismounted and bent down to pick up a stone when the shot had whizzed over his head, Jenny saw the duke's blue eyes darken and his expression become grim.

He placed a reassuring hand on the boy's shoulder. "Regrettably, it appears to be someone's shot going awry, William. I'm relieved you were not hurt."

William dug a finger into his collar his young mouth set in a firm line. "I explained to Miss Harrismith that the shooter might have stumbled and not realized where his shot went."

"I believe you are right," His Grace said. "But I intend to look into it and make sure it never happens again. Tomorrow, after breakfast, instead of riding, I thought we'd do a spot of fly-fishing."

William brightened. "Oh, yes, I should like that, Father."

"I shall come too," Barbara said.

Andrew shook his head. "I'm afraid you might not enjoy it, sweetheart."

Barbara began to fidget. "You promised to bring something back from London, for us."

"Dear heaven, in my haste to return I forgot! I will next time without fail, I promise."

"Are you going away again?" she demanded, finally revealing what really concerned her.

"No, sweetheart. Not for a while, it's to be hoped." He raised his eyebrows at Jenny. "We'll all go to the river tomorrow and have a picnic."

"A picnic!" Barbara clapped her hands.

"Now, I need to speak to Miss Harrismith for a moment. Perhaps you can find York on the map, which is where your governess hails from, isn't that so, Miss Harrismith? While she and I have words in the corridor."

He gestured to Jenny and crossed to open the door.

"I thought it best to report the incident right away, Your Grace," she said in the corridor. She hadn't expected the matter to bring him straight home from London, if that was what brought him here.

"My secretary considered it serious enough to notify me straight away, and rightly so," he said. "But it is likely to be just that, a stray shot, which I will investigate." He studied her face. "You brought William immediately home?"

"I did, Your Grace."

"Might there be anything you can add to William's account? No sign of anyone in the woods?"

She shook her head. "I expected someone to rush to see if we were hurt, but no one did. A bird was shot out of the sky, farther along the river about ten minutes later. In the afternoon, I went to inquire of the gamekeeper at his cottage, but when I couldn't find him, I decided Lord William and I would not ride until you had been consulted."

He nodded. "A wise decision, Miss Harrismith."

"I met Herr Von Bremen on the path to the gamekeeper's cottage," Jenny said. "He said he was returning from just having climbed that high hill to the north. He wished to view the surrounding countryside."

"Leave it with me, Miss Harrismith. Be ready with the children for our picnic at ten o'clock.

She hesitated. "You wish me to go too?"

He smiled. "You shall have to take care of Barbara, otherwise I fear I will be fishing her out of the river."

Jenny grinned and nodded. "We shall be ready, Your Grace."

She left the duke and returned inside. "I've found York, Miss Harrismith," William said, pointing to the map. He already looked happier.

"Oh, well done, Lord William."

"Can you tell us another story about your sister's animals?" he asked. They loved her tales featuring Beth's odd assortment of stray animals. But she remained uneasy about what was occurring back home in Yorkshire, and aware of how quick children were to sense a mood, sought to delay it.

"I shall, but now it is time for your baths, Nanny will be waiting."

ANDREW LEFT MISS Harrismith, whom he'd found to be perfectly sensible, and unlikely to exaggerate her account of the shooting, as Greta had suggested. He descended the stairs. Ivo was more intrepid than he gave him credit for if he'd climbed Spender's Bluff. It was not impossible to scale if one knew the right way to go about it. Evidently, Ivo had discovered the route, but somehow climbing steep hills didn't fit with his idea of the rather indolent man.

"Tell Clovis I wish to see him first thing in the morning," he instructed the footman. He must dress for a dinner which would be regrettably lacking in feminine company. A game of faro or billiards with Raymond and Ivo might serve to banish the worries from his mind for a few hours. First Winslow, and now this business with William, which was not easily explained. Andrew's plans for a comfortable retirement from his diplomatic duties had suffered a bad beginning. Hopefully, there would be nothing more.

CLOVIS CAME TO see Andrew in the library the next morning while he sought through the fishing gear that had just been brought to him.

"Have you been culling pheasant, Clovis?"

Clovis shook his head with a puzzled frown. "No, Your Grace. Needs to be done, I grant you."

"Someone discharged a gun near the river. Close to the bridle path. A shot came perilously close to my son."

Clovis' eyes widened. "Good lord! Who would do such a reckless thing?"

"That's what we must find out. And as soon as possible."

As Miss Harrismith had seen Ivo returning from Spender's Bluff, Andrew delayed questioning him, in the hope that the culprit would be found. He had no wish to ruffle Greta's plumage, which was becoming increasingly easy to do. Ivo had been an arrogant bore last night, annoying Raymond as well as Andrew, boasting about his prowess with women. Andrew must question him when he'd really love to throw Greta's bad-mannered brother out on his arse.

"Let me know if you hear of anything, Clovis. And check the gun room. I want to know if any guns have been taken out and fired."

"It will be done, Your Grace." Clovis scratched his head. "Odd business. Can't make head nor tail of it."

When the door closed behind Clovis, Andrew stared out the window taking scant notice of the gardeners clipping the yews. He considered the only other possible person to take a gun out would be Raymond. His cousin felt very much at home here. It was entirely possible he could have taken it upon himself to go on a hunt without requesting permission. Andrew remembered several similar experiences when they were lads. He had envied Raymond's devil may care attitude, back then. But their differences became more marked after Andrew inherited the dukedom and subsequently married.

Raymond's father, Andrew's Cousin Charles, was a reckless man. He died in an accident while racing his curricle when Raymond was a baby. While Andrew's father had been an upright, resolute man, who did not forgive the frailties of a young son. A respected speaker in the House of Lords, Andrew had a grudging admiration for him, but at the same time, was determined never to be like him. He suspected the choices his father made, ignoring Andrew's mother, who then became a society leader at Almack's along with Lady Jersey and had little room in her life for either her husband or her son, caused his father to be lonely. Andrew had wondered if he'd ever regretted anything. He'd certainly never spoken of it, nor approached Andrew to bring them closer.

Raymond's mother, his Aunt Augusta, expressed concern to Andrew about the manner in which Raymond lived in London. He didn't find anything unusual about it. Raymond lived like many sons who did not have the responsibility of an estate. With little to do, and readily available funds, they spent their time whoring and gambling. Andrew sighed and went to find him. His cousin was next in line after William, but perhaps it was fortunate that Raymond would not inherit the dukedom.

He went to join the governess and his children for a morning's fly-fishing. Cook was to pack a luncheon hamper which would be taken to the river in the trap.

Miss Harrismith, in her green habit, waited with the children at the stables. They rode out on horseback in the autumn sunshine. Barbara rode with Andrew and the other two followed behind along the woodland path. It was three miles to the best fishing spot for trout. When they arrived, George was already there setting out the picnic luncheon on the grass in the shade of an oak tree.

Andrew handed a rod to William and took up his own as Barbara and Miss Harrismith wandered over the meadow, picking the last of the wildflowers before the onset of winter.

"Where will we stand, William?" Andrew smiled at his son's enthusiasm and the precise manner in which he chose the fly and attached it to his line.

"Over there, the water flows better, Father. More chance of getting a bite."

"Quite so." He sensed William was eager to show his finesse at the sport.

They found a level spot to stand on the bank. William raised his rod into the air taking it back over his shoulder. He cast it into the water. The fly landed an impressive fifteen feet from the bank.

"That was very well done, William. The gamekeeper has taught you well," Andrew said as he cast his own line into the water.

A soft breeze toyed with the willow fronds and birds chirped around them. As the tension drained from Andrew's muscles, he realized how strained he'd been.

Barbara's laughter made him turn. A rabbit hopped away and disappeared into a hole. Miss Harrismith was grinning. Her eyes found his for a fleeting moment and she raised her hands to her chest as if to say, Isn't this perfect?

And it was.

He took a deep breath of country air scented with damp grass and mud as William yelled. "Father look! A trout has taken my lure!"

"Wait, take it slow, William, reel in the line. But if the fish wants to run, let it."

William played out more line and then began to reel in the struggling fish.

"You're doing well, William," Andrew said as he reached for the net.

William turned his glowing face to Andrew. "I've nearly got him!"

Andrew leaned forward. "That's a decent size."

William grinned. "Big enough to eat, Father?"

"Someone will certainly enjoy it. If I can get it into the net." Andrew laughed as he scooped the wriggling fish from the water. "I quite fancy eating it myself."

"You caught a fish, William!" Barbara ran over with Miss Harrismith following. "Ugh, it looks slippery and wriggles!"

"Oh, well done, Lord William!" Miss Harrismith examined the fish. "When your father has caught one or two, there will be a fish course served for dinner tonight."

"Are you so confident I will, Miss Harrismith?" Andrew asked wryly not missing the mischief in her smile. There was a touch of the minx in Miss Harrismith, and he found himself wishing she would allow him to see more of it.

"I feel quite optimistic, Your Grace."

He had never seen her this lighthearted and free, but the governess understood as he did how important today was, to calm his son after his frightening experience.

With the fish safely in a bucket, they sat down to their picnic. Andrew stretched his legs out over the grass and picked up a chicken leg from the plate. He took a bite and chewed. "I shall make an attempt to equal your achievement after luncheon, William."

"I might catch another, Father!" William grinned as he rose to take the bucket to the river to replenish the water, and ensure his prize catch made it to the kitchens still fresh.

Miss Harrismith buttered bread and placed it on the plates as George stepped forward to pour the lemonade.

"Wine? Miss Harrismith?"

"No thank you, Your Grace. I prefer lemonade."

Andrew leaned back on his elbows and watched her. Her head in the straw bonnet was bent over the hamper while she added bread and butter to the children's plates. The fresh breeze brought the scents of leaves and grasses, and the river. How very pleasant it was. Might he and Greta have days like this?

"Right," Andrew tossed the chicken bone onto the plate, drank a glass of chilled wine, and climbed to his feet, brushing down his breeches. "Back to the river to take up the challenge!"

William still chewing, darted away with a laugh, and Barbara crawled on the grass nearby picking more daisies. Andrew paused at Miss Harrismith's side. "I've been away too long, and need to make up for lost time with my children. Do you think I'm making headway, Miss Harrismith?" He leaned down and offered her his hand.

For a moment, as she climbed to her feet, their hands entwined, the shock of skin on skin. Andrew was conscious of how slim and delicate her hand was, fitted into his palm, and then he released her.

She had gone that pretty shade of pink. "Your children hold you in great affection, Your Grace, but I'm sure it's not my place to say so," she said. "You are a duke and my employer after all!"

He smiled. He enjoyed looking at her, her straight nose, the firm line of her jaw. She was firm in her opinions too, was Miss Harrismith. "I was a man before I was a duke, Miss Harrismith. And I want all the things every man wishes for."

He saw understanding and warmth in her eyes before she lowered her lashes.

Then William called from the river and he turned away, wondering why he'd felt the need to say it.

Chapter Seven

I T HAD BEEN such a perfectly lovely day. When the duke spoke of his wish to grow closer to his children, she'd almost melted into her half-boots. She smiled as she rested her head on the pillow. His Grace had caught two more fish, but declared William to be the winner, as his catch was bigger. The trout were brought back to Castlebridge and sent to the kitchens to be served to the guests for the fish course.

The children were tired but still chatting about the picnic when she left them with Nanny. Jenny was pleasantly tired too, and spent the hours before bedtime reading her Jane Austen novel, but her mind kept returning to the picnic. His Grace's laugh, the warmth and thoughtfulness he displayed toward his children. His gentle teasing, which had briefly included her. And more perplexing was the electric touch of his hand holding hers. She bit her lip. It was dangerous to sigh over him, and would only bring misery. She had to concentrate on why she was here, to care for his children.

Her candle snuffed, she pounded her pillow, and drifted off to sleep.

JENNY STOOD SHIVERING on the rug in her nightgown. Half asleep, something had drawn her from her bed. Through a gap in the curtains, the sky lightened to a rose-tinted gray. A glance at the clock told her it was almost dawn. She stood for a moment unsure why she'd woken in a panic, and then she smelt it. Smoke drifting in on the breeze. The gardeners burnt off dead leaves in autumn, but would they leave them smoldering overnight?

The nursery wing was directly below hers. As unease gripped her, she told herself the fire might be somewhere in the woods. Perhaps lightning struck a tree. Yesterday, the bad weather had hit after they'd arrived home. And last night there was a storm.

Unable to ignore it, she snatched up her robe and shoved her feet into slippers. On her way down the servants' stairs, the smell of smoke grew stronger. When she reached the corridor below, a trail of smoke wafted along the ceiling. No one appeared to be awake. Jenny ran to the nursery door and burst inside.

Here the smoke was denser. The curtains were well ablaze, sucked in and out of the wide-open window. Nanny sat in a chair her head nodding on her chest, the children asleep in their beds.

"Nanny!" Jenny yelled. She grabbed a jug of water from a table and ran to the window. Coughing, she doused the flames as best she could then pulled the curtains down to the floor and stamped out the remaining embers. The smoke dispersed as cold fresh morning air rushed in through the window.

Nanny Evans sat up drowsily, her cap falling over one eye, and her long braid of grey hair sitting on her shoulder. "What are you doing, Miss Harrismith? What has happened?"

"Did you leave a candle burning, Nanny?" Jenny asked, checking the sleeping Barbara. William was stirring.

"No, indeed I did not," Nanny said, sounding cross. "And why would I leave the candle over there? It's always placed here beside me."

William rubbed his eyes. "Is it morning?" He coughed. "What is that smell?"

"Not quite yet, William. The curtains were on fire. But it's been put out now."

William was not one to take anyone's word for something unless he saw it for himself. He left his bed and walked over to the blackened, smoldering curtains. "Was it lightening?"

"The wind blew the curtain onto a candle," Jenny explained.

"Well, it wasn't my fault." Nanny climbed unsteadily to her feet. "You won't tell the housekeeper it was, will you, Miss Harrismith?"

"Of course I won't." Jenny patted the elderly lady's shoulder. "All over now. A bit of a storm in a teacup, really." *But it had not been.* Flames had singed the edge of the rug. If that had taken hold, it would have burned toward William's bed. She didn't dare allow the thought to continue to its conclusion.

"I can't go back to sleep now," William grumbled.

"No, but keep warm in your bed. The servants will be awake. I'll send up chocolate and muffins," Jenny said. "I must go down and speak to Mrs. Pollitt." She didn't want to leave him, she wasn't sure why.

"What should I do, Miss Harrismith?" Nanny asked. She shivered and appeared exhausted. "I daren't go to my room at night. I fear I might not hear the children."

"Please, Nanny, do go to bed or you'll catch a chill. I shan't be long."

Relieved, Jenny saw Nanny go uncomplainingly into the adjoining room and climb into bed. A moment later, she was asleep again.

"Nanny snores," William said. "She keeps me awake."

"Shush. I doubt a herd of elephants in the garden would keep you awake," Jenny said.

He chuckled.

Jenny hurried up to her room to dress. First the gunshot and now this. She wondered what her father would make of it. He didn't believe in coincidence. Only in literature. He would always quote Shakespeare's *Othello* to underline his point. The candle had barely burned down. Surely, after burning all night it would be no bigger than a stub? She shivered and rubbed her arms.

Jenny's anger grew as she went downstairs. Poor Nanny was too frightened to leave the children at night because she'd become a little deaf. Her heart ached for her.

It had grown light when she entered the servants' quarters. A few of the staff were seated at the long table eating breakfast. In the kitchen, two maids and Cook bustled about in the pantries and worked at a large scrubbed table. A roast turned on the spit beneath the vast chimney.

In her room, Mrs. Pollitt, with her scraped back hair and thin lips appeared her most unwelcoming self when Jenny entered. But she paled and rose quickly from her chair after Jenny explained what had happened. "How fortunate that you discovered it, Miss Harrismith. I shall inform the butler and send the maids to clear away the mess."

"We require new curtains. I'm afraid the old ones are ruined."

"I will see to it. Mr. Forrester will advise His Grace."

"I must return to the children," Jenny said.

"Yes indeed, Miss Harrismith. Do go. I'll have some hot chocolate sent up."

The housekeeper made no mention of Nanny's carelessness and nor did Jenny. She doubted even the butler would broach it with the duke. But surely someone must deal with this, or more incidents could follow. Jenny paused, a hand clutched tight on the banister as another possibility struck fear into her. What if it hadn't been Nanny's fault?

As Jenny approached the nursery door, her thoughts threatened to spiral out of control. The possibility that someone had come into the nursery and set the curtains alight was nonsensical. She was being overly dramatic. These sorts of accidents do happen, she thought, not totally convincing herself.

ANDREW WOKE TO a knock on the door. Early morning light filtered in through the gap in the curtains. Forrester entered with a murmured apology.

"I am sorry to disturb you, Your Grace," Forrester said, approaching the bed, "but there's been a fire in the nursery."

"A fire—" Andrew's voice broke off, his breath drawn sharply through his teeth. He threw back the bedcovers and leapt from the bed, snatching up his dressing gown. Fire was never to be taken lightly.

"The governess caught it in time, but I thought you should be made aware of it immediately."

"Miss Harrismith discovered it, you say?"

"Yes, Your Grace. It was the curtains. The fire is out now, thanks to her."

"I'm relieved to hear it, Forrester," Andrew murmured. "Send my valet to me."

Once dressed, Andrew made his way to the nursery. He found Miss Harrismith sitting beside William's bed as he drank chocolate and ate a muffin. Barbara still slept as did Nanny in her bedchamber with the door closed.

As he greeted the governess, it struck him rather uncomfortably that he was coming to depend on this young woman.

"There was a fire, Father," William said, in between chews.

"A candle caught the curtain, Your Grace," Miss Harrismith said. "I thought it best to alert the housekeeper."

"Indeed. A candle was left burning all night?"

"Yes, an oversight. But placed near the open window. It caught the curtain."

Andrew went to the window; the curtains had been well ablaze, and the rug was singed. Unchecked, it could easily have taken hold and set the whole nursery alight. Disturbed, he swung around, and returned to William's bedside, as he fought to maintain a semblance of calm. "I'm grateful you were here, Miss Harrismith. Come and see me in the library at eleven."

"Certainly, Your Grace."

He ruffled his son's hair. "Never a dull moment, eh, William?"

William nodded, unperturbed, his mouth full of muffin.

Andrew descended the stairs. Nanny must be urged to retire. A nurse would be employed to replace her, but it would take time for her to become familiar with his children's needs. Nanny's loss was sure to upset them, and they'd had enough disruption already in their short lives.

He paused, a hand on the banister. In a household of loyal servants, he considered Miss Harrismith to be best able to care for his children. The efficient manner in which she had handled the gunshot in the wood showed her to be more than capable. And she had tried to warn him that Nanny was worn-out, which he'd dismissed out of hand. He clenched his jaw and continued down the stairs. His children and possibly others might have perished because of it.

Three hours later, the governess stood before Andrew's desk, neatly dressed in unadorned gray wool apart from the cameo which unfortunately tended to draw his eye to her chest, and seemingly unflustered by the dramatic events earlier. He drew in a breath. "I must apologize to you, Miss Harrismith." He rose and invited her to sit. "You did warn me that Nanny has been finding it difficult to carry out her duties." He threaded his fingers through his hair and took a seat opposite her. "I suppose I was thinking of Nanny as she used to be."

"Nanny Evans is a wise and caring soul, Your Grace."

"Of that I am sure." Nanny Evans had a special place in Andrew's heart having cared for him when his parents were so often away. He'd been left to his own devices as a child haunting the woods and the stables. His father, when he was in residence, seldom asked for him, and his mother was often caught up with social engagements which kept her in London.

"Nanny remains positive that she didn't leave the candle by the window. She always places it on the table beside her chair."

"Mm. Well, perhaps as you say she has become forgetful." He tapped his fingers on the arm of his chair. "I will ensure she is made comfortable in her retirement. But in the meantime, until the new nurse arrives, I would prefer you to move into the nursery with the children."

Relief filled the governess' gray eyes. "Certainly, Your Grace."

"The nursery maid will care for the children when you wish for time to yourself. I remain very much in your debt," he confessed. "I should have made a point of visiting the nursery. Understood what was happening there."

"I doubt you would have found anything unusual, Your Grace. Nanny merely becomes a little tired at times."

"Still. This could have been averted. I have you to thank for avoiding a disaster."

"I'm glad I was there," she said briskly. The delicate flush on her cheekbones gave clue to the depth of her emotions.

He found he wanted to draw her out more. To discover why she had responded so swiftly to his children's plight. "Yes, but your room is not on that floor. And surely you would have been asleep at that hour."

"Ordinarily, yes. But something woke me." A frown marred the smooth skin of her forehead. "And then I smelled the smoke."

"You kept a remarkably cool head in the circumstances," he observed. Curious how like a mother she seemed, always sensing when a child was in trouble. "You are the oldest daughter, are you not?"

"Yes, Your Grace."

"And your father is a widower."

She nodded.

"I assume you took some role in your younger siblings care?"

"Yes, I did."

"Did your mother pass away recently?"

"No, some years ago, Your Grace."

It appeared she had taken on the role of mother, raising her younger siblings. Such experience was invaluable. "Anything that you require you've only to ask, Miss Harrismith." He looked away from her full bottom lip. *This attraction would not do.*

"Well, I believe that is all for now."

After Miss Harrismith left the room, Andrew returned to his desk and shuffled papers, but couldn't banish the chill that filled his chest at the thought of a fire raging in the nursery. He would become more involved in his children's welfare. They must come before his work for the government, the demands of his investments and the running of his estate.

It was no good wishing things would have been different if Catherine had lived, he had to embrace the future. He smiled up at her painting which hung over the fireplace. How proud she would have been of her spirited daughter and conscientious son. It was admirable of William to be protective of his sister, but he and Barbara should feel secure within a loving family.

Andrew accepted he must marry again. And soon. He looked forward to introducing the children to Greta.

Startled, he glanced up as the door opened. As if his thoughts had drawn her here, Greta slipped into the room with her appealing smile, dressed in a flattering gown the color of primroses. She had not long returned from London. "You missed a wonderful play, Harrow," she said, crossing the carpet to his desk. "As I was invited to a card party, I stayed for another night. It was vastly entertaining. I'm sure you would have found it so." She ran a finger along the carved edge and her blue eyes sought his. "Have you missed me?"

Andrew chuckled. He moved around the desk to kiss her cheek. "I have. But I'm pleased you liked the play and regret I couldn't stay to enjoy it with you. May I make up for my neglect tonight?"

She smiled. "I should very much like you to try."

"That doesn't fill me with hope."

Greta traced the pattern on his waistcoat. "It is wise for a lady to keep a gentleman guessing," she said. "Once he is sure of her, he loses interest."

"I can assure you I haven't lost interest."

He gazed down at her. She was exquisite. Like a porcelain figurine. He lowered his head to kiss her mouth.

A knock came at the door and he stepped away from her. "Come."

The gamekeeper entered clutching his hat in both hands. "You wished a report on the gun room, Your Grace?"

"Ah, Clovis, yes." He turned to Greta. "I must apologize, baroness, matters are demanding my attention, yet again. Shall we continue this interesting conversation in the evening?"

"Certainly, Your Grace." She smiled and walked to the door. "And please don't concern yourself about me. Your cousin, Mr. Forsythe, has invited me to walk in the gardens with him."

Andrew stared abstractedly as the door closed behind her as Clovis spoke. "I've checked the gun room, Your Grace," he said. "Nothing missing, and no guns have been fired recently."

"You are certain of that, Clovis."

"Yes, Your Grace."

Andrew frowned. "It's a puzzle, then, Clovis."

"It is, Your Grace. I'll ride into the village, ask around."

"Good."

Something that had at first seemed like an appalling accident now had taken on a rather more sinister appearance.

Chapter Eight

J ENNY LEFT THE children with Mary, who had become the full-time nursery maid. Mary was sensible and efficient, and Jenny was confident they would be well cared for in her absence. She spent the next hour with Nanny, helping her pack her trunk before she left for London. Nanny was to live in one of the Duke's townhouses. "You'll be able to meet your old friends, the nannies you talked to in Regent's Park when you took the baby for an airing."

Nanny tucked a shawl into the trunk. "Few would still be in service, at my age those I knew are likely below ground. When a children's nurse is no longer useful, they're usually sent away to their relatives. If they're lucky enough to have any to take them in."

Overcome with compassion, Jenny slipped her arm around Nanny's thin shoulders. "I do hope you will be content there, Nanny, and not miss us too much."

"You are a dear girl." Nanny patted Jenny's cheek. The affectionate display surprised Jenny, for Nanny, although always kindhearted, was usually reserved and formal in her manner. "I am most fortunate, Miss Harrismith. I shall have my pension and a nice place in which to live. His Grace is a true gentleman. I should know," her eyes softened. "He was high spirited, but always a good boy. And so is William."

She drew her handkerchief out of her pocket and blew her nose. Tucking it away again, she glanced around the room. "There, I am ready. I shan't worry about the children because they have you."

"The children will write regularly and tell you how they go on."

Jenny kissed Nanny's papery cheek as two footmen entered to tie the cord around her trunk, then escort her down to the waiting carriage.

A moment later, a maid bustled in, her arms full of Jenny's clothes. "I'll bring the rest of your things down shortly, Miss Harrismith."

"Thank you, Alice." Jenny looked around the room. Her new bedchamber was roomier and more comfortable than the attic room, with a larger wardrobe, although her few clothes wouldn't fill it. The window had the same view of the southern aspect of the house as the nursery and the schoolroom. She looked down over the water feature to the trees in the park and the loop of carriageway. Down below on the carriage drive, the coach stood waiting. His Grace bent to kiss Nanny's cheek then helped her inside. The footman closed the door, put up the steps, and the coach drew away.

Jenny watched until the duke disappeared from view. Then she spun around. What thrilled her most was that the nursery was right next door, and the children were entirely in her care, at least until the nurse arrived. She metaphorically rolled up her sleeves. There were changes to be made. Nanny, for all her wisdom, was a trifle old-fashioned.

While Jenny took her allotted time off she sent the children with Mary to the schoolroom where William could read or draw. Barbara was learning to cross-stitch. Jenny loved to walk. Back in York she would tramp for miles over the dales, but with only an hour to spare, she could not venture far.

The gardens slumbered beneath the autumn sun, but the sharp breeze held the promise of winter. The smell of freshly scythed grass scented the air. Jenny picked a white lily that had been left hanging on its broken stalk. She would put it in water in her bedchamber. Flowers always made a room feel cheerier. She crossed the lawns to inspect the yews the gardeners had pruned into neat shapes.

"Good afternoon, Miss Harrismith. Are you contemplating nature?" Herr Von Bremen stood before her, smiling in that slightly whimsical manner, as if he found everything secretly amusing. She hadn't heard him come up behind her, his footsteps muffled by the dense grass.

"I was admiring the gardeners' workmanship." She wished he would go away. "The Castlebridge gardens are truly magnificent."

"Not a patch on those in Germany."

"It's almost winter, you are not viewing them at their best," she said, suffering an urge to defend the place that was now her home. "Those azaleas will be a bank of bright color in spring." She gestured to the shrubs beneath the library windows.

When she turned back, Von Bremen had moved closer. He reached out a finger to touch the brooch on her chest. "That piece of jewelry is most unusual."

Jenny stepped back, her hand covering the brooch. "The clasp is loose. The cameo was my mother's."

He tilted his head. "And she is gone, yes?"

"Yes, some years ago."

Suddenly, the library window behind her was thrown open. Jenny looked into the duke's frowning countenance. "May I have a word, Ivo?"

Something indecipherable flickered in Herr Von Bremen's eyes. "Certainly, Your Grace." He bowed his head. "We shall talk again soon, yes?" He nodded to her and walked away.

The duke remained at the window. "Why the lily, Miss Harrismith?"

Jenny jumped. She dropped the flower as if scalded. Did he object to her picking just one flower? "I thought it pretty."

"Baroness Elsenberg wishes to meet the children. Would you bring them to the yellow salon at four o'clock?"

"Yes, Your Grace."

The window shut. With a flick of the curtains he disappeared. Dismayed, Jenny made her way back to the schoolroom, her pleasant promenade of the gardens spoiled. The duke appeared to be annoyed. Did he think she was flirting with Herr Von Bremen? She flushed and bit her lip. For him to think poorly of her was the last thing she wanted.

"You wished to see me, Your Grace?" Ivo entered the library and sauntered over to Andrew where he stood before the fire, a book of his favorite poems in his hand.

Andrew eyed him and snapped the volume shut. Even the arrogant way the man walked irritated him. "Please sit, Ivo. Care for a Cognac?"

"I would, thank you."

Andrew crossed to the drinks set up a silver tray and measured three fingers of liquor into each snifter. He returned and handed one to Ivo, then sat on an armchair opposite him at one side of the fireplace.

Ivo studied Andrew over the glass. "You look like a man with something on his mind."

"On the day I went up to London shots were fired in the wood. One came perilously close to my son. It was in an area where no one is permitted to discharge a firearm."

Ivo raised his eyebrows. "And you believe it was me?"

"I don't know who it was. But I intend to find out."

Ivo swirled the Cognac in the snifter then tossed it back. "Well I'm afraid I can't help you with that."

"Were you out riding?"

He rubbed his chin. "With Greta in London? No. I was in bed, I imagine. Alone as it happens."

Andrew frowned. "And since you mention it, I would prefer you to leave my female staff alone."

A smile tugged at Ivo's mouth. "You mean the governess? Tasty little piece, isn't she?"

Andrew's blood boiled, Greta's brother or no, he wouldn't get away with that. "Whether she is or not, Miss Harrismith must be left to do her work. She is not here for your amusement."

"Very well, Your Grace." Ivo cocked an eyebrow. "I shall avoid the governess."

"And the rest of my female staff," Andrew added. "None are here to entertain you. If you wish for feminine company, I advise you to return to Town."

"Unfortunately, Greta might object to that."

Andrew found he didn't much care. "I'm sure your sister can be persuaded to part with you."

"Perhaps. She has little need of my company."

Andrew narrowed his eyes. "Which means?"

"Your cousin has been most attentive. But I shouldn't worry, Your Grace. He could never be your rival."

For a moment Andrew quietly studied him. The man was being deliberately provoking. Why, he had no idea. Andrew put down his glass and stood, gazing pointedly at the arrogant man, wanting him off his property and out of his sight. In another minute he might forget he was the host, and this man Greta's brother. "If you'll excuse me, I am rather busy."

Ivo stood. "I'm considering going into Oxford for a few days."

"My carriage is at your disposal."

Ivo nodded. "Then I shall leave tomorrow. I'll see you at dinner, Your Grace. We can make up a four for whist. Or might we play vingt-et-un for higher stakes?" At the shake of Andrew's head, Ivo held his rather delicate long fingers over his mouth as if to stifle a yawn.

The door closed. Deuce take it! The fellow needs a lesson in manners, Andrew thought.

At four o'clock, he entered the yellow salon where Greta sat alone reading a magazine, dressed in a blue gown the color of her eyes. She put down the magazine. "I had hoped you'd ride with me this afternoon, Harrow."

"Tomorrow, Greta. I promise." He seated himself beside her on the sofa upholstered in gold damask. "I must apologize. I have been a neglectful host. It was not my intention, but matters have conspired to keep me busy."

Greta frowned. "You have been preoccupied since we arrived. I find myself wondering what has caused such a change in you."

"There was a fire in the nursery."

"A fire? Dear me. Was it put out?"

"Yes, thankfully, by the governess."

"The governess. Now why am I not surprised? She is a schemer, Harrow, I did warn you."

He sighed. "You are mistaken. Miss Harrismith came upon the fire, she didn't cause it. Let us cease this ridiculous conversation. Allow me instead to tell you how eager I am for you to meet my children."

"I am sorry. Please forgive me." Greta poured Andrew a cup of tea and added lemon, just as he liked it. She handed him the cup and saucer with her pretty smile.

A footman admitted Miss Harrismith into the room. She led Barbara by the hand with William following. The governess ushered his children across the Axminster carpet. In their brushed and combed neatness they stood shyly before them. Andrew's deep love for them caught at him chokingly.

He cleared his throat. "Greta, allow me to introduce you to my son and daughter, William and Barbara. Children, please greet Baroness Elsenberg."

"How do you do." Greta held out a hand to William.

William bowed, but made no move to take her hand.

"And this must be Barbara." Greta quickly turned her face toward his daughter who had wobbled into a curtsey. "Your father speaks of you often. What a pretty kindchen you are."

"What is that?" Barbara frowned and turned to the governess for an answer.

Greta put a hand on the aquamarine and gold necklace at her throat. "A kindchen is a baby girl, Barbara."

Barbara looked shocked. "I am not a baby."

"No, of course you are not. It also means a young girl." Greta threaded her fingers through the gold chain.

Barbara edged closer. "That's pretty."

Greta sat up straighter. "Yes. It is very special to me."

Barbara leaned against Greta's knee. "Why?"

"It was a gift…" Greta shrugged and appealed to Andrew.

"It is bad manners to ask personal questions, Barbara." Andrew noticed that Miss Harrismith had retreated to stand by the door.

"Why's it *persnal*?" Barbara asked.

Greta gave a strained smile. "Because your father said it was, my dear."

Andrew tamped down a sigh. "Sit down, please, both of you. Have your afternoon tea. Miss Harrismith, will you assist the children?"

The governess hurried over. Murmuring to Barbara, she settled the child beside William on the sofa opposite Greta, and placed napkins in their laps.

Greta turned the conversation to a letter that had come from a mutual acquaintance of theirs. "They will be in London on Friday for only a short time," she said. "I do hope you will spare a few days to dine with them."

"I shall try to." Andrew's attention was caught by the governess in her demure gown, neatly cutting a portion of cake for Barbara, while quietly preventing William from overloading his plate. It reminded him pleasantly of their picnic by the river and he found himself smiling.

Greta sighed. "Please do, Harrow. The charms of the English countryside are all very well, but the company will be more entertaining in London."

The governess whispered something in William's ear. His son cleared his throat. "Are you fond of horses, Baroness?"

She turned to look at him. "But of course, Lord William. We kept an excellent stable in Germany."

"Did you have some Holsteiners? That is a fine warm-blood breed," William asked, his young face flushed with enthusiasm.

Greta raised her eyebrows. She shook her head with a laugh. "I didn't much care what breed they were as long as they obeyed me when I rode them."

William slumped in his chair.

Before Andrew could smooth things over, Miss Harrismith sat

forward. "If you'll permit me, Baroness. Lord William is most interested in the history of horses, particularly the Arab."

"How enlightening." Greta stared sharply at Jenny while her hand returned to her necklace.

Andrew sat back and crossed his arms pleased that his son was gaining in confidence. "A fascinating subject, William. Please tell us more."

William reddened and launched into a discussion of his favorite subject. As he began to describe the Byerly Turk, Andrew, with a degree of amusement, felt Greta sag back against the cushions beside him. He must take her to London to dine with her friends. This was all too unfamiliar. Once she became more acquainted with English ways, she would enjoy the Season in London as well as their time spent in the country. And surely, she would come to love the children. What woman could not? Why even Miss Harrismith, who sat listening intently to every word William uttered, while preventing Barbara from jumping up, was obviously very fond of them.

William came to the end of his discussion and gazed expectantly at Greta.

"Thank you, William. That was… most educational," Greta said.

Andrew smiled warmly at his son. "Your knowledge is impressive, William."

Barbara managed to evade Miss Harrismith and slid off the sofa. "William knows everything!" she declared in a loud voice.

Her brother grinned at her.

It pleased Andrew to see how fond of each other they were.

"Perhaps I should take the children for a walk as they've finished their tea, Your Grace?" Miss Harrismith suggested.

"Yes, thank you, Miss Harrismith."

When the door closed on them he turned to Greta. "Now you know all about breeding horses."

"I do hope so…" With a smile, she reached out to bring him closer.

The door opened, and Raymond strolled in. "Well, here you are. I could do with a cup of tea, I just rode from the village."

"Ring for a fresh pot, Ray," Andrew said. He rose. "I shall join you before dinner, Greta."

She pursed her lips and nodded.

"My secretary wishes to see me, but come to the library in a half an hour, will you, Ray? There's something I need to ask you."

Raymond turned from smiling at Greta. "Very well, Andrew."

Andrew left the room feeling unsettled. The sense of order he'd wished for in his life seemed further away than ever.

Chapter Nine

BIRDS FLOCKED IN the majestic oaks and elms as Jenny and the children strolled through the park. William swung from a low branch while Barbara gathered pink daisies to make a daisy chain. It was cool, but a lovely day. The trees were in glorious autumn leaf, the bronze, gold, and burgundy a bright contrast against the gray beech trunks and the silver bark of the birch. In the distance, a stag stood like a statue watching them.

Inevitably, their walk ended at the stables where they met Marcus, the new groom recently come from London.

"You'll be able to ride again tomorrow, Lord William," Jenny said, trying not to be disappointed that her brief sojourn on horseback had ended.

William patted a chestnut's neck when it thrust its head over the top of the stall door. "I wish Father would give me my own mount."

"Isn't Lavender your horse? You ride her every day."

William turned to frown at her.

"You have to be patient, Lord William. More things will come to you as you grow older and gain more experience. It wouldn't do to get everything you want all at once, now would it?"

William cast her a disbelieving glance.

She smiled. "Otherwise, what would you have to look forward to?"

She left William talking to the stable boy who perched on a stone wall polishing saddles and went in search of Barbara who had disappeared through the stable door. Inside, the air was heavy with the blended smells of hot horseflesh, saddle oil, leather, and feed. The little girl sat cross-legged on the hay-strewn floor with two young cats in her lap. She looked up, her face vivid with delight.

"You'll spoil your dress, Lady Barbara," Jenny said halfheartedly. She couldn't help being charmed by the sight as Barbara stroked the ginger cat while the gray and white cat tried to climb her bodice.

"Aren't the kittens *bootiful*?"

Jenny crouched down and stroked the gray one's silky head. "Yes, indeed they are."

William followed them inside. "I say, what nice cats. Which one do you like best, Barbara?"

"The orange one," Barbara said, hugging the purring animal. "I want it."

"It would be unkind to take it away from its family," Jenny began, doubtful that the children would be allowed to keep a stable cat in the schoolroom.

Barbara's big blue eyes flooded with tears. "Just for one night. *Please.*"

"You must seek your father's permission," Jenny said uneasily. She should handle this herself, but that meant she must say no. The duke would be irritated at being disturbed over such a trivial matter, and she'd already annoyed him more than once.

There was nothing for it. She straightened and held out her hand to Barbara. "Shall we go and ask your father?" Jenny didn't want to disappoint Barbara, when the children should have a pet. They had always had cats and dogs at home. She might annoy His Grace, but she doubted he could refuse his small daughter's wish.

"Would you like me to carry the cat?" William asked.

Barbara shook her head refusing to relinquish the soft purring bundle in her arms. In a slow and stately procession they left the stable yard and crossed the gravel drive. Entering the formal gardens, they approached the southern wing where the library was situated, and the duke might be found. If he wasn't there, Jenny would have to deal with the matter herself. Should he be entertaining his guests, she had no intention of entering the house by the front door. They would have to climb the staircase to the elegant salon with walls of gold silk, silk damask sofas and rich Eastern carpets, which was far too beautiful a room to receive two grubby children and an animal. A grin tugged her lips when she imagined the look on the baroness' face in response to that. If the lady had anything to do with it, Jenny would be dismissed on the spot.

WHEN CLOVIS ENTERED the library, Andrew looked up from his desk where his secretary, Mr. Anthony Bishop, hovered with the heated wax, while he signed a pile of letters.

Andrew frowned as he pressed his seal into the red wax. "Still confident it wasn't poachers, Clovis?"

"As much as I can be, Your Grace. None have been seen around these parts for a while. The magistrate who presides over the Oxford Assizes could have deterred them. He's had a few hanged in the past. The last were transported to a penal colony. Perhaps for this reason, they've begun to poach farther afield."

"Still, you'll keep an eye out. Check the areas where they used to set their traps."

"I will, Your Grace."

Andrew turned back to his secretary after Clovis left them. "How many more, Bishop?"

"Half a dozen, Your Grace, and there's that notice from the bailiff."

"Let's get to it, then."

Pen poised over a letter, Andrew glanced up with annoyance when someone scratched on the door.

Raymond walked in. "You wished to see me, Andrew?"

Andrew replaced his pen in the holder. "Yes. Bishop, can you give us a few minutes?"

When his secretary left the room, Andrew joined his cousin, who stood in front of a fine oil painting of mares and foals in a landscape. "I've always liked this one," Raymond said.

"Yes, a favorite of mine. Stubbs had a sure hand with horses."

Raymond turned to glance at him curiosity writ large on his face. "What did you wish to speak to me about?"

"Have you been hunting in the woods?"

His eyes widened. "No, why?"

"William came very close to being shot. Whizzed over his head."

"Good God! But who would be so careless? A poacher?"

"Clovis doubts it."

Raymond frowned. He raised his hands, palms up. "You don't think I could do a bloody reckless thing like that?"

"Ray, it's imperative that I find out who almost killed my son. You have a better chance of learning something from the staff than I do. They might be keeping knowledge of it to themselves, either afraid to come forward, or protecting someone."

He squared his shoulders. "You can rely on me, Andrew. I know I haven't been behaving quite up to snuff of late. But I would never endanger William's life. I'm fond of the boy."

Andrew laid a hand on his shoulder. "Yes. I know you are."

With a nod Raymond made for the door.

"Ray?" Andrew called before he reached it. He chose his words carefully. "You seem to enjoy the baroness' company."

His cousin swiveled. He frowned. "What makes you think…"

Andrew smiled. "Greta is lovely and charming company."

"Are you planning to marry her, Andrew?"

"Nothing's settled between us, but it's possible."

"Well, if you do, you're a lucky fellow. Don't worry. I'm not foolish enough to believe a lady of her wealth and rank would consider a suit of mine." He gave a half laugh. "I won't attempt to snatch her from you if that's what you fear."

Andrew chuckled. "I seem to remember that you weren't always so scrupulous."

"When we were youths, it was merely lighthearted play. A game with us back then, wasn't it? I'd say we ended up about even."

"You might have a slight edge. Unfortunately, life has become more serious since those days."

Raymond nodded. "I'll see what I can discover. It's likely an accident that no one is going to lay claim to. Some fool…"

Unsettled after Raymond left, Andrew wandered over to the window. In the garden, the governess led his children along the path. Was that a cat his daughter hugged to her chest? He threw open the window. "Did you wish to see me, Miss Harrismith?"

Her fingers toyed with her brooch, a high color on her cheeks. "Your Grace, Barbara has her heart set on taking the kitten to the nursery. Not wishing to upset her I've suggested she can take it to the schoolroom for a brief stay, with your permission."

"His name is Carrot," Barbara said.

"I thought one night couldn't hurt, but of course, it is your decision, Your Grace," Miss Harrismith continued. "As I've told the children."

"I imagine you would wish to hand such an important decision to me," Andrew said with a wry lift of his lips. He was rewarded with a slight widening of her darkly fringed eyes and a small lift of her lips while a brief moment of understanding passed between them. The minx has cornered me very neatly, he thought.

"We'll take good care of the kitten, Father," William said.

"Carrot doesn't seem a particularly appropriate name for a cat." Andrew fought a grin. "Is the animal male or female?"

"I have yet to ascertain the kitten's sex," Miss Harrismith said. Did he see a corresponding glint of humor in her eyes?

"Very well." Andrew nodded. He eyed the small cat whose kitten days were behind it and accepted he was outnumbered. "One night. And then we'll discuss Carrot's future."

His secretary cleared his throat behind him. "I must get these to the post box in time for the mail coach, Your Grace."

"Miss Harrismith, we shall talk further." Andrew nodded to the governess, smiled at his children, and closed the window.

Pen in hand he stared at the papers before him, but instead, he saw the smile curling the corners of Miss Harrismith's mouth. No, she was nothing like the old governess, Miss Tibb. Tabby he called her, behind her back. She not only lacked a sense of humor, she was rather fond of hitting him with a ruler and he'd been relieved when she was replaced with his tutor.

After Bishop hurried away with the signed and sealed documents, Andrew decided an investigation was required and made his way to the stables. He saddled Cicero and rode along the bridle path to the river.

When he reached the spot where the shot was fired, he dismounted and approached the tree that had been struck by the ball. He dipped a hand into his pocket, pulled out his pocket knife, and dug into the soft bark. The ball fell into his hand. Andrew turned it over in his palm. Clovis had been right. No guns had been used from the Castlebridge gun room. This ball was not one from here.

Grim-faced, he tucked the ball into his pocket with his knife and whistled to Cicero who had wandered over to a tender patch of grass. The stallion raised his head and trotted back to him. Andrew leapt into the saddle. This could not be delayed. He must go to London. If he left at first light, he would make it back by dusk, and meanwhile, Raymond could be relied on to entertain Greta. Although that made him decidedly uneasy. Was this a random attack by someone local? Or was it linked to the London murder? He wouldn't rest until he knew what he was dealing with.

When he returned to the house, he made his way to the schoolroom where Miss Harrismith arranged a basket for the cat while his daughter offered advice. His son was on the floor playing with Carrot.

"We shall bring the basket to the nursery at night," Barbara explained.

"Wasn't the kitten to remain in the schoolroom?" He found himself unable to put up much of an objection after witnessing the endearing scene.

Barbara frowned at him. "Poor Carrot would be all alone, Father."

"Of course. We cannot have that," he said mildly, a smile twitching his lips.

Miss Harrismith finished arranging the cat's bed and rose. "Is there something else, Your Grace?"

"Yes, I'd like a word." He strolled over to the pianoforte against the far wall, out of earshot of the children. Miss Harrismith followed.

His gaze took her in. The dove-colored cambric muslin dress she wore suited her, the brooch at her breast the only piece of jewelry, except for a watch hanging on a fine gold chain. He was struck again by her poise. He'd been surrounded by ladies dressed in the first stare of fashion all his life. Miss Harrismith's outfit was far simpler, and yet somehow, in his opinion she would not be out of place among them.

"I'd like you to take extra care, Miss Harrismith," he said, gazing down at her. "Until I've found out who discharged the firearm."

He eyes widened. "Yes, of course, I shall, Your Grace."

She studied him as closely as he did her. His visit was the flimsiest of excuses, but he found himself wanting to see her before he left. He folded his arms and leaned back against the smooth wood of the pianoforte. "Tell me more about your family. You have six siblings? Their names?"

She looked faintly surprised. "Jarred is my father's heir. He is a law clerk at the Inns of Court."

"He is not at university?"

"No. Unfortunately there was no money for that. Colin, who is twenty, serves in the navy. We haven't seen him for almost two years."

"Do any of his letters reach home?"

"Yes, we have been fortunate to have received two. The last a few months ago. He wrote of his new experiences. The exotic places he visits." Her lovely eyes sparkled. "He has eaten the flesh of a coconut! I've only seen a picture of one. It is a hard life, but he seems happy at sea." She paused, and he nodded to encourage her. "Arabella, or Bella as she is known to us, is seventeen. She is the beauty of the family and is to make her Come-out soon. Then Beth, who is a gentle soul of thirteen. She loves animals, and is always bringing home strays, rabbits, birds with broken wings, even a fox cub, which Papa would not allow her to keep."

Andrew smiled. "I can't say I blame your father for that."

Mischief sparked in her eyes. "No, but it was the snake that upset Papa the most. Beth brought it in in a box when the vicar had called. He spilled his tea in his lap."

He chuckled. "And the younger boys?"

"Charley is ten and practices sword play, as he intends to be a hussar, but he spends hours planning battles with his tin soldiers, so I suspect he might rise to be a general! Edmond is the baby at eight. He is a rather solemn little boy. My father believes he is destined for the church."

A change had taken place in Miss Harrismith as she spoke. Her gaze drifted away from him. He sensed that in her mind she was back at her home in York. Her love for her family shone in her eyes. While he had grown to admire her and was grateful that his children would be safe and content in her care, her presence here also bothered him a great deal.

"You miss your siblings," he said drawing her back.

She looked startled. "A little. But I've been too busy to think of home very often."

He didn't believe her. But she was a surprisingly independent young woman, and proud, he suspected. He wondered again why she had left them and come to Castlebridge. "If Arabella has a London Season, won't you wish to be there with her?"

"She won't be going to London."

"So, like you, that opportunity isn't available to her?"

"No. It is very expensive."

He thought it most unfortunate that these children were brought up in such a careless manner. The eldest boy not going to Oxford when he was obviously clever, not to mention the girls missing out on what every young lady wished for: a London Season, and a chance to marry well. He thought of Barbara who would enjoy the best of everything and was glad he could provide it for her. Didn't every father wish for that? A baron with an estate should be able to find the money from somewhere, and he wondered again what had happened to send this young woman, who so loved her family, far from home.

Barbara had wandered up to them. She ran her hands along the pianoforte keys striking discordant notes. "Will you play and sing for us, Miss Harrismith?"

William had joined them. "Can we have Greensleeves, please?"

Andrew smiled. "Yes, Miss Harrismith. Greensleeves, it is."

She looked adorably flustered. "If you wish, Your Grace."

He winked at William who grinned. "I do wish."

Barbara clapped her hands as the governess took her place at the pianoforte.

Miss Harrismith, her long slender fingers on the keys, began to play, her voice rising pure and sweet.

Barbara began to sing with her, then after William joined in, Andrew added his baritone.

He found himself rocked by a realization. This was what a family should be. Enjoying a picnic, or gathered together around the pianoforte. Might Greta sing as charmingly as Miss Harrismith?

When the music died away, and she rose from the pianoforte, he bowed his head. "Well done, Miss Harrismith," he said. "I must go." For the last half hour, he'd forgotten his concerns but now they rushed back.

Barbara and William had returned to play with the kitten. He ruffled Barbara's hair and placed a hand on William's shoulder, wishing he could sweep them up in a hug. "Be good for your governess, children." He expected them not to notice, they were so caught up with their new pet, but they both jumped up.

"Goodbye, Father," William said smiling shyly at him.

"Will you come and see the kitten again?" Barbara demanded.

"As soon as I can."

Andrew said goodbye to the governess and left them. It would not be tomorrow, he thought with regret.

Chapter Ten

I T TOOK A while for Jenny to settle Barbara; the child kept getting out of bed to check on the kitten which was curled up in the basket on the floor. Finally, both children dropped off to sleep, and Jenny retired to her bed leaving the nursery door ajar.

She must have fallen asleep. She and the duke were waltzing, he with the precision and grace of movement she'd come to expect, along with the strength and self-command which was inherently him. Suddenly, a dark shadow loomed over them. They broke apart, and Jenny, heart beating hard, backed away from some unknown terror.

A wail brought her awake. Jenny leapt out of bed and stumbled into the nursery. Barbara sat up in bed. "Carrot's run away."

"He can't have gone far, sweetheart." The candle lit, she turned to search the room. No sign of Carrot. In the far corner, William's bed was empty, the covers thrown back. With a sense of panic she discovered the door to the corridor stood open.

"William's gone to get him," Barbara said.

"He'll be searching the corridor." Jenny peered out into the shadowy hallway and called his name. Her voice echoed eerily back at her. She came back to the anxious little girl. "I'll fetch William and Carrot. You must stay in your bed, Barbara, until the footman comes. Promise me?"

Barbara sniffed and nodded. "You'll bring Carrot back?"

"Don't worry. Carrot won't have gone far." Jenny pulled the bell then ran into her bedroom and snatched up her dressing gown. She pushed her feet into her slippers.

She closed the nursery door behind her. "William?" Her slippers tapped hollowly down the dim corridor bathed in shadows. She should have taken time to light the lantern, but fortunately, enough moonlight shone in to light her way.

There was no sign of William as she walked along the corridor. Her calls were met with silence. She had come to the end of the corridor. The door leading down was locked. There was nowhere to go except up the stairs to the round tower unless he'd gone in the other direction and down the main stairs. In that case, he would safely return soon. But if he'd followed the kitten up... Jenny didn't hesitate. She entered the narrow stairs and began to climb as the wooden steps creaked and echoed emptily. At the floor above, the door was locked. She gathered what was left of her breath to call again. She should go back, but found she couldn't ignore the risk that he might be up there.

She entered the empty round chamber at the top of the stairs, and gasped for breath, her heart banging against her ribs. She hated heights and had never been tempted to come up to the tower. The door to the roof stood open, moonlight flooding inside. Surely William wouldn't go out onto the parapet? Why then was the door left open? Jenny stepped outside into a moaning wind, while praying that Carrot had led William down to the floors below, and he was now safely back in his bed in the nursery. The blast of cold air hit her, making her blink, and carrying with it a faint sound. Was it William? She yelled, but the wind snatched her voice away. Behind the battlements the narrow walkway led around the tower. There were wide gaps at intervals in the masonry. Up here the moonlight looked ghostly, but it did help her find her way. She tried not to look beyond the battlements to the inky blackness below. She called again, her voice hoarse. Was she being foolish? Should she turn back?

"I'm here." William's faint voice carried on the wind.

"Where?" She almost choked on a cry of relief as she moved along crab-like, leaning into the sloping roof and away from the dreadful drop, one stumble and... "Where are you, William?"

On the moonlit side it was easy to make her way, but when she moved back into shadow away from the moon, her steps became frustratingly slow. She'd almost circumnavigated the tower when she found him. Shock and panic gripped her, pulling her up. William was above her on the sloping roof, squashed into a narrow space beneath the finial. Carrot struggled and mewed piteously in his arms. If he slipped, he would tumble...

"I'm here now, William." She positioned herself beneath him and held up her arms. He had begun to climb down but there was still several feet between them. "I'll take the cat."

William's face looked as pale as the moon. He edged sideways down the slope. When he reached where Jenny had anchored herself, legs spread, ready to help him, he balked. The last bit required him to leave the roof and step down onto the parapet. It frightened her as much as he. "First, give me Carrot," she said, forcing calm authority into her voice.

He gasped. "I... I can't. The cat will fall."

"Cats are nimble. They have nine lives, didn't you know? I won't let him go. You can do it." She sucked in a breath as William leaned toward her, the kitten protesting. "That's right, now..." Jenny reached up and grabbed the kitten by the scruff of the neck. While Carrot wriggled and yowled, Jenny locked a vice-like grip on William's arm with her free hand as he dropped down. "That's right. Good boy!"

As pale as marble he stood beside her. Shaking, he struggled to speak. "I was afraid, Miss... Jenny."

"Of course you were, William. So was I! But you are so very brave. And it's all right now," she said briskly. "Hang onto me and we'll edge our way around to the door. Be sure not to look down."

Minutes later, they ducked their heads and almost fell into the tower room. William sank to the floor. Jenny's heart pounded loud in her ears as she shut the door. She dropped down close beside him and gave his arm a squeeze and then settled the cat more comfortably in her arms. The purring animal had decided not to put up any more resistance. "How did Carrot manage to get up here?"

"Carrot was on the bottom step," William said. "I snatched him and ran up here. I didn't want him to be hurt."

"Why did you think he would be hurt?"

"Because someone was in the corridor, Jenny. Something woke me. The nursery door was open, and Carrot wasn't in his basket, so I went out looking for him. When I found him on the stairs, I thought I heard a noise. Something moved in the shadows behind me, so I picked up Carrot and came up here. The door to the roof was open and Carrot escaped. I had to go after him."

Jenny dragged in ragged breaths to still her anxiety and calm her voice. "William, tell me exactly what you saw and heard."

"I thought I heard footsteps," he said. "But then you called out. Whoever it was, must have run away."

"But wouldn't I have seen them? They would have to pass by me in the corridor."

"I don't know, Jenny…" His voice broke. "I couldn't have imagined it, could I?"

"I'm not sure, William. The shadows can look like that sometimes. You didn't see who it was?"

He shook his head. "Just a dark shape moving away."

She gasped. "I left Barbara alone. We must go back."

They descended the stairs and hurried along the corridor to the nursery. "We mustn't worry Barbara with this, William."

"No, Jenny."

In the nursery, Barbara was sobbing and giving a garbled account to the mystified footman.

"It's all right, dearest. William and Carrot are here. They're both safe." Jenny forced some warmth into her voice while her mind was struggling with the possibility that someone intended to harm William. Too many coincidences, she heard her father saying.

She placed the kitten in Barbara's arms. The animal immediately kneaded a spot on the bed and settled down. Barbara yawned, lay back on the pillow and closed her eyes. Soon, she slept.

Jenny turned toward the footman. "George, can you have some

hot chocolate sent up for Lord William? The kitten escaped so you see we've had a bit of a scare. After you bring it, could you spend the rest of the night here?"

George, reassuringly tall and of a solid build, nodded. He bowed to William. "Of course, Miss Harrismith. I'll see to it, right away."

Jenny locked the door behind George. "Back into bed, William. After your chocolate you must try to sleep. In the morning, your father will deal with this."

"Father will be angry." William shivered as he climbed into bed.

"Yes he will be. But not with you, William."

THE NEXT MORNING, Jenny dragged herself from her bed. William was still asleep, exhausted by his experience during the night. She washed and dressed quickly.

George napped in a chair she'd placed by the door. She poked him gently on the arm and his eyes flew open.

"Thank you, George. I've rung for Mary. I need to speak to the duke."

The footman stood stretching his arms. "Glad to be of help, Miss Harrismith."

When Mary arrived, Jenny explained her mission, without telling her the reason. She hurried downstairs to the kitchen.

Cook stood before the mammoth stove stirring eggs. "I'm sorry to interrupt you at this busy time, but has His Grace breakfasted?" she asked raising her voice above the clatter of a pair of kitchen maids bustling in and out of the pantries, and a maid in the scullery, working furiously at their tasks.

Narrow-eyed, Cook glanced at her. Jenny knew that a governess was not viewed as part of the staff below stairs, and she did not have any authority here. It was a difficult position to be in. And the fact that she was a lord's daughter didn't help.

"His Grace has not eaten breakfast. Nor does he require any," Cook said.

"Why?"

Cook kept stirring the wooden ladle coated with egg. The strong smell of bacon fought for ascendency with the parsley. "Best you ask Mrs. Pollitt."

Jenny knocked on the housekeeper's door. Invited to enter she hurried inside. "I need to speak to His Grace, Mrs. Pollitt. It's important. Do you know if he's here?"

Mrs. Pollitt's features arranged themselves in strong disapproval. "Are you sure it is important?"

"I am not dramatizing the situation, Mrs. Pollitt." Jenny tried not to show her annoyance at the housekeeper's insinuation. "Something happened during the night that His Grace must be made aware of."

"And what was that?"

"Lady Barbara's kitten escaped and…"

Mrs. Pollitt clucked and held up a hand. "I don't see that it's anything to bother the duke with." She lowered her head over her accounts book. "His Grace has sent word that he will not require either breakfast, or luncheon. You might ask Mr. Forrester if you wish to know more."

"I shall. Thank you, Mrs. Pollitt."

Jenny left her, chewing her lip in frustration. Mr. Forrester was polishing silver plate and glassware in the butler's pantry. He informed her that the duke had gone to London, but would return tonight.

She had to be content with that. The children would spend the day in the schoolroom. Any outdoor activities must be curtailed to keep them safe. William would be like that caged lion they'd taken him to see in the Royal Menagerie at the Tower, she thought, as she climbed the stairs.

Mary had the children washed and dressed. They both sagged with tiredness. Barbara was playing with Carrot, dangling a piece of wool for it to catch in its tiny claws. William listlessly turned the pages of a picture book. "Did you speak to my father, Jenny?"

"I'm afraid he has gone to London. But I will tonight."

William wearily nodded his head.

Jenny sat down while she considered what she might do to keep them busy during the long day. The children's breakfasts arrived; hers came over an hour later, and was cold.

She sighed and picked up the milk jug, hoping it was just a mishap. They must be busy with the guests. That would be the reason. But after she pushed away the congealed porridge and cold toast, the concern that the staff were against her remained, and it made her feel homesick and terribly alone.

ANDREW ENTERED THE London morgue to be greeted by the foul odor of death. After explaining what he wished to see he was shown into an office. Minutes later, a box was brought, containing the ball dug out of his friend and colleague, Richard, Earl of Winslow. He removed the ball from his pocket to compare them. They matched.

As the carriage took him to his Mayfair house to wash away the stench and change his clothes, Andrew speculated about what he'd found. It could mean nothing. The ball was not unusual, except that it was of a better make than the cheap shot poachers and London footpads might use. But the one thing that he was sure of was that the gun had not come from the gun room at Castlebridge.

After he'd changed he partook of a light meal in his dining room, and then visited his club in Pall Mall. It was too early to find any friends at White's, and he wasn't in the mood for socializing in any event. He'd sent a footman around to Castlereagh with a request to meet him there.

Andrew sat in White's library reading the newspapers. Winslow's murder still made the front page. Although nothing new had been reported, the way he'd been laid out with the white lily caught the imagination of the public.

Castlereagh entered minutes later.

"Anything new on Winslow's murder?" he asked Castlereagh after their initial greeting.

Castlereagh shook his head, clearly frustrated. "What brings you to

London?"

"I've just come from the morgue." As another man entered the library, Andrew dropped his voice. "Someone on the estate fired off a gun near where William was riding. The ball lodged in a tree. On a hunch I dug it out, and it matches the ball they extracted from Winslow. It's a common enough belted ball from a Brunswick rifle. The Brunswick rifle uses a special round ball with raised ribs that fit into two spiraling grooves in the barrel. Castlebridge uses the Brown Bess which is a smaller caliber."

"Bloody hell! Surely no one would deliberately target William?"

"One would think not," Andrew replied gruffly. "I've questioned the stable staff and the guests. No one saw anyone carrying a rifle, but it stands to reason that whoever fired the shot didn't wish to be seen. My gamekeeper hasn't found any evidence of poachers." He shrugged in frustration. "But nor can I discount that possibility."

"Are you aware of anyone with a grudge against you? Someone who might get at you through William?"

It sounded so brutal that gall filled Andrew's throat. He took a sip of coffee. "One cannot escape upsetting a few people on one's journey through life. And I can't dismiss the possibility that it might be connected to Winslow's murder. But why William?"

Castlereagh raised his eyebrows. "If Winslow's death has something to do with the discontent stirred up by the Vienna Congress, it's unlikely they'd travel to Oxfordshire with the intention of killing your son. They'd murder the other delegates, or I'm afraid, they'd assassinate you. That's why we must watch our backs."

Andrew eyed his paranoid friend sympathetically. "I must depart for the country, I have guests who regard me as a poor host."

"The baroness?"

Andrew nodded.

"If she loves you, she will understand."

Andrew ran a hand through his hair. "I'm not sure she does love me."

"Really?" A smile toyed with Castlereagh's lips. "Most women fall at your feet in a dead faint."

Andrew cocked a brow. "And you used to scoop them up."

The Irishman's brief smile reminded Andrew of how rarely he saw it. "You've a shooting party planned. Is it to go ahead?"

"The birds have been allowed to breed for several seasons. They need culling." He frowned. "I may delay it until next month. Hopefully this matter will then be dealt with."

"Might be wise. It's a perfect time for them to make another attempt. And this time you could be the target."

Andrew nodded. "I'd rather it was me. That I can handle." He consulted his watch and put down his coffee cup. "Now I really must go, if I'm to arrive back before midnight."

"You're traveling the roads after dark. It will make you an easy target," Castlereagh said. "Why don't you stay tonight for the Carlton House dinner?"

Andrew shook his head. "I declined the king's invitation. I prefer to be in the country with my children."

"And the baroness," Castlereagh amended, eyeing him.

"That goes without saying."

"Who doesn't love you?"

"I didn't say that, precisely."

"Perhaps you aren't in love with her."

"Now you're going too far." With a shake of his head, Andrew rose to his feet.

Castlereagh stood and placed a hand on Andrew's shoulder. "It is only what your good friends will tell you."

"Mm. Sometimes friends can be the most annoying pests," Andrew said with a brief grin. They walked out of the club into the street where Andrew hailed a hackney. "Will we see you at Castlebridge if this business is quickly resolved and the shooting party goes ahead?"

Castlereagh sighed. "I will if I'm in the mood for company, but thank you, my friend. I hope you discover who is responsible for this disturbing business." He started off down the street. "Take very good care, duke," he called back and patted his coat and the two flintlocks he was never without. "Stay armed."

Within the hour, Andrew was in his coach on the road to Oxford. He wouldn't reach Castlebridge until well after dark. Never happy while traveling in an enclosed vehicle, he leaned back against the squabs and closed his eyes as Castlereagh's words, designed to provoke this very reaction, made him question his future. If Greta married him, was he capable of offering her enough of himself? After Catherine, he doubted he'd fall in love again. The deep well of sadness he carried in his heart would be difficult for any woman to overcome. He folded his arms. Perhaps Greta wouldn't care.

What did Greta feel for him? It was useless to speculate at this early stage of their relationship. But there was attraction, and some measure of affection between him and Greta. He didn't wish for more, did he? Greta was a social butterfly. If her social life was vibrant and the marriage bed satisfying, she would be content. He pursed his lips. He might be doing her a great disservice. She might want his love.

Chapter Eleven

F ORCED TO REMAIN indoors, the day seemed interminably long. Jenny had given up on lessons and instead chose the children's favorite pastimes to distract them. After they played a board game, she'd suggested reading "The Tortoise and The Hare," but they demanded one of hers. She made up a story about Heggie, the baby hedgehog one of her sister, Beth's stray animals, which even William enjoyed. The puppet show employing hand puppets she made from sewing button eyes onto old stockings held their interest for a time, but soon they became tired and restless.

After luncheon, Jenny decided the best course would be for them to have an afternoon nap. Barbara began to fret and was constantly distracted by the kitten, and William was close to falling asleep, but he repeatedly asked Jenny when his father would come home.

"I'm too old for naps," William protested as she settled him in bed. She handed him a book, but he only read one page before falling asleep.

Quiet descended. Still tense and worried by the frightening experience of the previous evening, Jenny opened her sewing-box, then sat in a chair and hemmed a shift. Did the staff suspect her of making up stories merely to see the duke? She'd had to distract William when he had noticed her breakfast had not been served. Her luncheon, however, arrived on time. So perhaps it would not happen again. If it was a comment on her conduct, she imaged it wouldn't be the last of it, because she was determined not to let another night pass without informing His Grace of the terrifying episode on the roof. She would not trust Forrester to tell him, for he could not have learned the whole of it from Mrs. Pollitt.

George stood guard at the nursery door, and as soon as the duke's coach arrived, no matter what the hour, she would speak to His Grace before he retired to his apartments.

After the children woke, the rest of the afternoon dragged on into the rose and purple light of evening. Jenny stood at the nursery window, her gaze caught by the golden ribbon of driveway lit by flickering braziers.

It approached midnight when the duke's coach, pulled by six handsome dappled grays, drew up before the front entrance.

Jenny cast a quick glance in the mirror and tucked a stray curl behind her ear. She looked tired and pale but her determination to seek help for the children did not falter. It was worth all the condemnation of the staff, and possibly the duke's anger to approach him at this hour. In the corridor, George rose from the chair to greet her. "His Grace has arrived, George. I'll go down to speak to him. I don't expect it will take very long."

"You do what you have to. I'll be here, Miss Harrismith." As she approached the stairs, George sat again, folded his arms, and leaned back.

Much of a footman's life required great patience, Jenny thought sympathetically, as she darted downstairs. For such strong, active young men that could not be easy. She began to form her thoughts into a cohesive description of what had happened to William, aware she needed to grab the duke's attention, when he would be tired from his journey.

Jenny considered it best to use the great staircase. She hoped she wouldn't meet any of the servants at this time of night. It was a foolish hope, for below in the entry hall, the butler, who would normally have retired by this hour, and a footman, stood with the duke. Her hand tightened on the banister as she descended. Forrester conversed with His Grace as he divested himself of his hat and greatcoat into the footman's arms.

The duke looked up and saw her, and his brow furrowed. He said something to the butler who in turn glanced up, then His Grace strode across the vast echoing marble floor. When she reached the bottom step, he held out a hand to assist her down.

His serious blue eyes surveyed her, his eyebrows raised. "Miss Harrismith?"

"Your Grace, I must speak to you." She took his large gloved hand in hers and stood before him, swallowing nervously. Her anxiety came more from the upsetting news she must tell him than the man. He exuded a kind of strength and power which she welcomed.

In fact, after the dreadful happenings of last night, she would dearly love to step into his arms and rest her head on his broad chest. The thought startled her, and she gazed up at him anxiously. His expression was hard to read. Concern, and something else, indefinable.

"What is it you wish to speak to me about, Miss Harrismith?"

Aware she'd become tongue tied, she glanced at the butler, whose stiff stance and frowning countenance conveyed outrage. "Might we talk…"

"Come to the library." The duke turned. "Go to bed, Forrester." He strode with her down the hall.

The footman preceded them and lit the candles. "Do you wish me to light a fire, Your Grace?"

"No need Jeremy." He turned to her. "I apologize for the cold room, but I don't anticipate this will take long, Miss Harrismith." He eyed her carefully as he smoothed a hand over his hair. "Who is with the children?"

"The footman, George."

He nodded. "Sit please, Miss Harrismith. This must be important, but before you tell me, I believe a drink is in order. What will you have?" He walked over to the drink's table. "Brandy? Or I can send for coffee?"

"Brandy, thank you." Jenny had never so much as tasted it in her life, but right now, she felt a definite need of it.

He nodded approvingly. "Good choice. I always find coffee disturbs one's sleep." He poured two glasses and walked over to hand her one. He sat on the chair on the other side of the fireplace. "Now, what must you tell me at this ungodly hour of night?"

Jenny held the balloon glass in both hands and took a hurried gulp. The brandy lit a fire in her throat and brought on a coughing fit.

"It's generally wise to sip it, Miss Harrismith." A slight smile tugged his lips.

"Your Grace." Jenny breathed deeply. When more confident of her voice, she launched into a hurried description of the episode at the tower from the beginning when she'd woken to find William gone.

He sat forward frowning and fired off a question. "Why did you assume William would go up to the tower? He might have gone downstairs."

"I wasn't sure, but if he'd gone downstairs, he would soon return. I couldn't take that chance."

He nodded. "Go on."

At the point where she and William regained the nursery to find George with Barbara, she paused for breath.

"Good God," he murmured, shaking his head. Obviously shocked, he rose to his feet, and stalked around the room. Then, retracing his steps, placed his glass on the table beside hers and stood looking down at her. "Is William quite sure he saw someone?"

"He is not entirely convinced. As I followed close behind him, I would have come across them, surely."

"Not necessarily," he said heavily. "There are secret passages all throughout this old house, Miss Harrismith. One on that floor leads down to the garden. As a child, I used it often." He frowned. "But I gave orders for it to be boarded up years ago after my son was born."

"Your Grace, I don't want to dramatize what could be a simple matter of the cat escaping, but coming after the episode in the wood…" Her throat was still horribly dry, so she took another deep sip of brandy which made her cough again. She wasn't getting any better at drinking it, but the liquor did add a warm glow to the spot where a cold chill lodged in her chest. "And I'm now unsure if it was Nanny Evans who left the candle burning and set the curtains on fire. I wondered at the time why the candle hadn't burned down to a stub." She searched his concerned face. "I hope I am right to have come to tell you delay."

"You did right, Miss Harrismith. I can hardly ignore the distinct possibility that someone has made three attempts to harm my son," he said. "If there's a villain's hand at work, then thank God you were there to thwart the attempts." He stood. "Come. I need to see my children."

They reached the top of the stairs. In the corridor outside the nursery, George rocked gently on his chair.

The duke raised his eyebrows, blue eyes incredulous. "You gave George a chair, Miss Harrismith?"

"He will be more alert if he's rested." Jenny didn't wish to point out the long hours the poor footman had remained at his post.

"Unless he's made too comfortable," the duke murmured. "Perhaps a nice warm shawl?"

At their approach, George jumped to his feet and bowed. "Your Grace."

"Keep alert, George, with a primed flintlock. Expect trouble. Jeremy will relieve you shortly," the duke said. "It will be the routine from now on. Forrester will be informed."

"Yes, Your Grace." George leapt forward to open the nursery door. The duke motioned Jenny inside and followed her.

In the dim light of the argand lamp Jenny now used instead of candles, both children slept deeply. William was curled up as if he suffered from bad dreams. Barbara lay on her back with the kitten stretched out beside her.

The duke stared down at William. He bent and gently eased back a lock of hair from the boy's brow. William stirred, and half opened his eyes. "Father?"

"It's all right now, William, go back to sleep. I'm here."

William murmured something indecipherable and rolled over.

The duke moved to Barbara's bed. The kitten raised its head and stared at him. It opened its pink mouth and yawned, stretched, and closed its eyes. The duke pulled the blanket up to cover his daughter's shoulder.

"Now, Miss Harrismith," he said, turning toward her. In the poor light, his eyes looked strained. "What shall we do?"

The duke didn't require an answer, and she couldn't have given him one. He approved of the arrangement she'd made with the footman, and he knew she was here for the children. That didn't need to be repeated. After a moment, he walked over to the door. He turned, a hand on the latch and searched her face. "I am asking a lot of you, Miss Harrismith."

"I'm up to the task, Your Grace," she said, more briskly than she felt.

He nodded. "I'm impressed by your courage, but this must not rest on your shoulders. While I get to the bottom of it, an armed footman will remain outside the nursery at night, and the schoolroom by day. Keep to your routine, but always with a footman to protect you. I will ride with William." He sighed heavily. "If anything bothers you, you are to come to me. No matter how insignificant you might consider it, or whatever time it is."

"Yes, Your Grace."

His gaze searched hers. "It's late. You must be tired. Good night, Miss Harrismith."

After the duke left, Jenny nodded to George, entered the nursery, and locked the door behind her. William propped himself up on his elbows. "Is Father angry with me for following the cat, Jenny?"

"No, William. He loves you and your sister very much."

She knew this to be true.

William lay down and closed his eyes. He was soon asleep.

In her bedchamber, she undressed and washed in cold water from the jug. She climbed in between the chilly sheets and rested her head on her arm, too harried for sleep. The duke was a man of deep emotions. A wounded soul. And now this! Why would anyone want to hurt him and his family? Could they have entered the house through some secret passage the duke had talked of? The thought that danger lurked behind the walls terrified her. She shuddered and pulled the bedclothes close.

MISS HARRISMITH'S EARNEST, worried face stayed with him as he made his way to the floor below and crossed to the north wing and his apartments. This situation was intolerable! Should he pack William off to his aunt in Northumberland? Trouble was, he disliked removing the boy from under his eye. Not knowing if he was safe. That he might be followed there. No, William would be safer at Castlebridge.

He reached the central hallway where the staircase swept down to the lower floor and found Greta waiting for him. Obviously angry, she approached him frowning, her hands on her hips.

"So it is the governess, Harrow? You hear such tales often enough. But I would have thought such behavior beneath you. It does make me understand why I've seen so little of you since I came here."

Andrew disliked being waylaid and accused unjustly, but an inexplicable stab of guilt made him snap. "You are eager to leap to the worst possible conclusion, Greta. And I am in no mood to deal with your temper. I may be lacking in my attentions to you, but if you remember, your behavior has hardly encouraged more from me."

She narrowed her light blue eyes. "I will not play second fiddle to..."

Before they were overheard, he grabbed her hand, flung open his sitting room door and drew her inside. "I was visiting my children."

"While they are asleep?" she mocked.

He gestured to a chair. "Someone is trying to hurt William."

She sat silently as he spoke of the three attempts on his son's life, designed apparently to look like an accident. "And they would have succeeded, if Miss Harrismith had not been there."

"I suspect the governess has exaggerated these incidents. After all, each one has a logical explanation. A wayward hunter's bullet? An inefficient nanny? A lost cat? This woman is cunning, she plans to snare you."

"Snare me? Ridiculous! You'll have to explain why you suspect that, Greta. But I don't know if I want to hear it." He had not expected her to be so cold.

"Miss Harrismith is a lord's daughter, is she not? There are dozens of young women like her, advancing on the Season every year with the aim of snaring a duke."

"You sound as if I'm besieged by young debutantes. I am not. And Miss Harrismith is not one."

"If you spent more time in England, you would be. I promise you their mamas are very aware that you are no longer married. None of those young fresh-faced ladies will find themselves actually living in a duke's house. What an opportunity! Miss Harrismith will keep coming up with reasons to turn to you for help. Next, we shall find her fainting in your arms." She raised her eyebrows. "You must have noticed that she's quite comely."

"She is here to care for my children. Her appearance has nothing to do with it."

"No? Perhaps not. But you will come to realize that I am right about her."

"This is nonsense, Greta. I don't intend to trivialize these attacks on my son. Please be patient as there's another matter of great import in London which may require my attention. When I see my way clear…"

"Then come back to London, with me."

He eyed her dismayed. "You would ask me to abandon my son for a few days of pleasure?"

"You are a duke, you can hire an army to mind him."

Impossible to make her understand. She wasn't a mother. He perched on the arm of her chair. "I am sorry for neglecting you. Fortunately, you have my cousin and your brother for company."

"Ivo has gone to Oxford for a few days."

"Good."

She tilted her head. "You don't like my brother much, do you?"

Andrew shrugged. "He's an insolent young buck."

"I admit he can be. But when you get to know him, you'll see the good in him. Our father was autocratic, and Ivo's life has not been easy."

"Neither was yours. Married to an old man at seventeen."

She shrugged. "I have nothing against Franz. The baron left me a comfortable fortune." She reached up and pulled Andrew down to kiss her. "Might we put this argument behind us and end the evening in a much more pleasing manner?"

She was inviting him into bed. He hesitated too long, aware he'd fail to do justice to their first time together. A murderous rage still consumed him, and all he could think of was his children's safety.

Greta released him and hastened to repair an awkward moment. "You are tired, after traveling to London and back, and now the silly governess waylaying you with this nonsense. Don't be tempted by Miss Harrismith or there will be a babe for you to deal with."

He caught his breath. Not only was it a cold calculating thing to suggest, it appeared she thought him capable of it. Disgust and disappointment rendered him silent.

She withdrew her hand from his and rose. "We'll talk again at breakfast."

"I'll see you to your bedchamber, Greta."

She shook her head. "No need. I know my way."

Greta's exotic perfume lingered after she left the room, but now he realized it had a cloying sweetness. She'd been toying with him. When they played whist she chose Raymond for her partner and lavished attention on him. How different it had been in Vienna; that elaborate, elegant world had suited her. They'd laughed, drunk champagne, and waltzed, and enjoyed the witty repartee of good company. Whilst here, she seemed out of place.

His mind returned to William. If it were Andrew they targeted, he would meet them square on and deal with it, but his vulnerable and brave little son? His stomach roiled. He'd get to the bottom of this, but right now he needed help, not an army as Greta had suggested, but someone adept at handling such situations.

Andrew's valet awaited him in his dressing room. Burton knew better than to make idle conversation while he attended to Andrew's clothes. He wished him good night and took himself off after Andrew distractedly dismissed him.

Andrew washed, cleaned his teeth, and climbed into bed. Rigid with an odd kind of leaden exhaustion, he lay down and forced his thoughts into some kind of order. Where to begin?

Check that passage in the nursery wing and make sure it was secure. He'd see to it himself this time. Employ a Bow Street Runner? No. That could prove awkward. If this had something to do with the Vienna Convention, however unlikely Castlereagh considered it, it must remain secret. Forrester must be made aware of the situation. He would know if any new staff had been employed in the last month. Beyond that… he ran a hand over his tired eyes; he had never felt so exposed, so helpless.

A thought came to him bringing him upright. "Strathairn!" His friend, the marquess, was the best man in all England to deal with this. He would write to him tomorrow.

Having found a possible solution, his tight muscles eased a little, and he allowed his thoughts to dwell on Miss Harrismith, whom he'd come to admire. She seemed mature beyond her years. It was in her manner, he decided, the way she held herself when many young women would be reduced to hysterics facing a situation such as this. So brave and resourceful, but her determined little chin had wobbled when she described the terrifying scene on the roof. If she came between an assassin and William—and there was always a chance that she might—she too would be in very real danger. A sudden chill ran through him.

He considered again the possibility of sending the children away to his aunt, however his austere aunt was unlikely to accept such a young woman into her household. Another excellent position would have to be found for Miss Harrismith. Not only did the idea seem flawed, because he would lose control of the situation, the depth of his dismay surprised him. Not only would the children lose their beloved governess, his brief moments with Miss Harrismith, when he was more like himself than at any other time, would be lost. He couldn't deny that the thought of not having her here at Castlebridge left him feeling decidedly empty.

He rearranged the pillow and turned over, finding sleep eluded him. Greta's accusation, however outrageous, held a modicum of truth, which didn't reflect well on him. From his experience, a woman's instincts were often proved right. They went to the core of the matter while a man sought to apply reason. What the devil was he to do? Nothing, he decided. Right now, William must remain uppermost in his thoughts.

Chapter Twelve

T HE NEXT MORNING, Jenny's breakfast was late again. The tray
didn't arrive until well past eleven when lessons had begun. The
food was cold the porridge congealed and smelling faintly sour. She
quickly replaced the cover over the dish. "Do you know, I'm not really
hungry," she said hurriedly, because William, smart boy that he was,
had leaned forward to inspect the food on her plate. "It's just as well, I
have put on a little weight."

The door opened, and His Grace strolled in.

"Father!" Barbara darted off her chair and ran to him. "Carrot was
so funny this morning. He got milk all over his whiskers."

The duke placed a large gentle hand on her head. "Did he, sweetheart?"

"Did Jenny tell you about how I climbed onto the tower roof and
rescued the cat, Father?" William stood tall but still looked pale and
tired.

"Miss Harrismith did, William. You are pluck to the backbone.
And very resourceful."

William went pink with pleasure. "I thought I saw someone in the
corridor. But Miss Harrismith thinks I must have been mistaken."

"Shadows can trick you, my boy. The way they sway about. It's a
reflection of the trees in the moonlight. Nevertheless, you did a
splendid job rescuing the kitten." The duke drew up one of the small
chairs and joined them at the table. "Let's see what you are up to."

Barbara giggled. "You look like a giant, Father."

He laughed. As he looked through William's workbooks praising him on his arithmetic, Jenny swept the offending breakfast tray away onto a small console table.

"What is that?" His Grace's sharp gaze missed little.

"Jenny's not eating breakfast," William said. "She thinks she's too fat. Jenny's not fat, is she, Father?"

"Not in the least." The duke untangled himself from the chair. He walked over to where Jenny stood blocking the tray. "Let me see."

She shook her head. "It really isn't necessary, Your Grace."

He raised a dark eyebrow. "You would refuse me?"

"I..." She met his questioning gaze and swallowed. "It's just my breakfast."

"At this hour?"

He put a gentle hand on her arm and moved her aside. When he lifted the cover a heavy frown creased his forehead. "When was this brought up?"

Jenny opened her mouth and then closed it again.

"It just arrived." William came over for a closer look. "Ugh, it looks all dried up."

Barbara pushed her way in past William. "Carrot might eat it."

His Grace turned to her, a spark of anger in his eyes. "I would like to speak to you in the corridor, Miss Harrismith."

"You're not angry with Jenny, are you, Father?" William asked.

His father ruffled his hair. "Certainly not, William. Go back to your books. We shan't be long."

The duke strode to the door opened it and stood waiting.

Jenny hurriedly complied. Outside, George's replacement, red-haired Jeremy, had left his chair. He bowed.

"Go for a walk for five minutes, Jeremy."

Once Jeremy had moved out of earshot, the duke turned to her. "My son now calls you Jenny."

Her heart sank. "It happened while on the roof, Your Grace," she said vexed that he'd noticed before she could address the matter. "I didn't have the heart to dissuade him so soon after the terrible shock he's had, but if you feel I should." She hurried on. "Although, I'd prefer to wait until he's a little more…"

He held up a hand to stop her. "If he takes comfort in it, I have no objection." He paused. "Has this business with your meal occurred before?"

"It really isn't important, Your Grace."

He folded his arms and frowned at her. "Do you ever answer a question in a direct manner, Miss Harrismith?"

Jenny sighed. "I am sure they will tire of it."

"I am not about to wait for them to tire of it," he growled. "Rest assured, it will not happen again."

"If I just ignore it…" Jenny rather feared that the duke's interference would make things worse. She'd scandalized them, she supposed, waiting to meet him in the middle of the night. But it would be a brave servant indeed who disobeyed him.

He waved a dismissive hand. The matter was not up for debate. "I had considered sending the children to their aunt until this matter is resolved," he said, almost to himself.

Jenny's heart began an odd thrumming. She would have to seek a new position, and worse, she would never see the children again. She studied his handsome profile as her fingers found her brooch. Was it only the children? Or the duke himself? And she considered herself sensible! At the flash of inexplicable loneliness she tightened her lips on a sigh.

"Of course, I would ensure you found a position comparable to this one," he said, guessing her thoughts.

"If you think it's best, Your Grace," she murmured, hating the idea.

"I've decided not to at this point. That is, if you wish to remain here with us? Under the circumstances I would understand if you do not."

"But I do. Very much."

"I am about to employ a guard to watch over you and the children until this business is at an end. Until then, don't go anywhere without the footman."

"William is used to visiting the stables alone. I shall have to tell him something."

"That he is to be William's new riding instructor. You have an argand lamp in the nursery. Light it and bring it to me."

In the nursery, Jenny picked up the tinderbox and lit the lamp, wondering why he needed a lamp in broad daylight. When she returned, the duke beckoned to the footman who hovered several yards away. He ordered Jeremy into the schoolroom and told him to remain with the children until they returned.

She watched the duke carry the lamp along the corridor toward the steps leading to the tower. He turned to her. "Come with me, Miss Harrismith."

Jenny hurried after him. A hundred paces farther along the lengthy corridor, he stood before a huge wall tapestry depicting the scene of a boar hunt. He moved it aside and pressed a panel in the oak wainscoting. Startled, she watched as the panel slid aside with a thud, to reveal aged, wooden steps wreathed in cobwebs winding downward. A dusty stuffy smell wafted out.

"I need to make sure the outer door is safely bolted." He turned to her. "You might wish to remain here. It's not a place ladies would care to enter, would you say, Miss Harrismith? His eyes gently mocked her. Annoyed at his inference, she leaned forward and gazed inside. It was horribly claustrophobic, and there could be rats. But she was curious, and she wasn't about to refuse a blatant dare.

"I should like to see where it leads, Your Grace."

A light sparked in his eyes. "Well? Come on then. Better for me to go first."

She edged forward behind him, calling His Grace's bluff, if that's what he'd intended, and entered the narrow staircase. It smelled of centuries of dirt, mice droppings, and worse. The duke, who barely had enough headroom, had already turned a corner, and disliking the idea of being left behind, she darted down after him. If mention of this should reach the kitchens, she would starve to death. Fortunately the footman was in with the children, and there was no one to witness it.

The creaking stairs led them down in a dizzying spiral, the duke negotiating them at speed, the lamp held high, throwing eerie shadows in his wake. "These were used for a stealthy escape during the Civil War," he said, his voice sounding hollow. "There was a bridge over the old moat not far from the stables which enabled them to ride away before they were discovered."

The narrow stairway was every bit as unpleasant as she'd anticipated. The weight of the solid old house seemed to crush in upon her. A cobweb stirred by the draft blew across her face and tangled in her hair. She emitted a small squeak of horror.

He turned and held the lantern up. "Are you all right?"

"A spider," she muttered breathlessly her hands raking through her hair, loosening hairpins.

He observed her with a grin. "The spiders are long gone."

"How can you be sure?" she asked with a shudder.

"Have you seen one?"

"I'm trying not to look."

Was that a chuckle? Annoying man.

"I thought you were made of sterner stuff, Miss Harrismith," he commented as he continued down.

"Everything except spiders, Your Grace." Which wasn't the exact truth. Spiders and dukes.

"Keep up."

She swallowed an impudent reply and closed the gap between them as he negotiated the narrow slippery steps with ease.

Finally they reached the bottom, and stopped before a solid wood and iron door with a big rusty ring latch, the heavy bolt at the top drawn back. Boards which had been nailed across to block access were cast aside on the stone floor.

"What in the world...!" The duke's bantering tone was gone. He crouched down and examined the boards, then rose to drag the door open. Stepping outside, he turned to hold the door open for her to pass through it. Jenny was only too pleased to leave the oppressive place, made worse by their discovery. The possibility that a dangerous person had orchestrated the attack on William came closer to reality. She could sense the duke's distress as she stood on the grass and gratefully dragged in deep breaths of fresh air.

"I'll have it repaired immediately, Miss Harrismith," he said not looking at her. "And I'll find out who is behind it."

Jenny had no answer. Her heartbeat was still uncomfortably fast. She looked around to get her bearings.

"Where are we, Your Grace?"

"This is the western side of Castlebridge, the moat would have been beneath our feet," he said.

They were quite alone and not overlooked by any windows unless someone peered down at them from the tower. From this angle, the door looked insignificant, its entrance shielded by a lilac tree and a high privet hedge. The stables were visible beyond the grove of limes which bordered the carriageway.

She attempted to order her hair, stabbing pins into her scalp. Had someone used those stairs with the intention to harm William? And opened the nursery door while they slept? A shudder raced through her.

"If someone came up that way they must be familiar with this house," she said trying to banish the apprehension from her voice. "And they would know about the kitten."

She hadn't fooled him. He turned to look at her. "I've frightened you," he said after a moment. "You must leave this to me, Miss Harrismith. Rest assured, you and the children will not be exposed to any more danger. I'll send a carpenter to board up the door. And this time he'll make a thorough job of it."

"Are there any other passages, Your Grace?"

"There are. But none on that floor. You should return to the schoolroom. It might be prudent for you to pick some flowers before you go back inside. Your absence could be noticed." He paused, and his angry blue eyes met hers. "White lilies seem to be a favorite of yours."

"Not especially, Your Grace," she said suffering a need to defend herself. "The one I picked was half broken off. Actually, it was the only lily left in the bed. The rest were just bare stalks."

His eyes turned to slate, and a muscle flickered in his rigid jaw. "No need to explain. I am not about to refuse you a few flowers. Bring the children to the salon at three o'clock. It's close to luncheon. You missed breakfast and must be hungry."

And with that, carrying the lantern, he strode away.

Jenny watched him pause to stare up at the tower high above them. He squared his shoulders and walked on as if whatever decisions he needed to make had been decided on. She was confident the duke would deal with this. That he would find this person. She had never known anyone like him. Perhaps only dukes had that degree of self-confidence. It made her feel a good deal better to place her trust in him and get on with her duties. She was sure the villain, for surely there was one, would be caught. His Grace was not a man to be trifled with.

ANDREW SOUGHT THE head gardener before returning to the house. He found him digging in the kitchen garden, stirring up earthy smells blended with sage and rosemary.

"Your Grace?" Startled, he whipped off his hat and dug his spade into the earth before bowing.

"Good day, Wilkins. Looks like rain doesn't it?"

"Might be just a shower, Your Grace. But I hope to get these beds finished before the weather turns."

"The white lilies in the garden near the library. Why were they cut?"

"Ah." Wilkins scratched his head. "Those were for the housekeeper. Mrs. Pollitt wanted to add 'em to an arrangement for the reception rooms, Your Grace. We are saving the hothouse flowers for the weekend party."

"Good." Andrew nodded, aware the man was nonplussed to find

him wandering among the vegetables holding a lantern and asking inane questions. If things weren't so grave, he might laugh at it. Perhaps Miss Harrismith would find it amusing too. "I won't keep you, the wind is picking up."

He sent the lantern back to the nursery and gave instructions for the carpenter to block up the door. Then he requested the housekeeper come to the library.

"When I visited the schoolroom, I took note of the governess' breakfast," he said when she stood before him. "Are you aware that Miss Harrismith's meal was not delivered at the proper time?"

Mrs. Pollitt flinched, and her gaze slid away. "It was regrettable, Your Grace. The kitchens were kept busy with the guests."

It was enough to tell him that she was quite aware of it. It had been a deliberate act designed to teach the governess some kind of lesson. Why? To keep her in her place? Because she had sought him out on several occasions? Anger shook him, and he glanced down at the papers on his desk to gain control, aware that any action on his part could make matters worse. "We have three guests, Mrs. Pollitt, I find myself in fear of what might occur when we have fifty," he said mildly. "I'm relying on you to make sure it doesn't happen again."

She firmed her lips. "It won't, Your Grace."

"I am glad to hear it. You may go."

She curtsied and hurried from the room.

Andrew rose. Luncheon was about to be served in the dining room. He had yet to see Greta today. She was unhappy with him, and somewhat to his surprise he suffered no urgent need to smooth things over. She'd displayed a regrettable lack of sympathy when he'd expressed concern for his son's safety, and her insinuation that he might consider bedding the governess left him wondering if he really knew her. She obviously didn't know him. Why had she drawn such a long bow? Had his behavior concerning Miss Harrismith stirred Greta's feminine instincts? He could explain that he'd come to rely on the governess, but that would only make matters worse.

And then there was Greta's brother. Had he returned from Oxford? It would be good to know what he'd been up to there, but it was pointless to ask him. Ivo would tell him what he chose to, shifty individual that he was. Could he have returned late last night and used the stairway? Or was his concern for his children making him chase after shadows?

Worry was causing him to behave unlike himself. To invite Miss Harrismith to join him in that stairway was not only rash, the impulse bordered on the irrational, and decidedly reckless if anyone should get wind of it.

Even worse than that, when he questioned his actions, his thoughts skidded away. Foolish to feel somehow lighter in her calm presence. She handled everything dealt her with surprising composure for someone so young. Except when confronted with spiders.

He smiled in spite of himself. Ridiculous to think of the young governess as his comrade-in-arms, and yet he did, because there was no one else he could turn to. It hurt to admit Raymond must be considered a suspect, but he had been behaving differently since he came. Might he wish to step into Andrew's shoes and win Greta? Saddened by his suspicion of his cousin of whom he was fond, he shook his head. Irrational, no doubt about it.

A footman was sent to York to deliver a message to John Haldane, Marquess of Strathairn, at his estate, where he would be in residence now that parliament was in recess. He knew that Strathairn spent all his spare time there tending to his horses. Andrew hoped for a swift reply, with either an offer of assistance or some expert advice. Until then, he would personally keep an eye on his children.

The most important thing was to have Bishop write to the guests and advice the shoot had been postponed.

Chapter Thirteen

J ENNY RETURNED TO the house cradling a large bunch of yellow irises the gardener had kindly cut for her. She greeted Jeremy at the schoolroom door and entered to find the children sitting at the table with Mary. William his head lowered over his book, was busy drawing, while Barbara and the cat played with a ball of wool Nanny had left behind.

As Jenny put the flowers in water, their luncheon arrived. A lamb pie, vegetables in season, bread and jam, and tea for her, a treacle pudding, and milk for the children. She ate the tasty food with good appetite, while Barbara told them one of her rambling stories about a barn owl they'd seen on their walk the previous week who had lost his hat. William laughed and asked what kind of hat it was and where did he lose it. This led to a lengthy discussion peppered with his sister's giggles.

Despite the distressing incidents of the last couple of days, William appeared in good spirits, having convinced himself that Carrot escaped by accident and there was nothing in the corridor except shadows on the wall.

After luncheon, a footman took Barbara for her dance class while William had violin instruction in the music room. It left Jenny free to plan further lessons. A book open before her and her pen poised over her notes, she stared out the window at the gray-blue expanse of sky dotted with small dark clouds like smoke from a giant's pipe. It had been an extraordinary few days. Especially this morning.

She rubbed her arms recalling the horrid cobwebbed staircase, the sour air, and His Grace, agile for a big man, his long legs carrying him speedily down, as if to tackle the culprit at the bottom. The lantern light gleamed on his thick dark hair. Then the discovery of the barricade ripped from the door and cast aside. His blue eyes filled with rage.

The children were to have a guard accompanying them everywhere they went. Although relieved, she couldn't help sighing. Would the peaceful existence they'd once enjoyed ever return? She shivered at the thought that he might easily have carried out his wicked plan in the nursery while they slept.

Jenny considered each incident in turn: first the gunshot, then the fire, and Carrot's miraculous escape through the closed nursery door. Each of them could have been intended to appear like an accident. Who would benefit by William's death? She started. Mary had told her that the duke's cousin, Mr. Forsythe, was next in line to inherit the dukedom after William. Would the duke suspect his own flesh and blood? She rubbed her arms, suddenly chilled. It would be wise to keep the children from being alone with him.

At three o'clock, she took the children to the salon where they were to take tea with their father. Baroness Elsenberg and Herr Von Bremen were seated with the duke when she ushered the children inside.

"Thank you, Miss Harrismith," His Grace said, as she settled the children on the pale gold damask sofa. "They'll be returned to the schoolroom at half past four."

The baroness gave Jenny another of her hard stares, and Von Bremen offered his brazen smile. Jenny curtsied and left the room.

With the need for fresh air and exercise, the notion of a bird's eye view of the duke's estate appealed to her. Jenny set out along the path toward the distant hill the German had claimed to have climbed. She had conquered her irrational fears about being alone in the woods, aided by the knowledge that she'd left the unsettling Von Bremen in the salon.

It took her close to half an hour before she left the dense woodland and emerged into the fragile autumn sun. She kept the hill in view as she walked along a fence and crossed a style onto a wide pasture where a cluster of black-faced sheep cropped the grass. A small hut was nestled beside a chestnut tree. She gazed through a window, finding it empty. Most likely used for feed, and shelter in bad weather.

Jenny continued at a brisk pace until she came to the foot of the hill which towered above her. A rocky ridge half way up seemed the farthest one could climb, the rock face above it so steep even an experienced climber would find it difficult to scale without the proper equipment. She recalled the composed, elegantly dressed man who met her on the woodland path. Von Bremen hardly looked like he'd just indulged in a dangerous climb up a rocky escarpment. When they almost bumped into each other, and he sought to steady her, he carried no rope or pick with him. Might there be an easier way to climb the hill from the far side? It looked to be a long way around, and difficult to get to, with no obvious path through the brambles.

She consulted her watch. She would run out of time if she didn't start back, and would be late for the children.

ANDREW HAD FORCED himself to face his own shortcomings by the time he entered the salon. He smiled and came to take Greta's hand. Whatever doubts he now had about her as a possible wife, he admitted he'd been neglectful of her, and hardly the swain she'd come to expect, which prompted her outburst. He still held out a hope that on further acquaintance she might grow more comfortable with his children on further acquaintance. He'd thought at first they made her nervous, but now the suspicion arose that she was not particularly interested in them. But perhaps in time she would come to know and love them, especially if she had a babe of her own.

In their short time together, he and Catherine had produced two wonderful children. Catherine's constitution remained delicate after a childhood rheumatic illness, and the doctors warned her against childbirth, but she had been adamant. To Catherine, life without children wasn't worth living. After a long, troubled labor she gave birth to William, and they were so thrilled to have a healthy boy that when she'd begged for another, Andrew finally agreed. And then he had lost her.

After the children had joined them for tea, the atmosphere in the salon became less strained, mainly because, surprisingly, Ivo got on well with them. His artful mocking pose dropped away, and he conversed on their level, laughing at some silly nonsense with Barbara, and engaging with William in quite a knowledgeable discussion concerning Archduke Karl von Hapsburg who had established a stud farm for breeding his own Spanish horses near Lipizza in Italy. He promised to tell William more.

Andrew watched his son's animated face as he listened intently, interrupting occasionally to ask Ivo questions. It hadn't occurred to him until recently that he would want more children. Now faced with the possibility, he discovered he'd like at least two or three more. He broached the delicate subject with Greta in an undertone while the children were in conversation with Ivo.

"I have no desire to become a milch cow, Your Grace," she murmured, looking horrified.

Ivo turned from where he talked to William and coughed.

Greta glared at her brother. "A baby would be most pleasant," she said smiling at Andrew. "A good nursery staff allows one to continue life as before. But I have no intention of becoming one of those women who give birth to a dozen. What would that do to my figure? Husbands are often unreasonable. They wish for babies to fill their nursery, but do not want their wives to get fat. Or else they seek a woman's attention elsewhere. Fortunately, the baron had grown-up children and did not wish for more." Aware perhaps that her comments had fallen flat, she shrugged. "And giving birth can be dangerous."

Andrew smiled and nodded while he tried to deal with what he considered to be the final blow to their relationship. "It is a sad fact and happens far too often, Greta." He rose. "You will wish to change for dinner."

He held out his hand. "Come children."

"Your Grace!" Greta hurried after him to the door. "Might we have a quiet word?" She glanced back at Ivo who was scowling at her. "Alone?" Her blue eyes implored him. "We have hardly had a moment since I came here."

Before he could agree, a knock came at the door.

"There is someone to see you, Your Grace," Forrester said at his austere best. "I've put the, ah, gentleman in the anteroom."

"His name?"

"Irvine. Says the Marquess of Strathairn sent him."

"Good. Send him to the library, Forrester."

Andrew turned to Greta. "I'm sorry, I must see this fellow. Lord Strathairn has a racehorse of mine at his stud. He has sent his man to advise me on my stable."

She gave a huff of annoyance and turned away.

"Have either George or Jeremy return the children to the governess, Forrester."

"Very well, Your Grace."

Andrew strode away without a backward glance. He needed time to order his feelings before he spoke to Greta again. He feared they would not make a good fit.

In the library, a short, powerful looking man turned to greet him, hat in hand.

"Take a seat, Mr. Irvine."

Once they were seated, Andrew got right to the point. "I should like you to be my children's guardian until such time as I can be sure they are safe from a possible threat."

"If it pleases Your Grace." Irvine removed a bulky letter from his pocket and handed it to Andrew before seating himself.

Andrew sat and unfolded the pages.

Harrow, my dear friend, Strathairn wrote. *It troubled me greatly to hear of your concerns. I can't imagine anything more frightening than to have your child in danger. I shall be there for the shoot, but until then, I have sent Miles Irvine. He fought under Wellington and then worked for the Crown. He was by my side when we sought a very dangerous French foe intent on wreaking havoc on England. You would remember the attempted attack on King George–Prinny as he was then, at St. Paul's cathedral. I would happily place my life in his hands. Irvine was badly wounded during that mission and decided to give the game away and become an apothecary, but he likes to keep his hand in. He has agreed to do a short term of duty, at least until I arrive, and we can work together to see what's afoot. Please God, the matter will be dealt with quickly! I'm sure you'll find him satisfactory.*

You can count on all your friends, Andrew. I am quite sure that Fortescue and Montsimon would come to your aid at a moment's notice. Please let me know. We are here for you.

Andrew put the letter down, with a warm feeling of relief. He studied the man seated before him. "I am very glad to have you here, Mr. Irvine."

Irvine narrowed his dark eyes. "Nasty business, Your Grace. If you'll tell me what you wish of me, I'll get to it."

"My footmen will remain stationed outside the nursery and schoolroom doors. You are to ride with my son every day. He will be told you are here as his riding instructor and to assist with my horses. My stable master, Ben, will supply you with the stable books. Read them if you will. Then if my son should ask you any questions," he smiled briefly, "and I suspect he will, you will have a knowledge of the horses we have here, physical marks, breeding, performance, staying power, etc. And the gun room is at your disposal. The butler has the key."

Irvine patted his coat. "Carry my own, thank you, Your Grace."

"Good, a footman will take you to your lodgings. You will be introduced to the stable staff and eat with them. But first I'll explain exactly what has occurred and what else I wish you to do. You'll work directly with me."

Irvine widened his eyes. "You, Your Grace?"

"Yes. The butler and the governess are the only ones who know why you are here. For all intents and purposes that is to discuss the racing interests I have with Lord Strathairn, and the possible purchase of more bloodstock. That gives you access to the stables without any suspicion attached to your visits. Do not speak of this to anyone else. I gather I can trust your discretion?"

"You can. It will be my pleasure, Your Grace."

"Good man."

After giving Irvine an account of recent events, Andrew returned to his desk and took a page of bond from the drawer. He trimmed his pen, dipped it in the inkwell and began to reply to Strathairn's letter. He thanked him for his support, stated how he looked forward to seeing him, then requested another favor. Could he make inquiries about a German gentleman, Herr Ivo Von Bremen, who was staying at Castlebridge with his sister, Baroness Elsenberg, particularly in relation to any dissident groups known to be causing problems on the Continent.

He called for his secretary to send it off immediately.

Chapter Fourteen

WHEN THE CHILDREN returned to the schoolroom, Jenny asked them if they enjoyed their time with their father.

"Herr Von Bremen knows all about the Spanish horses in Italy," William said. "He has promised to tell me more about them."

"He was funny. But I don't like the baroness." Barbara glanced up as she dressed a doll in a new gown.

"You don't yet know Baroness Elsenberg," Jenny said. "In time…"

Barbara shook her head determinedly curls swinging. "Do you like her, William?"

William frowned. "Father does."

Barbara's worried gaze flew to Jenny's. "She's not going to be our new mother, is she, Jenny?"

"I don't know, poppet," Jenny said. "That is a matter for your father. Rest assured he will want you both to be happy with his choice."

Barbara firmed her lips. "I wish he would marry you, Jenny."

"Yes," William said. "I want that too."

"Don't be silly, children. I am a servant. Now, no more of this nonsense. After you've spent more time with the baroness, I'm sure you'll grow to like her." They both looked so unhappy, she searched for a distraction. "Shall we play Jackstraws before supper?"

"Yes!" William said.

"Get them please, Lord William," Jenny said. "Will you play with us, Lady Barbara?"

Barbara pouted. "William always wins."

"Yes he does. But let's try to beat him, shall we?"

With a grin, Barbara put down her doll.

William tipped the sticks out onto the table. They were soon absorbed in taking away each one in turn without moving the rest.

Jenny watched him, chuckling as he successfully removed another stick with nimble young fingers. She had not warmed to the baroness either, not that it was any of her business. It would sadden her to see the duke marry someone who took him away from his children. But she really should give the intelligent man some credit. Despite the baroness' beauty he would not act unwisely.

Barbara cried out as the pile collapsed at her attempt to remove a stick and William won again.

Jenny shook her head at the smug victor as she hugged the little girl. "Never mind, poppet, we shall try again soon!"

After the children had finished bathing, Jenny dressed them in their night attire. They sat by the nursery fire drinking hot chocolate while she read the German story about a young girl's favorite Christmas toy, the nutcracker which comes alive and, after defeating the evil Mouse King in battle, whisks her away to a magical kingdom populated by dolls. The duke had brought the English translation back with him, along with some other toys. The story proved popular with both William, who liked the battle scene, and Barbara, who was fascinated by the kingdom populated with dolls. She came to the end and closed the book.

At the suggestion of bed, William protested as he always did.

"You don't want to be tired tomorrow when riding with your new instructor," she said.

That worked like a charm. She tucked them both in and they soon fell into the restful sleep of the innocent.

Mary called through the door. When Jenny unlocked it, the maid came in carrying a copper jug of hot water which she added to the children's cooling bathwater. Jenny indulged in a bath whenever she could, but she would rather a tepid bath than ask the footmen to lug up buckets and be accused of rising above her station again. She just knew what the housekeeper would say about that. It proved to be the perfect solution for too often in the cold weather ablutions were merely a thorough wash with a flannel before darting beneath the covers.

The nursery settled into a peaceful silence broken only by the children's soft breaths. She let Mary go, promising to tidy things away when she'd finished. Jenny lay luxuriating in the warm water with a bar of plain soap. She longed for the scented variety her mother had favored, but added a little lavender water to the bath instead. She soaped her long hair and rinsed it, then climbed out and stood shivering by the nursery fire. With the towel wrapped around her, she knelt before the hearth to dry her hair.

Some moments later, a knock sounded on the nursery door. With a start, Jenny jumped up. Whipping off the towel, she hurried into her dressing gown, and pushed her feet into slippers. Was it Mary again? She always called out. The belt tied tightly Jenny stood listening at the door, concerned she would wake the children. "Is it you, George?" she whispered.

"I should like a word, Miss Harrismith, if I may."

The duke! Jenny flushed. She could hardly keep him waiting while she dressed. She tightened the dressing gown more securely around herself and unlocked the door.

The draft flattened the nursery candle and made the corridor sconces flicker. In the poor light, His Grace's shoulders looked tense. A shorter man, dressed plainly in brown stood at his elbow, with George waiting a few paces away.

"I regret having to disturb you at this late hour, Miss Harrismith," the duke said. "But I wanted to introduce you to our new guard, Mr. Irvine as he is to begin his duties first thing in the morning. Everyone, except you and Forrester believe he is here in connection with my stables."

"How do you do, Mr. Irvine." Jenny's worries eased slightly at the sight of the bulky, grim-faced gentleman. He appeared most competent, without saying a word.

"Pleased to meet you, Miss Harrismith," he said, a smile softening his rugged features.

"George will remain on duty this evening," His Grace said. "Mr. Irvine will ride with William while I give Barbara a riding lesson on her pony. Would you bring my daughter down to the stables at eleven?"

"Certainly, Your Grace."

Jenny was acutely aware she was naked beneath the robe. Her damp hair hung down to her waist. She flicked a curling lock back over her shoulder and resisted tightening her belt, her fingers curling nervously over the bow.

"I have caught you at a difficult time. I do apologize." He stepped back. "Tomorrow then." After a few words to George who would be relieved by Jeremy at midnight, both men departed.

Would the duke think her indolent to be in her nightclothes so early? Although it grew dark earlier as winter approached, the children had only just gone to sleep. She frowned and raised her chin. Well, her time was her own after all.

With a nod to George, Jenny retreated into the nursery and shut the door, smiling and light-hearted for the first time in days. She crept across the carpet to check on William. He slept soundly on his back, arms and legs flung out, as did Barbara, who lay with a small hand curled over the coverlet, Carrot beside her. Jenny tucked her in and went into her bedroom to douse the fire. The nights were growing colder, and although the schoolroom fire was lit during the daylight hours, she would never leave a fire burning in the nursery at night.

She removed her dressing gown, donned her nightgown, and shivering, climbed into bed wishing for the bedwarmer she had at home. Taking up the splendid novel by Miss Austen, she removed the bookmark and settled down to read by the argand lamp, but her thoughts kept returning to the duke. She wished she knew what he thought finding her in a state of undress, but with the candlelight behind him, his face was cast in shadow. She'd found no condemning note in his voice, however, as he informed her of the new arrangement then ushered Mr. Irvine away.

ANDREW PAUSED ON the stairs to advise Irvine of the direction he wished him to take when he rode with William. "My son will want to ride to the river. But I prefer he does not, for that was where the shot was fired. Take the bridle path to the west as far as the first fences. Do not allow him to cross the meadows to the river. He is to ride one of the smaller horses, the gray mare Lavender, is quite docile, although he may protest, he is keen to ride one of my hunters."

"Very well, Your Grace."

"Should I be unavailable, you can seek Forrester's advice. I don't intend the housekeeper, Mrs. Pollitt, or the staff to learn why you are here. For all intents and purposes, you are a new member of my stable staff. I prefer to keep it that way."

Andrew said goodnight to Irvine and made his way to the drawing room.

He found a game of faro had just finished. Greta glanced at him sharply. "You are joining us, Your Grace? One might ask what has kept you." She took up her wineglass and sipped her wine, her blue eyes suspicious.

"Forgive me. A matter with the staff," Andrew said refusing to be drawn.

Naturally, that failed to satisfy her. He knew what she was thinking, but as he was unable to dissuade her of it, and indeed had no desire to, especially in front of his cousin and her brother, he kept silent. He suspected anything he said to her now would fall on deaf ears. It was an uncomfortable business which he would soon have to deal with.

"You are just in time for the next hand," Raymond said.

Andrew eased his shoulders, discovering Irvine's appearance made him enormously relieved. As if a weight had been transferred from himself to Strathairn's man. He anticipated the sensation would be brief, for tomorrow, he would return to his constant state of vigilance. Tonight, he could relax in the knowledge that Miss Harrismith would remain alert. She had not unlocked the door without confirmation of who was on the other side of it, despite knowing George would be there.

"Right," he said, "if you are game, gentleman, let us continue. Raymond, you are banker. I shall now endeavor to remove a goodly amount of yours and Ivo's blunt." He smiled at Greta, but she looked away. She had come here on his invitation. It behooved of him as a gentleman to offer some explanation which wouldn't matter should it reach Ivo's ears. As he suspected everything did.

He poured himself another glass of claret from the drink's table and took his seat before the board. Greta perched on the sofa arm next to Raymond to watch.

Andrew's gaze flickered over her. She wore an exquisite evening gown the color of lilacs threaded with silver, with diamonds at her throat and ears, her pale hair dressed in an elaborate chignon by her French maid.

Although undeniably lovely, Greta failed to banish the image of the governess from Andrew's mind. He should have been repentant to have caught Miss Harrismith in dishabille, but found he wasn't. Not a bit of it. Her face had flushed becomingly in her rose pink dressing gown. She'd unwittingly offered him a brief glimpse of a slim lower leg and ankle; her masses of curly brown hair half dry down her back. Initially embarrassed, her relief to meet Irvine quickly banished any self-consciousness. It would not have occurred to her that she looked so appealing. He found the absence of artifice beguiling and accepted that he was beyond the pale.

He gave a deep regretful sigh, a little guilty about Greta, because of the direction of his thoughts. She'd accused him of fancying Miss Harrismith. And dammit, he did! He'd known such men who took their governesses to bed. Andrew had disparaged such behavior as the lowest of the low. And while it was only thoughts and not deeds, he still accepted what a hypocrite he'd become.

He laid down his chips centering them at the corners of four cards.

Raymond protested, and Ivo chuckled.

Greta kept silent and avoided eye contact. Andrew toyed with the stem of his wineglass. It proved to be an uncomfortable evening, and he did not look forward to the conversation between them which would likely follow. He couldn't blame her for being angry. Circumstances had disrupted their plans for spending an enjoyable time together, and while he was so worried about William, he could not make himself care. Upheaval sometimes revealed people in a more honest light.

He and Greta would not suit, of that he was now quite sure. He acknowledged he'd been different in Vienna when his life was a giddy round of social gatherings. A charming world ruled by etiquette and oftentimes a brittle gaiety. Laughter, noise, and color swirling beneath crystal chandeliers, while some momentous matters were argued over in an antechamber and others gambled away their fortunes in the adjoining room.

But this was what he was, a man who preferred the quiet and the freedom of the country to Town. Who wished to enjoy his children while they were young. They would not thrive in the polluted air of London. The man he was before Catherine died. And whom he wished to be again. Not the social animal Greta thought she knew. He wasn't about to change his mind, but he wished to handle the matter tactfully at the appropriate time.

As if she heard his thoughts, or sensed his cooling ardor, she leaned over and rested her hand on Raymond's shoulder and spoke to him in a seductively low voice.

When Raymond chuckled, and patted her hand, Ivo cast Andrew a measuring glance.

As the evening continued, Greta continued to flirt outrageously with his cousin and Raymond seemed under her spell. Ivo made several attempts to distract them but failed. It was Greta's way of gaining his attention, Andrew understood, and making him pay for his careless disregard of her, so he chose to ignore it. Trouble was Raymond had begun to take it far too seriously.

Chapter Fifteen

A FOOTMAN WAS soon to arrive to take William to the stables. The boy was so excited at the prospect of a new riding instructor, Jenny had to urge him to eat his breakfast.

"He'll let me canter, and maybe even gallop," he stated with great confidence as she did up his coat buttons.

She smoothed back his dark hair, so like his father's, and put on his hat. "Do you think so?" William had yet to meet the severe-looking Mr. Irvine.

"But I'd rather ride with you, Jenny," William added quickly.

"My, but you are going to be a charmer when you're grown, my lord," she said with a smile. "Even though I don't permit you to canter?"

"Well you did once, Jenny."

How could she forget that frightening day as they raced away through the woods?

Someone knocked. Three taps, a pause, and then one more. The secret signal she and the footmen had concocted between them.

"It's Jeremy." She opened the door. But it was Gerald, a footman who seldom ventured into this wing of the house. "I am here to take his lordship down, Miss Harrismith."

"Where is Jeremy?"

"He is on another errand. He gave me the signal."

"Will you wait, please, Gerald?" Jenny closed the door. "Barbara, come here and I'll put on your bonnet. We will walk down with

William to the stables. It's a little early, but you can play with the gray cat until your father arrives."

Barbara needed little encouragement, she rushed to give Carrot a smothering goodbye hug as the kitten lay in its basket.

Gerald walked down with them, then bowed and left them at the stables where Mr. Irvine stood waiting with two saddled horses. One was the gray mare, Lavender, William was usually assigned.

At the thunderous expression on William's face, Jenny had to admit she was relieved not to have to wrestle with him. He had set his heart on riding a big gelding. But one glance at William's new riding companion told her that he would handle William without difficulty.

The two rode away. Before they disappeared into the trees, William glanced back with a sulky expression which brightened as he looked past her.

Jenny turned to find the duke walking into the yard. She drew in a breath. He wore a double-breasted indigo blue waisted coat, that fitted his narrow waist and broad shoulders, his breeches of pale leather clinging to strong thighs. His top boots polished to a high shine, he carried a crop and black hat in gloved hands.

"I'm afraid Lord William is a trifle disappointed, Your Grace," she said with a faint smile as Barbara came to deposit the gray cat at her feet.

"Look Father, isn't she sweet?"

"Yes, Barbara." The duke nodded to Jenny. "I told Irvine to allow William a canter once they were clear of the wood."

"Oh, he will be thrilled!"

When his glance swept over her, her hand went to her brooch, recalling the previous evening when he'd found her inappropriately dressed. "Lavender won't get up much speed," he said. "I see no harm in it in any event. William handles the horse well. If, that is, he's watched closely and isn't left to his own devices, and decides to jump a fence."

She nodded, disconcerted. She was pleased for William, but something about the duke today made her pulse race, perhaps it was how handsome he looked, or was it how he looked at her?

"Father, can I take this cat to the nursery? She misses Carrot," Barbara said, breaching the silence that had settled between them, and saving Jenny from uttering an inane comment about the weather, the only thing she could think of. The duke's presence had an absurd effect on her today.

"Put down the cat, Barbara," he said. "One is quite enough in the nursery." His Grace held out his hand to his daughter, his eyes twinkling. "One too many you might say," he said as an aside to Jenny, then gave her the benefit of his devastating smile she saw so rarely. "Look Barbara, here is your pony."

Barbara released her father's hand as Jem emerged from the stable leading the small piebald and skipped toward him, but her father, in two quick strides, took hold of her hand again.

Jenny enjoyed the tender sight of him lifting his small daughter onto the saddle while the groom held the pony's bridle. She turned to leave.

"Miss Harrismith?"

"Yes, Your Grace?"

He bent over the stirrups. "You are handling this worrying business exceedingly well. I am relieved and very grateful."

"Thank you, Your Grace." Her cheeks heated, and her pulse galloped, pleased he didn't see her foolish smile.

He straightened and handed the rein to Jem. "Barbara will be ready to return to the house in an hour."

She sank into a small curtsey. "Very well, Your Grace."

His brows flickered down. He turned and walked after the groom who led Barbara's pony from the stable yard. The duke's praise meant far more to her than it should. What an idiot to soak up every kind word he bestowed on her, she thought appalled. She was like a silly green girl mooning over her first love.

As she made her way across the cobbles, the baroness appeared with her brother, and Mr. Forsythe.

So beautifully dressed, Baroness Elsenberg made Jenny uncomfortably conscious of her serviceable fern green wool morning gown. It had never been a thing of beauty.

Her crop tucked under one arm, she tugged at her York tan gloves, and strolled over to Jenny. "Miss Harrismith. Here you are again. In Germany governesses are seldom seen," she said. "And never without their charges."

Jenny curtsied, with a stiff smile. "His Grace has just taken Lady Barbara for a riding lesson, Baroness."

"And you are not with them? How surprising." Tapping the crop against her leg the baroness strode off to join the men waiting by the mounting block, while the groom, Marcus disappeared into the stables to fetch their horses.

Jenny swiveled and walked away, bewildered by the anger in the Baroness' pale eyes.

"Miss Harrismith." Herr Von Bremen approached her.

"Yes, sir?"

He came too close. It would be seen as rude should she step back away from him although her instincts told her to. "You must excuse my sister," he said. "She is rather short-tempered this morning."

"I hardly think that concerns me, sir," she said, attempting to hide her disquiet.

He bent toward her. "Do you know your gray eyes are as clear as water? Are you as principled as you appear, Miss Harrismith?"

"I believe I am." Surely he didn't expect her to deny it? While she wondered what lay behind his extraordinary question, she just wanted to escape him. But how, without seeming rude? "I walked over to see the hill you spoke of, sir." she said in an attempt to draw the conversation onto something less personal.

His expression grew pensive and a blond eyebrow lifted. "And did you climb it?"

She forced a smile. "No, of course, I didn't climb it. Did you really reach the top?" she added a touch of breathless wonder, then waited to see what he made of it.

He chuckled. "I'm afraid you've caught me out in a lie. I failed.

Gave up halfway. I'm inherently lazy, Miss Harrismith. Too much effort required."

"I considered the climb impossible without the aid of a rope," she said. "Is there a better way to scale it from the northern end, perhaps?"

"Mm. That might be easier, yes." He observed her closely, making her fear she'd said too much.

"Well, I doubt I'll make the attempt."

"Perhaps you might inquire of the duke, you seem to be on excellent terms with him."

Jenny drew in a breath. "My only concern is that His Grace finds my work satisfactory."

He nodded. "You are fond... of the children, yes?"

"But of course." She glanced over his shoulder. "I believe the baroness wishes to ride."

He turned to find his sister and Mr. Forsythe on horseback. She was talking animatedly to the duke's cousin, who listened intently.

With a nod to Jenny, Von Bremen walked away.

Jenny hurried from the stable yard before he changed his mind and called her back. She found him and his ambiguous comments disturbing and hoped he had not returned when she came to fetch Barbara.

ANDREW RESTED A booted foot on the bottom rail of the paddock fence and smiled at Barbara, chattering nonstop in her sweet voice as Jem led her around the paddock. She wasn't a bit afraid of horses. He was proud of his spirited child, who seemed at such an early age to have an unequivocal way of looking at life. She either liked something, or she didn't. And if she loved you, she did it with gusto, as with her brother. When she called to him, he nodded his approval with a smile. He had discovered the joys of being a father, and to watch her grow into a lovely woman like her mother, but physically stronger, with confidence to face the world, would be an everlasting delight.

The pony behaved well as if affected by the enthusiasm of her rider. Ponies were often bad tempered, but since this piebald had befriended Andrew's horse, Cicero, she'd become a favorite in the stables.

Jem led Barbara back to him, and Andrew lifted her down. "Did you enjoy your ride, sweetheart?"

"Yes. Rosie did too," she said matter-of-factly. "Can I see Misty, Father?"

He took her hand. "For a few minutes. Miss Harrismith will be waiting to take you up for luncheon."

Barbara frowned. "Why couldn't Jenny come and watch me ride my pony?"

He raised his eyebrows. "Did you want her to?"

"Jenny would like it."

"Oh? Well next time we shall invite her." He would have liked that too, but unwise perhaps, to expose the governess to any more of Greta's unfair criticism.

Miss Harrismith waited in the stable yard. With a thoughtful nod in her direction, Andrew released Barbara into her care and walked over to mount Cicero. He had promised to meet Greta, Ivo, and Raymond as they had decided to ride to the waterfall. Not something he cared to do, but his neglect of his guests had begun to weigh heavily upon him.

When he reached the river he met Ivo riding back.

"You didn't wish to see the falls?"

"No. I've had enough. They'll be along in a moment."

"I'll go and meet them."

"You'll find me in the billiard room, Your Grace. Perhaps we might have a game later." Ivo rode away.

Andrew turned Cicero's head and rode on.

A half hour later, his horse picked its way down through the glade where the stream flowed over a waterfall. Below, water swirled around a deep pool and rushed on. The air was damp. Birds swooped and called as he made his way down. Ferns grew lushly along the path.

He could see no sign of Greta or Raymond. Ivo had given him to expect to meet them on their way back.

When he reached the bottom, he dismounted and stood to watch the water cascade down the rocky cliff sending wide ripples over the surface of the pool, the spray dampening his skin. The roar filled his ears, but from somewhere came the sound of laughter.

Andrew led his horse by the rein along the path through dense woodland thick with vines and bramble. Around a bend two horses were tied to a branch.

Moments later, Greta, patting her hair, climbed the steep slope with Raymond.

"It's lovely here," Greta called to him. "I thought perhaps you weren't going to join us."

"Well here I am," he said pleasantly.

Raymond failed to meet Andrew's eyes.

Had his neglect sent her into Raymond's arms? Greta could easily walk away from a flirtation, but Raymond? Andrew very much doubted his cousin would handle it well. As for himself, he searched his own heart and found only indifference.

They mounted and rode single-file silently along the narrow forest path. By the time they reached the river, Andrew had already dismissed the incident from his thoughts. Instead, it was Miss Harrismith's compassion and concern for his children he preferred to dwell on, recalling her earnest face and her obvious affection for them. But there was something else, he found himself thinking about her at the oddest times. In fact, if he was being honest, he was thinking about her quite often.

When they reached the wider path leading to the carriage drive, Greta drew her mare alongside Andrew's.

As if he sensed a quarrel, Raymond dropped back behind them.

Greta stole a glance at him. "Harrow, I hope you don't think anything untoward occurred between Mr. Forsythe and me."

"No. Should I have?"

She gave a bemused laugh. "I rather hoped you might be jealous."

Andrew was suddenly profoundly sick of the games. "It looks like rain. We should hurry." Cicero needed little urging and cantered along the path. He hoped for Raymond's sake Greta put a stop to it, before it went too far.

Chapter Sixteen

AFTER LUNCHEON, JENNY set William some grammar to do while she taught Barbara her alphabet. It had been difficult to settle the boy down. He still bubbled over with excitement about his canter with Mr. Irvine. "He's an excellent rider, Jenny," William said for the third time. "Perhaps we'll gallop next time, Lavender was itching for it."

"I don't think so, William."

"Oh? Well. You should have been there, Jenny. When Herr Von Bremen rode up to us, Mr. Irvine, quick as a flash, wheeled his mount around to face him." He dragged in a breath. "And he placed his horse between Herr Von Bremen's and mine." William laughed. "Poor Herr Von Bremen was most astonished."

"Oh, yes, I can quite see how he would be. What did he do then?" Irvine was up to the task it seemed.

"He inquired if Mr. Irvine was our new groom."

"And what did Mr. Irvine say?"

"That he was here to instruct me in riding and advise my father on his stable. He came from the Marquess of Strathairn's horse stud in Yorkshire, you know, Jenny. I would love to go there and see his horses."

The Marquess' estate wasn't such a distance from Jenny's home. "He has had great success with his horses."

"Mr. Irvine said the Marquess' racehorses have won many trophies."

"And did Herr Von Bremen ride back to the house with you?"

"No. He rode off. He looked angry. But why would he be, Jenny?"

"I'm sure I have no idea. But this isn't getting your work done, is it?"

She turned back to Barbara who had continued chanting her letters in the background. "My, but you are quick to learn, Lady Barbara."

"This says b-o-y boy. See? I can read to myself. You won't have to read to me anymore, Jenny."

"You can! But I like reading to you. Don't you like it too?"

Barbara nodded. "When I'm sleepy, specially."

Jenny paused as the special knock sounded. "Now who can this be?"

She opened the door to find George stepping aside for His Grace.

The duke came into the room. "Was it you who conceived the signal, Miss Harrismith?"

"Yes, it seemed a good idea." She wondered if he thought she was dramatizing the situation, but every time someone knocked she wanted to know whether it was friend or foe who stood outside that door.

"It certainly cannot hurt." He had changed into a charcoal gray coat and buff trousers, the blue stripes on his waistcoat a perfect match for his eyes. "Am I interrupting lessons?"

As if it mattered. She smiled up at him, pleased to see him, far more than she should be.

He held a brown paper parcel tied up with string.

Both her charges were now out of their seats to better inspect it. "What have you brought, Father?" William asked.

His Grace handed the package to him. "A toy I bought in Vienna I'd forgotten to give you."

William tore away the paper. Barbara squealed. The toy was a simple wooden handle with a cup at the top. A string was attached at one end to the handle and the other to a small ball.

"This is how it's done." The duke took it from William. He flicked it in an attempt to get the ball to fall into the cup. After several failed attempts he handed it to William.

Jenny lowered he head and tried not to grin.

"Practice makes perfect, William," his father said raising his eyebrows at Jenny, a smile lifting a corner of his mouth.

William and Barbara darted off around the room engrossed in the toy.

The room was soon filled with the clatter of ball meeting handle, and their groans, when it failed to fall into the cup.

His Grace drew Jenny aside. His serious blue eyes sought hers. "I have yet to speak to Irvine. Did William's ride go well?

"Very well," she said quietly. "Apparently, they were met by Herr Von Bremen. Mr. Irvine took precautions and wielded his horse around to shield Lord William. The German gentleman seemed angry and rode off."

The duke turned. "William? Where were you and Mr. Irvine when you met with Herr Von Bremen?"

"It was over toward the gamekeeper's cottage, Father. We'd just cantered across a field. The one with the big old oak split down the middle by lightning," William said, without raising his head from the toy.

"It does sound as if Mr. Irvine knows his business," Jenny said.

William and Barbara burst into laughter. "I've done it, Father." William proudly brought the toy to his father to show the ball sitting in the cup.

"Well done, William," his father said. "Now give it to your sister and return to your work."

William handed it over, but began to instruct Barbara with the voice of experience.

"I can do it, William," she said turning her back on him. The ball was flying in all directions, and Jenny hoped it wouldn't do any damage either to Barbara or the vase of flowers on a nearby table.

"It is an excessively noisy toy," His Grace said, with an apologetic laugh. "I hope you won't curse me for it, Miss Harrismith."

"How could I when it gives them such pleasure? Nevertheless, I shall confiscate it shortly."

He nodded, smiling down at her for a moment. "A wise decision." He stirred himself. "I must go. William, you will breakfast with me tomorrow. Time to learn the social graces."

An eager light leapt into William's blue eyes. "Before my ride, Father?"

"Before your ride." He gave Jenny a conspiratorial wink and walked out the door. The room suddenly seemed empty and left Jenny as well as the children a little unsettled.

"COME IN, MR. Irvine." Andrew gestured to a seat. "My son approves of you, it seems."

Irvine smiled. "Well, I have a youngster at home, Your Grace. And the wife wants several more."

Andrew smiled. "Then you'd best return to the apothecary business. But not quite yet, I hope."

He smiled. "No, I like a challenge."

"That reminds me," Andrew said, "of the fine job you and Strathairn did protecting the king."

"It was Lord Strathairn, Your Grace. I was injured."

"Nevertheless, I'm sure you took a part in it. Tell me what occurred during the ride with my son. Did you see or hear anything unusual?"

"Only the German gentleman."

"Where was he off to? Did he say?"

"Said he liked looking around. Our woodlands are different to his country. Bit of a birdwatcher apparently."

"Is he indeed?" Andrew struggled to equate Ivo with birdwatching.

"He wished to join us, but I fobbed him off. Looked a bit annoyed at that. Asked me if I was a groom. When I explained that my business here concerned your horses, he left."

Andrew nodded. "Good work, Mr. Irvine. Take a different route each time, but avoid the river path."

"Yes, Your Grace."

When Andrew returned to the library, he found his secretary, Bishop, had placed a pile of letters on his desk. When he leafed through them, he found one from Strathairn. He picked up the letter opener and slit it open, perusing it quickly. Strathairn had investigated Herr Von Bremen. No evidence was found that he was connected to any German dissident groups. Ivo had spent a good deal of the last few years in Paris where he was known to be an inveterate gambler.

The last paragraph caught Andrew's attention and set up a new line of thought. *Although the baroness had been left a comfortable fortune,* Strathairn wrote, *it is believed that Von Bremen, who handles her money, has been gambling it away.* It seemed clear that Ivo had a very good reason to push for a marriage between him and Greta.

Andrew dropped the letter onto the desk. Ivo was doomed to disappointment, but he did feel more than a little sorry for Greta who had confidently avowed she'd been left a very comfortable stipend. He suspected she had no idea of the state of her finances. He deliberated whether to warn her, but he'd be hard pressed to explain how he came to learn of it.

Chapter Seventeen

THE NEXT MORNING, William returned from breakfast in high spirits. His father had talked about his schooldays at Eton and his time at King's College, Cambridge. William grinned. "Father liked cricket, but not Latin. He hated porridge too, so he didn't make me eat it, Jenny. I could choose from any of the dishes. I had bacon, eggs, and sausages. I didn't like the kidneys. Jeremy brought me toast and pots of jam. I tried three but liked the strawberry best."

Too much of a good thing, perhaps. She hoped the large meal wouldn't make William sick while riding, especially if Mr. Irvine permitted another canter. His usual porridge and toast might be improved on, however. She didn't approve of a bland diet for active children.

With Barbara skipping beside her, Jenny walked with William to the stables. They entered beneath the great arch bearing the Duke's coat of arms, into the stable yard where Mr. Irvine waited.

Without a murmur of protest, William was mounted on the small gray mare, and he and Irvine walked their horses out of the yard.

Barbara tugged on Jenny's hand. "Let's visit Misty."

Inside the stables, the gray cat sat atop the loose box wall. Barbara reached up to entice her down, but the cat leaped into the straw. A series of tiny mews rose up.

"Look Jenny! Misty has babies," Barbara cried. "Can I cuddle one?"

Four tiny kittens, two gray, two ginger, yet to open their eyes, nudged Misty's belly.

"Not yet, Barbara, they are too new. You know, Carrot might be their father."

Barbara's blue eyes widened. "Carrot must be sad."

"He might be. What shall we do?"

"We must bring Carrot back," Barbara ordered.

"Very well. We'll go and fetch him. He can come and visit us anytime."

As they crossed the cobbles, the duke's cousin, Mr. Forsythe, rounded the corner. "It's Miss Harrismith, isn't it?"

"Yes, sir."

"Hello, Barbara." He bent down to her. "Where is your brother?"

Barbara smiled up at him. "William's riding. We are going to get Carrot."

He raised his eyebrows. "Carrot?"

"Carrot is a cat," she explained.

"Oh? Of course it is, how silly of me. It sounds like an important mission, so I shall say goodbye." He paused. "I shall come and see William later."

He walked away. Tall and dark with deep blue eyes, Mr. Forsythe reminded Jenny of the duke, although in her opinion he lacked the duke's elegance. He seemed perfectly pleasant, but she was determined not to leave him alone with William.

"Pretty!" Barbara pulled away from Jenny, her attention caught by a bright blue butterfly fluttering over the ground, just as Baroness Elsenberg passed by them with a cool glance.

Outside the stable the baroness stood close to Mr. Forsythe. He briefly touched the lock of golden hair resting on her shoulder. It seemed an intimate gesture, and the baroness made no attempt to rebuff him. Their laughter floated across to where Jenny stood.

The butterfly flew away. Jenny turned to leave and found Herr Von Bremen crossing the cobbles. His attention seemed to have been caught by his sister and Mr. Forsythe. He lowered his gaze to Jenny. "Miss Harrismith. We are forever destined to bump into each other."

"I beg your pardon, sir." Jenny attempted to slip past him.

"Lord William has gone riding with that man, Irvine?"

"Yes. Mr. Irvine is instructing Lord William in the finer points."

"I intend to visit the schoolroom this afternoon. William wishes to know more about the Lippiza horses."

Jenny gave an inward sigh. "I'm sure he'll be pleased."

Herr Von Bremen's gaze settled on hers. "And will you be pleased to see me, Miss Harrismith?"

"Father!" Barbara detached her hand from Jenny's and ran to clutch the duke around the leg. "Misty has kittens!"

He widened his eyes. "I thought the cat's name was Carrot. And wasn't it a male?"

Barbara gazed up at him adoringly. "No, silly. Misty. She's a girl cat!"

It pleased Jenny to see the child openly affectionate with her father. "Ah, well that explains it!" With a fond smile, His Grace bent to tug gently on her blue bonnet ribbons.

When he straightened and nodded to Jenny, however, his gaze was cool. "I see the groom awaits with your horse, Ivo. Ask him to saddle Cicero, will you?"

"Certainly." Ivo bowed his head. "Until this afternoon, Miss Harrismith." He walked away.

"What is to happen this afternoon?" The duke demanded.

"Herr Von Bremen is to visit the schoolroom. Lord William wants to learn more about the Lippiza horses."

She saw his fingers tighten around his crop. "As long as it is only about the horses, Miss Harrismith. It is not my policy to have my guests mingle with the staff."

Her first instinct was to protest, but she could only watch open mouthed as he strode away toward the stables and the waiting threesome. It was the second time he'd been irritated when she was in the company of the German gentleman. Was it her, or Von Bremen who had annoyed him? Or both of them? It was frightfully unfair, and it cut her to the quick to think he might believe such a thing of her. Did he compare her with the former governess? Might he expect her to run off with the German, or perhaps a footman? Annoyed at not being able to defend herself, she tied her green bonnet ribbons firmly then clasped Barbara's hand.

SOME HOURS LATER, Andrew returned to the stables after putting Cicero through his paces. The chocolate brown stallion was always up for a good gallop. Ivo and Raymond had joined him when the path offered a good straight run. Then, laughing, they'd ridden back to Greta, who grumbled that a sidesaddle was too restricting.

As they walked the horses home, Raymond recalled his holidays at Castlebridge while the old duke was alive. "It was jolly fun, wasn't it, Andrew? We got up to all manner of high jinks. Remember when we hid in the priest hole in the library? My mother looked for us every-where. She almost had a fainting fit when we burst out in front of her. Her maid had to run for the smelling salts."

Raymond was the only one apart from himself who knew every secret place in the old house. But Andrew couldn't bring himself to believe his cousin would harm William. All his attention seemed focused on Greta, who so far had done little to deter him.

When he'd brought Greta here, Andrew had expected it to be the perfect opportunity for them to grow closer. But the opposite had occurred. It was Ivo who tried to bring them together. During their evenings Ivo made sure he partnered with Raymond at cards. And today, he'd distracted Raymond by riding alongside him and engaging him in conversation, which left Andrew and Greta alone. The man wanted the marriage, of course, if he was rolled up and needed an infusion of funds.

Trouble was, Andrew felt disinclined to be convivial. In fact, he'd begun to wish them all to Jericho, especially when Greta encouraged Raymond to make a fool of himself. He'd been struck by a dismaying realization. Greta's beauty and charm had blinded him to her less attractive qualities. He hadn't considered it particularly important that he wasn't madly in love with her when they were courting in Vienna. But coming home had changed him. Here at Castlebridge, where he'd once been so content, made him want that life again.

Society being what it was, men often did not marry for love. Instead they took a mistress. But it would not suit Andrew to escort a beautiful wife to dinner parties and balls and have her flirt with other men. Or for him to have a mistress. A hollow life which did not attract him at all. As soon as he could he would put an end to his and Greta's association, although he was sure she already knew it. It was just Ivo who did not.

Andrew dismounted at the stables. The others handed their horses over to grooms and called goodbye. He raised his hand in farewell as the earlier scene which had taken place here with Miss Harrismith caused him to feel some regret. What had got into him? He'd been unjust. She'd done nothing to warrant him cautioning her. He sensed she would have liked to object, but she merely raised her chin, while beneath the brim of her poke bonnet, her gray eyes had darkened with reproach.

He led his stallion into the stable stall and took a moment to lean over the loose box wall to see the kittens. Dashed cute they were, but before long the stables would be overrun. Good ratters, they would turn out to be, perhaps some of his tenants would like them. Squire Grimshaw's daughter, Sally, might like one for a pet. When the kittens were a little older he would ride over and invite her to choose one.

He settled Cicero into the stall and took down the curry brush from its hook. Working with the ease of long practice, he swept it over the horse's back. Miss Harrismith didn't appear to welcome Ivo's attentions. But to Ivo, flirting with a pretty woman was as natural as breathing, despite Andrew's warning to leave the governess alone. He was a good looking man, Andrew had to admit, with the same golden hair and cornflower blue eyes as his sister. Would Miss Harrismith find him so?

Andrew brushed over Cicero's withers. He wondered what was needling him. What harm could Ivo do in the schoolroom with an armed footman outside the door, just supposing he wished to? Andrew frowned. He still didn't want the man anywhere near Miss Harrismith.

He rubbed Cicero between the eyes, put down some hay for him and went in search of Irvine.

Chapter Eighteen

I N THE SCHOOLROOM, the quiet afternoon was disturbed, first by
Herr Von Bremen, who, after greeting Jenny in the playful manner
she'd come to loathe, pushed back his golden hair with a hand and sat
down with William. He launched into a description of the white
Lippiza horses and soon had the boy hanging on his every word.

Jenny drew Barbara into a quiet corner to read to her. The child
curled up on Jenny's lap on the rocking chair and immediately fell
sleep.

"A charming scene," Von Bremen said. "Your lap looks most inviting."

Jenny glared at him while William chuckled.

They were interrupted again when Mr. Forsythe entered. "Miss
Harrismith." He nodded to Jenny and turned to the children. "High
time I visited you two scallywags," he said. "William, how do you go
on? I remember the last time I was here, you had some splendid
drawings of horses. Do you have any more?"

"Yes," William jumped up. "I am going to draw some Spanish
horses, like the ones Herr Von Bremen has been telling me about."

Flushed with excitement at the two men displaying such an interest in him, William ran over to the bookshelves to fetch his
sketchbook. He handed it proudly to Mr. Forsythe.

Jenny watched as Forsythe flicked through it, making random
comments. He seemed kind, but she wasn't prepared to trust him.
"Jolly good work, William." He gazed around. "Now where is this

Carrot I've heard so much about?"

At the mention of the cat's name, Barbara opened her eyes. "Carrot is in the stables with his family."

Jenny had expected tears when they said goodbye to Carrot, but the little girl had accepted it without a qualm. "You will find Carrot with Misty and her newborn kittens, Mr. Forsythe," Jenny explained.

He smiled. "There are kittens? Then I shall certainly visit them."

The door which Jenny had barely shut, opened again, and the duke strolled in. He raised his eyebrows. "Quite a gathering. You're here too, Ray."

"Came to see the children," Mr. Forsythe said.

He looked uncomfortable and Jenny wondered why.

"Father, Herr Von Bremen has been telling me about Lippiza horses," William said.

The duke nodded. "There might be something on them in the library."

"Could there be, Father?"

"Perhaps Miss Harrismith would search for it."

"I'd be happy to," Jenny said.

The duke opened the door. "Miss Harrismith? A word outside?"

"Of course, Your Grace."

While attempting to decipher the critical glance Herr Von Bremen had cast her, Jenny settled Barbara down on the chair with a picture book.

His Grace had wandered a little way along the corridor, his arms behind his back. He paused in his stride for her to join him. "Are you managing the change in routine?"

"Yes, quite well. Lord William is enjoying his rides with Mr. Irvine. Apparently, the gentleman is showing him a few of the riding skills he learned during his time fighting Napoleon. And there are no longer any complaints about riding Lavender."

"Good. Nothing has happened to concern you?"

"No," she had begun to trust that they were at an end. "Is it possible that they were just random accidents?"

"I can't afford to think that, Miss Harrismith. And neither can you. We must remain alert."

"I plan to, of course."

His gaze sought hers. "We must not let anything, or anyone, distract us from our vigilance."

She flushed, and her fingers toyed with the brooch on her bodice. "I am aware of that," she said shortly.

"I am confident of your good judgement. But things happen... Should you be invited to go for a walk with any gentleman, other than myself, of course, I prefer you did not."

He turned and continued along the corridor. The former governess's behavior obviously still played on his mind. Did he think all women were so irresponsible? She bit her lip, he would be right to have that view, she supposed, having left her home to take up this position.

She frowned and hurried after him incensed at the injustice of the veiled criticism. "I am not in search of a husband, Your Grace," she said, her anguish making her sound horribly stiff. "If that is what lies behind this conversation."

He swung around, his eyes troubled. "Why ever not, Miss Harrismith?" he asked in a gentler tone.

She gasped. "Why? Because I value my trusted position here."

His dark brows snapped together. "You are skilled at evasion, Miss Harrismith. Most women wish to marry, do they not?"

"I did, once..."

"What changed your mind?"

If only he didn't sound so concerned. She feared he would make her cry.

"London Seasons and dowries are expensive."

"I understand."

And yet she feared he didn't. "I cannot blame my father, there are four children still at home. Bella and Beth yet to see married."

"However this fails to explain why you have chosen this life instead of marriage."

Why was he so intent on discovering the reason? How much could she tell him? "I refused a gentleman's generous offer and my father was so angered by it he told me to leave home."

"You refused?" His quizzical blue eyes met hers. "Despite knowing you would be placed in service? And with the knowledge that the marriage might have aided your siblings? But why?"

The question she hoped he wouldn't ask her. Jenny bit her lip, her heart galloping. "I'm afraid I shall not tell you the reason, Your Grace."

He arched his eyebrows. "You won't?"

"No." Amazed at her effrontery she pivoted to hurry away before she burst into tears and almost tripped over her feet.

He took her arm to steady her, his fingers strong and warm through her sleeve. "Miss Harrismith! I'm sorry I've upset you. It is your safety that concerns me, and I confess a wish to understand what brought you here. Of course, I consider myself most fortunate that you did come, but…" He shook his head. "We will say no more about it. Allow me to escort you to the schoolroom."

She trembled, and her deep gasps drew in the duke's fresh smell of starched linens and soap. The touch of his fine wool sleeve beneath her hand rattled her further, and she was unable to think of anything to mend her rude outburst, struck by a fear that he was not done with her. That he would prod her with more questions.

But he said nothing more. Was it bemusement that rendered him silent? Surprising indeed that anyone as lowly as a governess would deliberately withhold information from him. But would he now let the matter rest?

At the door he released her arm and stepped away. "I've enjoyed our talk, Miss Harrismith."

He had not of course. The fact that she'd been unhelpful to the point of rudeness, hovered for a moment in the air between them. But to tell him the truth and have him make inquiries, which she suspected he might, for he was a man who wished to right an injustice, could subject her family to unwanted scrutiny, and possibly retaliation.

Jenny suffered a spark of anger that a woman in her position must endure and remain silent or suffer the consequences.

"You're very welcome, Your Grace." She sank into a curtsey.

"I can't remember anyone putting a curtsey to such good use, Miss Harrismith," he said dryly.

He turned to George who'd sprung up from his chair and stood to attention beside the schoolroom door. "Inform the two gentlemen in the schoolroom that I am leaving. I shall go downstairs with them."

The gentleman accepted their marching orders with good bonhomie. Relieved, Jenny watched them descend the stairs with the duke.

Inside, the schoolroom had become blessedly quiet.

Enough excitement for one day, William and Barbara were both tired, and she was exhausted. More from emotion than too much activity, for the day had passed with little physical exertion. She feared she would not sleep well. The duke remained uppermost in her thoughts. It was as if he wished to search her very soul. She had frustrated him. Well, so be it. She would not tell him the truth if he locked her in the dungeon. No one must ever know for that could harm too many she loved. Tomorrow, during her time off, she would search for that book in the library, hopefully while the duke was out riding.

ANDREW ENTERED HIS apartments to change his clothes before joining his guests in the salon. As his valet fussed around him, he raised his eyebrows at himself in the mirror. Why did he wish to embroil himself in Miss Harrismith's affairs? Questioning her in that way had been totally inappropriate. His intention had been to warn her against the two gentleman who'd decided for some reason or other to visit his schoolroom, but it had somehow become more of an interrogation. It was just that it didn't sit well with him, he reasoned, to see her, a lord's daughter, in such a position. Little more than a servant, she must yearn for the life she was born to live. While he liked and admired her, there was little he could do to help her, unless she was honest with him. But she had refused point-blank to enlighten him. Even though it had obviously distressed her to oppose him. His questions got him nowhere, and he remained as much in the dark as ever. But something had happened to drive her from her home, and damn if he didn't want to know what that was, but if he wasn't careful, his children would lose someone they'd come to love, and there'd been no one else who'd meant that much to them since their mother died. Even Nanny Evans hadn't been so loved. Until Andrew married, and that might be some years away, they needed Miss Harrismith.

Was it the attractive Miss Harrismith who had drawn the two men to the schoolroom? Ivo might have been there to flirt, damn the man, but Raymond? He was smitten with Greta. No, Raymond had come for the soul purpose of visiting the children, something he'd never bothered to do before. Ordinarily, he'd treated Andrew's children with good-humored tolerance, but also a casual disinterest. And Andrew found himself wondering why that had changed.

He had gone to the library to find the book he'd promised William, but his search was abandoned when the butler brought a message from London.

He cursed under his breath, fearing the worst. And as he read it his fears were realized. Another murder, this time Lord Stonebrook, shot at his country estate in Hertfordshire, found dead with a lily on his breast. A search party had only discovered his body this morning. His lordship had been missing for some days. Andrew's presence was urgently required at Whitehall.

His first concern was leaving William. But Irvine coped well, and Andrew could rely on Miss Harrismith to be cautious. He would be back at Castlebridge by morning, as he intended to ride through the night. He sent word to the stables to saddle Cicero, then made his way to the salon.

Greta rose at his entrance. "I hoped to have a word with you, Harrow, before the others arrive."

"Greta. I'm called to Whitehall. I must leave immediately."

She frowned. "Won't you take me with you?"

"Not this time. I am sorry. These are matters over which I have no control. I'm riding Cicero. I'll be back tomorrow."

"What is the urgency?"

"A matter of national importance."

Dismay darkened her eyes. "I shall await your return. Don't let me keep you. We shall talk tomorrow."

"Yes, tomorrow." A talk they must have. He bowed and left the room.

Miss Harrismith was bathing Barbara when the footman admitted him to the nursery. William lay on his bed reading a book.

"Father!" Barbara squealed. "The soap makes pretty bubbles."

"So it does, sweetheart. A word, Miss Harrismith." He drew the governess away out of earshot.

"I have been called to London. I'll be back first thing in the morning."

She nodded gravely while keeping an eye on his daughter splashing about in the hip bath. "Very well, Your Grace."

"William may ride with Irvine as usual." Although there was a cautionary tone to his voice, she showed no sign of alarm at him leaving her alone in sole charge of the children.

"George will accompany us to the stables," she said. "After his lordship's ride we'll spend the day in the schoolroom."

Within an hour he was riding along the toll road toward London.

Whitehall was a miserable affair. Another member of their close group gone, and still no one arrested.

While Castlereagh's spies had unsuccessfully searched London for the culprit, Lord Stonebrook had been shot on his estate. It had rained since, and no usable evidence was found. Both men were brutally murdered with no discernable motive, apart from the prince's warning about the dissatisfaction building in Germany. Had a group come to London to inflict revenge on the delegates? Castlereagh was convinced of it.

The danger was no longer confined to London. And as most men had retired to their estates for the hunting season, they would all have to be doubly careful. Andrew wanted to get home, he wouldn't be happy until he was there again, despite most believing the attacks on William were unrelated.

Andrew left as soon as he could, riding out under the moon, a loaded pistol tucked in his greatcoat pocket. Clouds sailed across the moon and for a few minutes darkness descended. Andrew fought to quench his impatience as he rode Cicero down Headington Hill. Castlereagh had been right, if anyone wanted to pick him off now would be the time, while nothing stirred, and barely a light flickered in the town up ahead.

Chapter Nineteen

AFTER BREAKFAST, GEORGE accompanied Jenny, William, and Barbara to the stables.

Irvine waited with the two saddled horses. William ran to him and mounted and in a few moments they rode away.

Barbara tugged on Jenny's hand. "Can we visit Carrot and Misty?" she asked for the umpteenth time.

"We shall be fine now, thank you, George," Jenny said.

The footman left them, and she and Barbara entered the shadowy interior.

With a loud sigh, Barbara settled down on the straw to pet the cats. The tiny kittens still hadn't opened their eyes, but were bravely venturing farther from their parents. Carrot leaped down and stalked something at the back of the stables while Misty kept a sharp eye on them.

While Barbara was absorbed with the cats, Jenny perched on a hay bale. The groom, Jem grinned at her when he emerged from the harness room and began to saddle horses for the baroness, her brother, and Mr. Forsythe. She heard the German pair arrive, their voices raised in argument. They had spoken in their own language. Suddenly, Herr Von Bremen spoke English in a savage undertone. "Did you really believe the duke would fall in love with you if you flirted with his cousin? You are too used to men falling at your feet. The duke is no fool, neither is he like that weakling you married."

The baroness replied with a burst of outraged German which

quickly ceased as the groom led the horses out.

"Here is Mr. Forsythe!" she cried. "Shall we ride to the river?"

"You may ride wherever you like," her brother growled.

The sound of a horse galloping from the yard drew Jenny to the door.

"Where has your brother gone off to?" Mr. Forsythe asked the baroness.

She shrugged. "Ivo is in a temper. It is better. We can enjoy our ride. Just the two of us."

Forsythe smiled. "Indeed."

Jenny watched them ride away.

Barbara squealed. "Jenny! One of the babies, the gray one with the white on its head, has disappeared! Misty can't find it!"

The tiny kitten had somehow escaped. On her knees, Jenny felt around in the straw with Misty anxiously looking on.

Barbara watched, breathing heavily, as Jenny located the warm furry body beneath the straw and carefully withdrew the mewing kitten. She returned it to its worried mother.

"No harm done," she said to the anxious little girl beside her.

Another hour passed as Jenny sat with Barbara while they watched Misty cleaning her babies with her pink tongue. William should be back soon.

A flurry of hoof beats sounded in the stable yard.

Jenny walked to the stable door as William rode in. He was alone his face stark with terror. Jenny ran out to him. "Mr. Irvine's been shot. I think he's dead," William said trying bravely to hold back his tears. Jenny held the horse's rein as he dismounted. "There was someone after me, Jenny," he gasped, struggling to speak. "I rode as fast as I could to get away."

She turned and stared toward the woods. "Did you see who it was?"

"No, but he's not far away," William said, half gasping, half sobbing. "I heard him coming behind me."

Her first thought was to take the children back to the schoolroom.

But George wouldn't be there. He was to fetch them here in another half an hour. What if this fiend waylaid them before they reached the nursery wing? Where could they go? Had Mr. Forsythe escaped the baroness? He had the run of the house, and would know every nook and cranny. He'd been careful to make each attempt on William's life appear to be an accident. Why had he become so reckless? Trying again and again as each attempt failed. This time because the duke was absent, he obviously saw another opportunity.

The gamekeeper, Clovis would help them, and he would have a gun. Jenny called out for Jem, but he'd disappeared, the stable deserted. She grabbed Barbara's hand. "Come with me, William."

The way to the gamekeeper's cottage led in a northerly direction, away from the path William had taken with Irvine. She hurried the children along. Barbara quickly tired, so Jenny picked her up. "Lead on, William."

"Poor Mr. Irvine," William said his voice shaking. "We were riding across the same meadow as yesterday. I didn't see anyone, but I heard a shot and Mr. Irvine fell from his horse. There was blood on his head, Jenny. I turned my horse and heard another shot as I galloped into the trees. I didn't go the usual way. I took a rough overgrown path that's never used." He dragged in a breath. "I think it must have confused him, because after I rode into the trees, I didn't hear him anymore."

"That was quick thinking, William. It is fortunate you're such a good rider," Jenny said, her chest so tight her breath came in gasps.

"Who would want to hurt Mr. Irvine?"

"I don't know." Jenny imagined he would stick close to William, and the shot struck Mr. Irvine instead of the boy. The thought horrified her, but pushed her to walk faster, her arms growing tired.

"Where are we going?" Barbara wailed.

"On an adventure, my pet."

They struggled on, the pace far too slow for Jenny's liking, but she couldn't push the exhausted and frightened boy, and Barbara clinging with her arms around Jenny's neck made walking cumbersome. She listened for hoof beats and glanced behind them for any sign they'd been followed. So far, the woods were still and silent. But their pursuer was on horseback, how long before he found them?

Finally, they reached the gamekeeper's cottage. Jenny put Barbara down and banged on the door. Silence. He wasn't there and might be gone for hours. She could have screamed with frustration. Instead, with a murmur of disappointment, she continued on, praying the children would manage the distance.

"Where are we going now?" Barbara cried.

"To a pretty meadow with flowers and adorable lambs," Jenny said, trying to arrange her more comfortably in her arms, Barbara's legs hugging her waist.

It seemed like they had been walking for hours. There was still no sound behind them as they reached the meadow. Barbara perked up briefly at the gamboling black-faced lambs, and Jenny put her down. Ahead, stood the small thatched roof hut beside the giant chestnut tree. The door creaked when she opened it and led them inside. A makeshift ladder led to a loft.

Barbara made a face. "Pooh! It smells."

"You can sit on my lap," Jenny said. "It's a game. We must wait here until your father finds us."

"What sort of game," she asked sounding interested.

"Hide and seek," Jenny said.

"I like that game. William and I play it, don't we, William?"

"At Great Aunt Augusta's house," William said. "Will Father know where to look for us, Jenny?" William's voice rasped. He swiped at his nose with his sleeve and sniffed, then sank onto a sack of grain.

"He will find us, William. I am sure of it," Jenny said firmly. "And then all this will be over. We'll go home and have a nice meal." She wished she could be sure of it.

She glanced through the small window and thought there was movement among the trees. It might be a deer, but it wouldn't do to count on it.

She eyed the ladder. Two lengths of rope with wooden rungs attached by crude clasps. It looked decidedly flimsy and unsteady. She stared up into the dark space in the low roof. "Let's play another game. This one is called climb the ladder."

William needed no urging. He went up the rungs like a monkey. Jenny placed Barbara in front of her and helped her up it. She wasn't sure how she managed to get the little girl into the loft, but after a struggle, she did. Once the ladder was pulled up and stowed out of sight, she settled Barbara on her lap. "Now, whatever we hear, we must stay very quiet, or we lose the game."

Winning appealed to Barbara, and she lapsed into silence, leaning against Jenny.

An hour passed with only the chirp of birds in the oak and the bleating sheep.

Barbara's body grew heavy in Jenny's arms. She had fallen asleep. Beside her, William sat quietly, listening as intently as she was.

The clip clop of a horse and rider sounded in the distance. They came closer, cantering over the meadow. Jenny stilled not wishing Barbara to wake. She put a finger to her lips but was confident that William understood. The poor little boy now knew that the world wasn't always a safe place.

The rider pulled up his horse outside. A thump of boots hitting the ground, then the door banged back against the wall. Jenny's stomach tightened, and she felt sick. It wasn't His Grace. He would call out. Heavy breathing rose from below. The intruder's footsteps stopped. He must have been peering up into the loft.

Jenny leaned back against the wall in the shadows and tried not to gasp. She feared the tension in her body would rouse the child in her arms.

With a muttered curse, the man banged out of the door. Minutes later, he rode away.

William kneeled at the window.

"Don't let him see you."

"He's gone. Ridden back into the trees. I wonder who it was?"

"I don't know. William, only that it wasn't your father."

William gave a small shake of his head. "No, I could tell it wasn't

Cicero. I know the tread of Father's horse."

And she would know in an instant if it had been His Grace. Even before he spoke.

Jenny suppressed a shiver. In the silence when the man had stood below as if listening for them to betray themselves, Jenny sensed an evil presence.

IT WAS GONE ten o'clock in the morning when Andrew rode up the carriage drive toward the house. He dismounted and led his tired horse around to the stables.

George and Jem stood in the yard, then hurried over to him, clearly worried about something.

Andrew tensed. "Where is Miss Harrismith and the children, George?"

"That's just it, Your Grace. We don't know. They weren't here when I came to collect them. But Jem says Miss Harrismith was here earlier, wasn't she, Jem?"

Jem nodded. "With your daughter, Your Grace. They were playing with the cats. But when I returned from an errand to the kitchens, they'd gone, and Lord William's horse wandered loose in the yard."

Icy fear flooded through Andrew's veins. "Did you check the schoolroom and the nursery, George?"

"I went straight there. Mary said they'd not been back. I asked around, but no one knows anything. Mrs. Pollitt has had the house searched."

A horse came slowly into the yard, the rider hunched over its neck.

"Irvine? You're hurt!" Andrew ran over to him.

Irvine swiped at the blood dripping down his forehead as he dismounted. "Someone shot me. Meant for William. Is he here, safe?"

"No. He's gone, and so has the governess, and my daughter. It appears they did not return to the house."

Andrew pulled out his handkerchief, he folded it into a pad and handed it to Irvine, before blood seeped into his eyes. "Where did this happen?"

Irvine nodded his thanks and held the handkerchief in place. "We'd taken a different route, but on the way home, William suggested we go back to the meadow where we were yesterday. He wanted me to show him more of my maneuvers, and that was the best place for it." He groaned. "I should have refused. You did say not to go the same way twice. He lay in wait for us, the mongrel."

"Did you see him?"

"No. He hid among the trees. Where could William be, Your Grace? Please God, I haven't let the lad down."

"You've done no such thing, Irvine. I'll find them. Have that wound attended to. You're remarkably lucky it didn't kill you."

Irvine pushed his shoulders back. "I'll not rest 'til they're found. Let me go with you, Your Grace/"

Impatient to be gone, Andrew nodded. "I'd appreciate it. Jem, go and round up the grooms, the coachman and the stable master," Andrew ordered. "Get them out searching. Then you take the path to the river. Irvine, if you're sure you're up to it, take the western path. I'll go north to the gamekeeper, see if he's seen them."

"Right you are, Your Grace," Jem said moving away smartly.

Andrew led Cicero inside, quickly attended to his needs, then saddled Storm Cloud. He rode to the gamekeeper's cottage. Clovis was outside, chopping wood, smoke coming from the chimney.

Andrew quickly explained and fired off a few questions.

"Wasn't here earlier, Your Grace," Clovis said. "I haven't come across the governess or the children. "Saw the baroness, though, riding near the river. She was alone."

"Alone? Not with her brother, or Mr. Forsythe?"

Clovis shook his head. "No. No sign of either of them."

Andrew found it hard to think as he struggled to tamp down the fear. Go on or go back? Miss Harrismith had told him how she'd walked over to Spender's Bluff. If something had frightened her and forced her to run with the children would she choose a familiar route?

"Should I try to find them, Your Grace?"

"No. Remain here. If the grooms or Mr. Irvine turn up, let them know my direction. But tell no one else."

"Right, Your Grace."

Andrew nudged his horse's flanks and rode on. Had he made the right decision? What else could he do?

Chapter Twenty

EXHAUSTED AND FRIGHTENED, Barbara clung on to sleep. Jenny hugged the small, warm body, all her senses alert. William had given up trying to peer out of the tiny dusty window, and sagged back on the floor, silenced by the shock he'd experienced. One tended to forget how young he was, he was such a force of nature, appearing so confident, when of course, he wasn't. She loved both children so much, they might have been her own. Had she made the right decision? Should she have attempted to reach the butler, or the housekeeper? Her first instinct was to get them away. With the attacker following on William's heels, she'd been afraid he might lie in wait amid the copse of limes that bordered the carriage drive, and attack them before they reached the house. Or even in the house itself. The man must be mad, what could he possibly gain from such violence? Another thought struck her, might he now pose a danger to the duke?

She breathed deeply to calm herself. The children had missed luncheon. They would be hungry. How long could she keep them here? If they weren't found soon, they must risk emerging into the open and make their way back to the house. Perhaps the gamekeeper would have returned and could help them. They'd send word and wait there. But what if this fiend was lurking somewhere nearby?

Jenny wasn't sure when she first heard it. The sheep bleated and alerted her. A horseman. She daren't move. If she woke Barbara, the little girl could give them away. William heard it too, the rhythmic thud of a horse cantering across the meadow. She held a finger to her lips, and William, his face as pale as snow, nodded.

One rider. A clatter of a horse's hooves on the stones outside, then the thump of someone dismounting. Please God let it be His Grace. Would he be angry with her? Had she failed to take proper care of the children? She didn't care. Just let it be him. Her eyes filled with tears and a lump formed in her throat. The rusty hinges squeaked as the door opened.

"Miss Harrismith? William?"

Hot relief swept through her from head to toe. She smiled at William.

William leapt up to lower the ladder. "We're up here, Father."

In a minute, the duke was with them crowding the small space.

"Thank God." He dropped to his knees and held his arms out to William. The boy needed no urging, he moved silently into them, and his father folded them around him, one hand on his head. "It's all right now, son."

William's shoulders shook. "Mr. Irvine is dead, Father."

"No, William, Irvine is quite well, apart from a headache. He is out searching for you." His smiling eyes met Jenny's. "Well done, Miss Harrismith," he said quietly.

Barbara woke. "Father, can we go home? I don't like this place, it's dirty, and I'm hungry."

"Yes, sweetheart." The duke's voice broke.

To see the strong, honorable man brought low, made Jenny's eyes flood with tears. She searched for her handkerchief, plucked it from a pocket and blew her nose.

The duke came to his feet as a rider approached. He pulled his pistol from beneath his coat.

William's eyes widened.

Barbara wriggled. "Father..."

"Hush, poppet. We have to be as quiet as a mouse," Jenny whispered.

"Mice squeak," Barbara observed.

The duke crossed to the window and peered out. "It's Irvine."

Jenny took a deep shuddering breath and smiled at the anxious children. "We'll be just in time for luncheon. I'm quite peckish."

"I'm hungry too," Barbara said crossly. "And my bonnet is squashed."

"Let me put it on, sweetheart," Jenny said. "I'll fix it up nicely when we get home." Her hands stilled at the sound of another horse galloping across the meadow, scattering the bleating sheep.

William turned from the window. "It's Jem, Father!"

"Good." The duke held out his arms to Barbara. "Let's go down and greet the gentlemen, shall we?"

WITH THE MEN'S pistols handily placed, tucked into their trousers, and their vigilant gaze on the woods, they rode back to the stables.

A crowd had gathered: the footmen, grooms, and the butler, stood around in groups. They cheered as Andrew, holding Barbara within his arm, left hand on the reins, guided Storm Cloud into the stable yard. Behind him, Jem rode with Miss Harrismith, while Irvine followed with William.

Ben hurried over to help them dismount. "I'm relieved you're all safe, Your Grace."

"Has anyone else returned, Ben?"

"Only the baroness. Her ladyship was most upset. She wishes to see you."

"Let's get the children back to the schoolroom, Miss Harrismith." Andrew gestured to the red-haired footman. "Come with us, Jeremy, return to your post outside the door. Forrester? Inform Cook, the children, and the governess who is the heroine of the hour, shall require a hearty meal."

Miss Harrismith looked slightly flustered as she took the children to the nursery to wash and change their soiled clothing. Andrew found he wasn't ready yet to leave them, and helped with their clothes, tying

Barbara's ribbons, and buttoning her shoes. The little girl patiently held out her small foot. "We don't have to go back to that nasty place, do we, Father?"

"Never, sweetheart," he said huskily.

Miss Harrismith met his gaze as she helped William into his coat. It wasn't over. He still didn't know who this monster prowling the estate was. Where were Ivo and Raymond? He intended to find this man and when he did....

In the schoolroom, he took Miss Harrismith aside. "I'd like to learn more about what happened. I'll return as soon as I can."

She nodded briskly, only her tear-stained cheeks gave away any emotion. "As you wish, Your Grace."

It astounded him how she'd quickly returned to her composed self, something he'd begun to suspect was a way of hiding her true feelings.

Greta waylaid him on the stairs. "I expected you to come to me. They told me you arrived back from London at ten o'clock."

"There was another attack on William, Greta."

"Was there? I heard the shots while I was riding, I declare I almost lost my seat! Did you find the man?"

"No. Where were you?"

"I was returning to the house."

"Alone?"

"Yes, I—"

"Where is Ivo?"

"Ivo rode off in a bad temper, he might be anywhere." She waved an impatient hand. "All these questions! It is your cousin I wish to complain about."

Andrew gritted his teeth. "Oh?"

"Mr. Forsythe accosted me. We had dismounted to take in a pretty spot by the river. I didn't expect him to pounce on me. He... he tried to seduce me!"

"What happened precisely?"

She placed a hand on her bosom. "He tried to remove my clothing." She stared at him, her mouth thinning. "You don't seem particularly concerned, Harrow."

"What happened after you refused him?"

"He mounted and rode away, and I came back to the house. I was completely unnerved. I thought he might be the shooter. I have no idea where he is now. I hope he's left the estate. I refuse to set eyes on him again."

"I'm sorry Raymond took such liberties, Greta. I need to find him. Excuse me."

Andrew descended the staircase before she could utter another word. He strode back to the stables where Irvine waited, a bandage on his head. Neither Raymond nor Ivo had returned.

"You are coming with me? Shouldn't you rest, Irvine?"

"I can rest when I'm dead, Your Grace. I want the man who did this to me, and I want him even more because he tried to hurt William."

"Glad to have you." Andrew instructed the stable staff to take precautions against any possible trouble. Once he'd saddled a horse, checked both pistols, he and Irvine rode out searching for the two missing men.

After they crossed the lane that skirted Castlebridge and headed east, Raymond appeared riding across a field. His cousin hailed Andrew and rode up. "Have either of you seen the baroness?"

"Why?" Andrew asked coolly.

Raymond was red faced and flustered. "The darndest thing. We'd ended up alone together, because her brother had taken himself off somewhere. After dismounting at the river, she welcomed a kiss." His eyes flew to Andrew's face. "I accept you're angry with me, Andrew, but I hope you can understand. She wound me in a silken net, beguiled me." He shrugged. "I couldn't help myself. When she raised her face to mine, I had to kiss her, but then she suddenly flew into a pet. Called me an abuser of women! Demanded I assist her to mount. Then she rode off into the trees, saying she was going to find Ivo and have him deal with me."

"According to Greta, who has returned to the house, you tried to take off her clothes and ravage her."

Raymond gaped. "Deuce it! I didn't. I swear on my sainted aunt! I admit to having behaved appallingly where you're concerned. That I doubted the depth of your feelings for each other, is really no excuse. But to have ravished her like a common trollop? I wouldn't," his voice broke. "You must believe me!" He swiped off his hat and raked his hair. "I'll leave. I'm deeply sorry, Andrew."

"We'll discuss this later, Ray. I need to find Ivo. Someone tried to kill William. This time they made no attempt to make it look like an accident. They shot Irvine."

Astonished, Raymond turned to Irvine. "It's happened again then?" He paled, alarm in his eyes. "You can't think it's me?"

"Where did you go after leaving Greta?"

Raymond waved his hand in an easterly direction. "I was searching for her. I was afraid she'd get lost, and I wanted to have it out with her before she came back here and accused me."

Andrew nodded at Irvine who held a gun in his hand.

Raymond stared at the pistol. "Is Irvine going to shoot me?"

"Irvine will escort you back to the house. We shall speak, later." Andrew turned his horse's head and rode away.

Raymond called something after him. Andrew wheeled the horse around.

"I saw Herr Ven Bremen riding toward the house from the river," his cousin yelled again, before Irvine gestured with the gun for him to move on.

Andrew struggled to believe that Raymond was behind these attacks. Was it Ivo? But what motive might he have? Strathairn had been sure the German was not connected with any dissident groups; indeed he rarely returned to Germany. Ivo and Greta had been staying with Andrew when Winslow was shot in London. And it was doubtful he could have killed Lord Stonebrook either. Then there was the attempt on William's life in the tower, while Ivo was supposedly in Oxford. Despite all this, and the lack of any discernable reason for such violence, Andrew still found himself suspecting the man. There was something slightly unhinged about Ivo. He should have thrown him out long ago.

Andrew rode along the river for an hour but found no sign of him. Perhaps Ivo had returned to the house.

He rode into the stable yard as a big, fair haired man leapt down from his phaeton.

Andrew dismounted and hurried over to greet him. "Strathairn, the sight of you is good for sore eyes!"

"Thought I'd come down and see how you and Irvine go on," the marquess said, striding over to shake Andrew's hand.

"I'm very glad you did," Andrew warmly shook it. "There's been another attack. Irvine was injured, but he isn't badly hurt. He holds my cousin, Raymond, under guard. I'm about to search for Von Bremen." He turned to Ben who hurried out from the stables. "Any sign of the German gentleman?"

"No, Your Grace."

"I must go and find him," Andrew said. "Forgive me if I don't have time to offer you a whiskey."

"Saddle me a horse, I'm coming with you," Strathairn said.

A reluctant smile lifted Andrew's mouth. "I was counting on that. I'll send for a couple of rifles."

Chapter Twenty-One

J ENNY WAITED IN the schoolroom for word from His Grace. She tried to keep her mind on the story she'd asked William to read to them, but she found it difficult to concentrate. William did too. He kept fidgeting and losing his place. Finally, he put the book down. "I have read all these books! Jenny, can we go to the library and find another on horses?"

"I will go later. Your father ordered us to remain here."

Barbara had become fretful and needed a nap, so she took the children back to the nursery where Mary was sorting clothes.

Jenny settled Barbara down and handed William another picture book. He pushed it away looking miserable. He had been through so much, she wanted to comfort him, and it wouldn't take her but a quarter of an hour to find a book to please him.

"All right. I'll go down to the library. But you must stay here, please. I shan't be long." She expected the duke to be away from the house, but she changed her dress and tidied herself before the mirror.

Satisfied with her appearance, although her face was far too pale, she left Mary in charge, instructed George not to allow William to leave the nursery, or anyone to enter except His Grace, then went downstairs.

Was the duke still out looking for the gunman? Was it his cousin? How dreadful for him. A shiver passed through her. Would he be in danger? A footman admitted her into the empty library. As the familiar smells of old tomes greeted her, she searched the shelves and removed two books she found on horses, one particular one was on Arab horses which William was sure to enjoy. Pleased with her find, she returned by way of the servants' stairs, the books clasped to her chest. On the next floor, she found Von Bremen waiting.

"Ah, there you are, Miss Harrismith."

She clutched the banister, suddenly afraid. "What do you want?" She tried to sound indifferent, but her nerves were too on edge.

He flicked her chin, and she stepped back shocked by the intimacy of such a gesture. "Still sticking that out at me," he said. "We are going on a little journey."

"I am going nowhere with you." His odd expression scared her. She moved to pass him. "I am needed in the nursery!"

Suddenly, there was a gun in his hand. "Downstairs." He waved the gun. "Go."

"It was you?" Jenny stiffened with fear and stumbled down a step. How to escape him? She opened her mouth to scream.

A hand brutally covered her mouth. "I wouldn't do that. I'll shoot my way out of here. Be sensible, miss governess. Come with me quietly and no one will get hurt." He gave her a shove.

She feared he meant it. They continued down the stairs. "It was you who tried to kill William?"

"I've nothing against the boy. It's his father I hate. As a result of the meddling Vienna Congress my family lost much of their lands when the country borders were moved. I was willing to overlook it if he married Greta. But he was losing interest in her." He prodded Jenny hard in the back with the gun. "Because he'd set eyes on you, Miss Harrismith."

She dismissed it as the ramblings of a mad man, but it made her no less afraid of him. "But why hurt William?"

"If the duke lost his heir, he'd be keen to marry to replace him. And there was Greta who would comfort him and persuade him how much he needed her. A man in grief is easily manipulated. Greta's beauty would do the rest. A visit to his bedchamber in the night, and before long, it would happen. You were a problem though. It was my intention to seduce you, but you only had eyes for him."

"You must be mad." She turned to face him. "The duke is my employer."

"What does that have to do with anything?" He shoved her. "Keep moving!"

"What are you suggesting? I am merely the children's governess." They were almost to the kitchens. Perhaps there she could find someone to take a message to the duke. His gun prodded her in the back again.

"He hasn't bedded you, yet," he said conversationally. "I would know if he had. You are an innocent, Miss Harrismith. Your eyes look through me like glass."

"What good am I to you? Let me go. I promise I'll say nothing." The kitchen noises reached them as he motioned her down.

"While I've got you, His Grace won't set the hounds on me. If you're good, I'll let you live."

Jenny's breath shortened. A kitchen maid cut up vegetables while another was at the stove. They shrank back at the sight of Von Bremen's gun. "Not a word," he said to them. "Or I'll come back and deal with you."

He shoved Jenny out into the kitchen garden causing her to stumble. "My horse is over in those trees. Quickly!"

They made their way past the vegetable beds to the gate in the ivy-covered wall. He leaned around her and pulled it open. "Out."

They were in the open. Would a gardener see them? But there was no one around. "The maids will raise the alarm," she said.

"I trust they will."

He wanted them to be found. The man was mad. In among the trees a saddled horse was cropping grass. Von Bremen untied the reins and scooped Jenny up onto the saddle. The horse shied nervously as he vaulted up behind her. He was wiry and strong. One arm encircled her waist as he slapped the reins and kicked the animal. They took off toward the woods.

"You won't escape." She tried to pull her gown and petticoat down over her legs.

"I have a plan," he said in her ear. "I've been studying the terrain for just this purpose. One should always be prepared, yes?"

"I think your plan, whatever it is, is doomed to failure, Von Bremen."

His hand painfully squeezed her waist. "You'd better be careful what you say. I am not nice when I'm angry."

"What about your sister?" she asked, hoping to distract him.

"Greta will return to Germany, disgusted with me, no doubt."

"Don't you intend to join her?"

"I think not. I'm afraid she will be distraught when she discovers her coffers are almost empty. Gambling is such a curse, you know. And the salons in Paris such a lure." He sighed, his breath stirring her hair. "Pity Greta did not manage to get the duke to the altar. It would ease the pain of losing all her money, and she was most fond of him."

"You won't get away with this you know. They'll hunt you down."

"I have friends in London. They asked me to join them in their venture. I didn't wish to then. I am inherently lazy, Miss Harrismith, and I prefer the life in Paris, but now that my pockets are to let, I will meet up with them. They will be only too happy to have my help, especially after I've killed the duke for them."

Jenny wanted to scream at him, but she stayed silent. They were riding fast along a woodland path, heading north. Who were these people in London? She didn't understand what he was talking about. But somehow she must stop him. "You don't need me now. You'll go faster without me."

"Not quite yet." He chuckled, squeezing her waist again. "I will deal with Harrow first. The death of a duke will be quite a coup."

Appalled, Jenny prayed the duke wouldn't find them. "Castlebridge estate is enormous, it could be days before he rides this way."

Von Bremen pulled up the horse.

Jenny's hope that he had decided to put her down, soon faded when he grasped the lace on her collar and tore it away. "Give me your brooch, Miss Harrismith."

She covered it with her hand. "No!"

He reached around and pulled it roughly from her breast, breaking the loose catch. Then stabbing it into the lace, he tossed it onto the middle of the path.

"You may come to regret that," she said, her voice rasping in her dry throat. "His Grace will kill you."

"He won't know what hit him," he said, as he nudged the horse into a canter.

They rode on in silence, skirting the gamekeeper's cottage. Jenny considered yelling for help, but feared Von Bremen would merely shoot Clovis down. On reaching the meadow where the sheep grazed, he continued on past the small hut where Jenny and the children had hidden from him.

When they came to Spender's Bluff, he reined in. Jumping to the ground, he reached up and pulled Jenny roughly down from the horse.

"Surely we're not going to climb up there?" she asked, incredulity banishing the fear.

"Not all the way." He nudged her forward.

Half dragging her, Von Bremen forced her up the slope to a rocky shelf formed by huge boulders, forty feet or so below the cliff top. Above, the bluff towered over them, and beyond birds wheeled about in the sky.

His hand digging into her arm, he pushed Jenny down onto a rock, bruising her thigh. Then he reached into a crevice and withdrew a long shape wrapped in oilcloth. He uncovered a rifle and began to load it.

"You've had that gun here all the time?"

"I put it here the day you met me on the path. After I shot at William."

"And missed. The duke will have no trouble dealing with you."

Von Bremen backhanded her across the face. "The boy bent over at the precise time I fired. I'm an excellent shot, I assure you."

Jenny's eyes watered, and her mouth hurt. She licked it tasting blood.

He shook his head. "There, I told you not to make me angry."

She edged as far away from him as she could on the rocky ledge. "You are a monster. Why do this? Leave now and you can get away. If you're caught, you will hang. That's the law in this country."

"I won't be caught. Be a good girl. Sit quietly there behind that boulder. He's not to see you until I want him to. And if you move, Miss Harrismith, I have a knife in my boot, and will use it!"

She licked her sore lip again and didn't doubt it.

He checked his rifle. Her heart dropped at the sight of the guns he'd stored there. He squatted down beside her, but his eyes remained on the path leading back the way they came.

As STRATHAIRN'S HORSE was being led out, a footman ran into the stable yard.

"Your Grace! Miss Harrismith has been abducted," George cried. "She was on her way back from the library with a book for Lord William when the German gentleman grabbed her. They left the house through the kitchen. The maids are in hysterics! He threatened them with a pistol."

"Good lord! Was Miss Harrismith injured?"

"Didn't seem so, Your Grace."

"Did the maids see which direction he took?"

"No, Your Grace, they were too frightened to move until Cook returned. But one of the gardeners saw him with Miss Harrismith while he was working in the orchard. Said they headed in a northerly direction."

"George, go and tell Mr. Irvine. He's upstairs in the coach house with Mr. Forsythe. We're riding out, heading north."

Strathairn was already in the saddle. "Any idea why he would go north?"

"No." Andrew mounted Cicero. "He probably avoided Clovis'

cottage. Wouldn't have wanted the gamekeeper to see him. That way leads to Spender's Bluff. Ivo's been there before."

"Can he leave the estate lands that way?"

"Not directly. He would have to ride some miles to cross the river. Perhaps I'm wrong, but it's the only thing we have to go on."

They rode to the gamekeeper's cottage. On reaching it, Clovis informed them that he'd seen no sign of them. Andrew prayed his hunch was right. Miss Harrismith! If Ivo hurt her Andrew would tear him limb from limb. "I find myself totally at a loss," Andrew confessed. "How could someone be so wicked as to try to kill my son? And for what reason has he taken Miss Harrismith? The man must be deranged."

"He clearly is unbalanced," Strathairn said. "And such men can be extremely dangerous and unpredictable. We need a plan if we are to get Miss Harrismith back unhurt."

"John, I must tell you with the rage I'm feeling at the moment, I don't intend to bring him back alive," he said, desperation shaking his voice.

Strathairn's eyes narrowed. "And nor you should."

They'd traveled another mile when a pair of riders appeared a way behind them. Andrew and Strathairn reined in to wait. Moments later, Irvine and Raymond rode up. "Thought you might like some extra hands, milords," Irvine said.

"Indeed we would, Irvine."

Raymond's pale face was grim. "We'll get him, Andrew. Have no fear!"

Andrew glanced down. "Wait! What's that lying on the path?" He reined in and dismounted, then stooped to pick it up. A cameo pinned to a piece of lace. "It's Miss Harrismith's brooch." He buried his cold fury, his mind becoming cool and clear. "We're on the right path, gentlemen."

"Might it have come off during a struggle? Raymond asked.

"No, Ivo dropped it there. Miss Harrismith wears the brooch on her bodice, not her collar. He wants us to follow him, gentleman. Let's oblige the fellow."

The small hut where Miss Harrismith hid with the children stood empty. They rode on. When Spender's Bluff rose in the distance, Andrew reined in, as a suspicion answered the question he'd been asking himself. Why here?

"He must have a rifle," he said to the men. "It's possible he's holed up on that shallow ridge waiting to ensnare us in a trap."

"Is there a way to get up there?" Strathairn asked.

"No. If he's there. And I believe he is. He's chosen well. Rock at his back and a good view of the path leading right to him."

"We need some way of drawing his fire," Raymond said. "You can nab him when he has to reload."

"He may have more than one firearm. Miss Harrismith must be our first consideration. We'll take it slow and careful," Andrew said, aware of how reckless Raymond could be. "We make an excellent target if we show ourselves."

Chapter Twenty-Two

JENNY SHIVERED. THE sharp breeze toyed with her hair and chilled her neck. What did Von Bremen have in mind for her? Her thoughts were in turmoil. He sat so close to her she cringed at the touch of his arm against hers. He'd grabbed her when she'd tried to move away. His breath smelling faintly of liquor stirred her hair as he explained how he intended to ambush the duke. "He has to come that way. I'll bring him down long before he reaches us." He grew silent for a moment. "I'll have to take something with me, some sign that I've killed him. My compatriots don't trust easily," he said to himself. "Pity I don't have a lily." He turned to her. "That's what my friends are in the process of doing, killing the delegates, and then adorning them with a white lily. Clever, eh?"

"What delegates and why lilies?"

"Delegates to the Vienna Congress, of course. The lilies show that the murders are linked. They will be listened to, and respected, and their actions will bring about change." He frowned at her. "But this is nothing for you to worry your pretty head about."

He was telling the truth, she decided, she remembered the duke's look of surprise when she picked a lily in the garden. So that was why His Grace had been urgently called to London.

As he rattled on, Von Bremen became boastful and over confident. Jenny hoped it would prove to be a weakness. How could she warn the duke? As no opportunity had presented itself, she would have to wait her chance. In the distance a flock of birds rose into the sky.

"He's on his way. Won't be too long, now!" The German grew excited. His words tumbled over one another as he began to describe how much he would enjoy his time in London with his friends. "They live high on the hog in Seven Dials in a tavern. Women and wine are laid on, and they can carry out their plans without interference. Even if Bow Street came after them, there are so many narrow laneways to escape into, they would never be found. But the constables won't come after them. The magistrate has nothing to go on except the lilies. Bought them in Covent Garden markets. Can't trace them there. Maybe more delegates have been killed. I haven't been in touch with them since I went to Oxford."

He smiled strangely, and it occurred to her again that his frenzied state was due to madness.

"You did go to Oxford?" she asked to keep him talking.

"Do you doubt me? They directed a letter to a pub there because I wanted to be kept informed. When I saw the way the wind was blowing, I purchased more guns and still returned in plenty of time to lure the boy to the tower. Crept in, in the dark. No one saw me."

She curled her fingers into her palms and tried not to let him see how much he disgusted her. "So it was you who opened the nursery door and let the cat out?"

He kept his eyes on the path. "But of course. Who else? I placed the animal on the stairs leading to the tower. I planned to follow the boy up and send him over the side. It would have looked like an accident. The duke would be broken-hearted, Greta would console him, and you know the rest!" He turned to glare at her. "It would have worked perfectly but for you. You really are a thorn in my side, aren't you?"

"I didn't see you when I came after William. Were you in the hidden stairway?"

He chuckled. "I was."

"How did you know of it?"

"When Forsythe told me about it, I went down the stairs, and took a look around. It was perfect for my plans, so I removed the boards over the door. Forsythe knows everything about the old house. But he was a nuisance, looking at Greta with calf eyes. She couldn't resist flirting with him and trying to make Harrow jealous. I told her it wouldn't work. The duke is not the kind of man to fall for that. But would she listen to me?" He scowled. "She enjoys her effect on men, does Greta. Woman can prove a fearful nuisance when they don't listen to their betters."

"And the nursery curtains? Was that you too?"

"Yes. You got in my way there too, didn't you?" He studied her briefly. "I should have dealt with you much earlier. You are to blame for this, yes?" His expression turned nasty.

"I thought you liked William, taking the time to tell him about the Spanish horses."

"I thought it might give me a chance to get closer, but you were always there, the eagle-eyed governess.

"I detest the duke's privileged life," he snarled. "What's one child, he would have another one with Greta."

Jenny stared at him horrified. The look he gave her made her suppress a shiver. "What do you intend to do with me?" she asked fearing the answer.

"I shall let you go, of course," he said his eyes gleaming. "You will be the one to tell everyone how the duke was killed, and why."

Jenny didn't for one minute believe him.

"I'm sorry I broke your pretty brooch," he said, reaching out to touch the tear in her bodice. She slapped his hand away.

"Don't touch me."

"No, I'd better not. Have to keep watch," he muttered. He eyed her. "You'd better keep still, or you'll regret it. I can stick a knife in your ribs. That will keep you quiet."

Jenny wrapped her arms around herself and stared into the woods through the rock crevice. At the first sign of the duke, she would call out and warn him.

"He's close now," Von Bremen said in a high pitched voice. He aimed his rifle at the path just as a horseman appeared riding full pelt toward them.

Jenny screamed, but a second later, the German discharged his gun. Sobbing, she watched in horror as the rider fell to the path and lay still.

Von Bremen turned to her. Without a word, he raised the butt of the rifle and struck her on the chin. A sharp pain then blackness descended.

"RAY! FOR GOD'S sake. You fool." Andrew jumped from his horse and dragged the injured man away from Ivo's line of fire.

"Does he live?" Strathairn asked dismounting.

"Yes. Hit him in the shoulder." Andrew padded the wound with his handkerchief. "He's bleeding heavily. We must get him to a doctor."

Raymond opened his eyes and gave a painful grin. "Gave me a chance to make amends," he said, then collapsed unconscious in Andrew's arms. Andrew gently laid his cousin onto the ground.

"I'll take him there," Irvine said. He bent down and scooped Raymond up as if he weighed little more than a boy, then settled him over his horse. "Lord Strathairn is a superb marksman. If he can get a clear shot, the man is dead. Good luck, milords." Irvine mounted and turned the horse's head, riding away with Raymond hanging limply before him.

"Miss Harrismith's scream gave Ray enough time to take evasive action." Andrew gazed through the branches at the rocky escarpment. "Please God, the devil hasn't hurt her. We'll have to act quickly. Ivo has chosen this place with care. It's impossible for us to reach him without placing ourselves in the line of fire. How best to get this villain, John?"

"He's holed up there on that ridge, all right," Strathairn observed, squinting into the sun. "Is there a way to reach the top of the cliff?"

"It's a taxing climb, but yes, on the eastern side where it's more timbered."

"We need to take him before he starts bargaining with the governess's life," Strathairn said, checking his guns. "I'll go."

"No, better I do. Won't know if I have a clear shot until I get up there." Andrew shielded his eyes to view the straggling trees atop the cliff. "Seems there's a straight drop down to that ridge. I can't see anything to impede a shot. Not from this angle at any rate. If there is it will prove a prime distraction, at least. And give you a chance to take him out while he's busy defending himself..." He turned around. Strathairn had gone.

Andrew gave Strathairn time to make his way around to where he could more easily climb to the top. Then he decided to invite Ivo to use up all his ammunition. "You've jammed yourself in, Ivo," he yelled. "You can't win. Surrender, and I'll ensure you won't hang for this."

"You don't expect me to believe that, Harrow," Ivo shouted. "No way I'll hang, because you'll be dead."

Bent double, Andrew changed his position. A few seconds later, a shot sent up a flurry of leaves where he'd just been crouching.

"You're outnumbered," Andrew yelled, and moved again. Another shot rang out. No pause to reload. How many guns did Ivo have? An arsenal? Andrew yelled again, and the answer came swiftly. Too close for comfort.

From his new vantage point, Andrew's eyes raked the top of the bluff some sixty feet from the ground. Strathairn's head appeared. He seemed to be lying on his belly, his rifle aimed downward. Did he have a clear shot?

"Let Miss Harrismith go and I'll come out, Ivo," Andrew yelled.

No answer. He couldn't see her or any movement among the rocks. His gut twisted. Had the German hurt her? Fear and fury gripped him. Time to give Strathairn a bit of covering fire. He raised his rifle and aimed above the rocky shelf. His shot sent fragments of rock cascading down with a rumble. It was greeted by another shot from Ivo which came within a whisker of Andrew after he dropped to his knees.

Another blast echoed off the rock cliff, but this time it was from Strathairn's rifle. Andrew waited, his pulse thudding in his ears.

Silence.

Strathairn edged back away from the cliff and disappeared. Had he managed to bring Ivo down?

No answering fire, but Andrew couldn't wait, he had to get to Jenny. He tossed down his rifle, snatched up a pistol and burst forth, leaping over the bracken and rocks and began to climb. Nothing stirred. On reaching the ledge, he shoved his pistol into the back of his breeches and vaulted up, edging around the rocks. Ivo lay sprawled out, his eyes staring sightlessly, surrounded by guns and ammunition. Not far from him was a slim feminine form, her brown curls spread out around her, lying as still as a statue.

"Jenny!" On his knees, Andrew gathered her in his arms. He gasped as her head rolled back.

Her eyelashes fluttered but failed to rise.

"Alive! Thank God!" Andrew murmured as his heaving chest eased.

Strathairn appeared behind him. "Is Miss Harrismith badly hurt?"

"He hit her. There's a nasty bruise and swelling on her chin. She must have fallen and knocked her head." Andrew was vaguely aware of how much his voice shook. It earned a sidelong glance from Strathairn. "I need to get her home."

He hefted her slight body in his arms, her long hair escaping its pins, and began to make his way down the rocky slope with Strathairn following. "A fine piece of shooting, Strathairn," he said over his shoulder.

"Lucky I didn't follow the shot down," Strathairn said. "Had to lean out and wedge my feet into the tree roots. I would have called out after I'd shot him, but I wasn't sure he was dead, and I didn't want you to break cover."

"I am extremely grateful, my friend." Andrew was aware that a tremor still shook his voice. Was he blighted to lose those he cared for?

No. God could not be so cruel. Greta! She had lost her brother, and would be devastated by what had happened. Andrew's rage at Ivo was too raw, his thoughts were all for this innocent young woman in his arms.

Strathairn glanced at him again, his eyes questioning. "Glad to have got the devil."

When they reached where the horses were tied up, Strathairn assisted Andrew to lift Jenny onto his saddle. Andrew mounted behind her. She lay limply within his arms so deeply unconscious that it scared him. He kicked the horse's flanks and rode for home. "Jenny, Jenny, sweetheart, don't die," he murmured. "I couldn't bear it."

Chapter Twenty-Three

HER HEAD ACHED. Jenny opened her eyes. She'd never been in this bedchamber before. Gold silk tented above her, the damask bed hangings drawn back from the ornately carved four poster. The walls were an intricate pattern of gold and blue, the carpet like thick cream, a swathe of gold silk dressed the windows.

Confused, she closed her eyes again. The image of a rider falling from his horse brought her up on her elbows with a gasp, before she sank down again, trembling. Wisps of recollection jostled in her brain. Was it the duke? Had Von Bremen shot him? That His Grace might have been hurt, or worse, brought tears to her eyes. She had the strangest dream. The duke had spoken to her. "Jenny, sweetheart, don't die, I couldn't bear it." His urgent voice came out of a fog which hid his face from her, yet she knew he was close, because she was held snug and safe in his arms. She frowned. Was it a dream?

The door opened, and a woman entered, dressed in unadorned gray linen, her brown hair pulled severely back from her face. She crossed to the bed with a look of inquiry. "You're awake, then, Miss Harrismith. You gave everyone quite a turn." She stood before the bed, hands clasped at her waist, her brown eyes stern. "I am the nurse, Miss Green."

"How do you do, Miss Green." Jenny wanted to ask about the duke, but feared it would come out wrong somehow. That this stringently observant woman might suspect she cared too much. "How are the children?" Jenny attempted to sit up again, but her head still spun, and she lay down, grateful for the soft pillows.

"Perfectly well, but demanding to see you. When you've recovered, I shall permit it."

"I'm quite recovered and should like to see them now," Jenny said. "Do you know who brought me here?"

"I'm told it was the duke. But servants are inclined to speculate. They say His Grace entered the house with you in his arms." She looked faintly disapproving, whether of the servants, or her, or indeed, her employer, Jenny wasn't sure. And neither did she care. The duke was alive! Was it as she remembered? His strong arms around her, his clean manly smell, being carried light as a feather, her fears falling away. But the rest of it, his passionate words, were they real, too? Dare she hope he cared for her? Or should she protect her heart from a foolish dream? Who knew what tricks the mind could play on one?

At the fireplace, Miss Green pulled the bell sash. "You will wish for tea, and something to eat."

"Thank you, I would appreciate a hot drink. How long have I been here?"

"I arrived two days ago when everyone was in a fluster over the accident. The housekeeper took me straight to the nursery. My time has been taken up with the children, who want for discipline, and the nursery, which has required my attention to set it in order."

"They are beautifully behaved children, and have suffered a shock," Jenny said, frowning at the woman. She ignored Miss Green's suggestion that the nursery required ordering. It hardly mattered. "His Grace wasn't hurt was he?" She needed to be sure.

"I don't believe so. Why would he be?"

"I'm a little confused." *Who had been shot and fell from his horse if it wasn't His Grace?* She wondered just how much the staff had been told. Fortunately, Miss Green displayed little interest in probing her for information about her apparent accident.

She must eat to gain her strength and assume her duties. Jenny cautiously pushed herself up on the pillows. Her head no longer spun, but still ached, and her chin hurt most dreadfully. She touched it gingerly and then discovered another sore spot on the back of her head. How did that happen? She must have fallen onto the rocks. "Some bread and cheese would be welcome, thank you."

Miss Green shook her head as if Jenny was one of her charges. "Something more substantial than that, I should think. You've barely eaten a mouthful since the day before yesterday."

Jenny seemed to remember someone assisting her to drink a little broth, but had no idea who it was.

George answered the bell. "The servants have been worried about you, Miss Harrismith. I trust you're well now?"

It surprised her, did the staff really care? "I am rallying, thank you, George, but there are gaps in my memory."

"The house is abuzz, but no one knows for sure what happened. I imagine His Grace will tell you more although he is about to depart for London with Baroness Eisenberg. His Grace asked to be advised when you had awakened."

The baroness! How foolish to have forgotten. She would be greatly distressed by her brother's wicked behavior. And naturally, His Grace would be there to comfort her. So very foolish of her to forget the elegant, beautiful, woman. "Oh wait, George. I must tell him…" She put a hand to her head finding it hard to think through the pounding of her temples. "I'm sure there's something I must tell him."

"Best give yourself time, Miss Harrismith. The body has to heal." The Nurse turned briskly to address George. "Miss Harrismith requires hot water, tea, and a light meal, I recommend coddled eggs."

After George left them, Miss Green smoothed the bedcover and arranged Jenny's pillows. Then she brought Jenny a mirror and comb from the bureau. "Now I must return to my charges."

How efficient she was. Jenny hoped she would become more congenial on further acquaintance. It was important for the children to warm to her. "Of course, please tell them I miss them and bring them to see me soon," she said faintly, resisting the urge to leave the bed and dress. Her limbs seemed to have turned to lead.

With a brisk nod, Miss Green left the room. If she'd been surprised to find Jenny in one of the guest bedchambers, she hadn't revealed it.

The cozy bedchamber in the nursery was now Miss Green's. Jenny would no doubt return to her old attic room. She should not be here in this luxurious bedchamber as if a guest of the family. She held up the mirror, and gazed at the unsightly purple bruise on her chin, where Von Bremen hit her. Grimacing, she ran the comb gently through her tangled tresses, trying to avoid the sore spot on her scalp. Her hairpins had vanished, and as she braided her hair what Von Bremen had told her came back in a rush. The duke must learn of it! Had the German escaped? Or was he captured? Could the duke already have learned about the men hiding in the tavern in Seven Dials? Von Bremen confessed it all to her because he intended to kill her when she was no longer useful to him. She shuddered remembering his mad eyes.

An hour later, after a good wash and a hearty meal of eggs, ham, and bread, washed down with hot tea, she felt considerably better. She was about to throw back the covers and leave the bed when a light tap on the door made her start. "Yes?" She pulled the covers up over her chest, hoping it would be the duke.

Miss Green popped her head around the door. "Shall I send in the children, Miss Harrismith?"

"Please do, Miss Green!"

After the nurse left them, William, and Barbara ran across the carpet. When Jenny patted the bed, they climbed the step and settled beside her. "Are you better now, Jenny?" William asked. "Father said you'd had a fall."

"Yes." Jenny touched her chin. "Silly me."

"It's purple," Barbara observed coming close to examine Jenny's chin, her sweet breath touching her face. "Does it hurt?"

"Not so much now," Jenny said with a smile.

"Father said they caught the man who shot Mr. Irvine," William said. "Mr. Irvine's gone home now." He looked disappointed.

"I'm sorry I wasn't able to say goodbye to him," Jenny said. "Such a good man."

"A nonpareil," William said with conviction. "Like Father and

Lord Strathairn. The marquess has invited me to visit his horse stud to see his Arab stallion."

"That's splendid, William."

Barbara seemed unusually quiet. "And how are you, my pet?" Jenny asked.

The little girl plucked at the bedcover. "Miss Green is sleeping in your room, Jenny. And I'm not allowed to visit Misty and Carrot. Their babies will be all grown up."

"No, they will still be quite small. Shall we visit them tomorrow?" Jenny asked her.

Barbara smiled and nodded.

"Miss Green is to care for you both in the nursery, but I am still your governess, and we will do all the things we did before." Jenny suspected that she and Miss Green might have a few disagreements in the future.

"I found the books you dropped on the stair. It must have been when you fell and hurt yourself," William said.

"Did you find them interesting?"

"Yes! Did you know that in the desert the Arabs never used a bit on their horses? They were considered so smart they didn't need it. They took their horses into their tents when the sand storms hit, too." William's eyes were alight with interest. "Father's horse, Cicero is an Arab stallion. He has the arched neck and the high carriage of the tail."

"Your father's stallion is a beauty!" An image of His Grace riding the magnificent horse made her pulse race. She was a hopeless case. She must stop this, or life would become unbearable.

"Did you know Father is going to London?" William asked.

"I'm sure it won't be for long," she said, hoping he would not leave the children for a lengthy time. Jenny hoped the duke hadn't already left. She must tell him what she knew.

JENNY! WHEN ANDREW discovered her lying so pale and still, fearing her dead, it had rocked him. Then, learning she would live, he'd buried his head in his hands and uttered up a prayer of thanks. He was forced to admit that she'd come to mean more to him than merely a servant in his employ.

The events that followed, left him little time to dwell on the state of his emotions. Once the doctor assured him that Jenny was not seriously injured, Andrew was forced to turn to other matters, while all the time, wishing to go to her, to confirm in his own mind that she was well, and on the mend.

Greta had accused him of murdering her brother and demanded to be taken to London where she would arrange passage to Germany with Ivo's body. Andrew promised to ensure her safety and comfort until she sailed.

Irvine, anxious to get home, had left immediately, with Andrew's grateful thanks and a remuneration for his trouble.

Not long after Irvine left, Andrew saw off Strathairn in his phaeton. He was to return to his lady wife, Sibella, at his Yorkshire estate. He explained to Andrew that Sibella was not keen on him taking up the reins of his old life and placing himself in danger. "She lived through my time working for the Crown and now requires assurance that I'll come home at night." He grinned. "And I am to please relay a message. She plans to have words with you when next you meet, for sparking my interest and sending me from home."

Andrew smiled. "Please beg the marchionesses' pardon, and say I am very grateful that you came, and have every hope that when we meet again, it will be over a glass of champagne."

"Sibella will forgive you anything, Andrew," Strathairn said with a grin, as he gathered up the reins. "She's too fond of you to remain cross for long."

With a laugh, Andrew waved Strathairn off as he drove his prime pair of bloods down the carriageway.

Andrew visited Raymond's bedside to reassure himself that his cousin would live. Although he'd lost a lot of blood, the doctor was confident that Raymond would make a good recovery.

Andrew would always be grateful for his cousin's brave action when he'd so courageously drawn Ivo's fire, and as soon as he was able, told him so.

"I'm relieved you brought that bloody mongrel down," Raymond muttered.

"I would have preferred you not to get shot. But heaven knows what might have happened if we'd all ridden into a trap. Ivo had an arsenal up there."

"I'd like to know what was behind it all." Raymond yawned. "But I expect you have Greta to deal with." He grimaced. "I didn't do what she accused me of, but I'm still heartily ashamed."

"Let's leave it in the past, Ray. I don't want the baroness to come between us."

A smile lit Raymond's eyes, but it wasn't long before he drifted off to sleep.

Andrew returned to the library, wondering what Castlereagh was dealing with in London. He could offer nothing to help him. Ivo's attempt to kill him and William seemed unconnected to the other two murders, for nothing the mad German did made sense. Unless Jenny knew something that would help fill in the pieces of the puzzle when he was able to see her. The doctor had dosed her with laudanum and kept her asleep for most of yesterday and he'd had had to curb his impatience. He just needed to see her, for his world had turned upside down when he feared she wouldn't be in it.

"Miss Harrismith has woken, Your Grace." George stood before the library desk some hours later, where Andrew sorted through some pressing matters with Bishop, before he took Greta to London. "She has asked to see you before you leave."

"Have the children been in to see her?"

"Yes, a few moments ago."

Andrew finished a letter and put down his pen. He stood. "The rest can wait, Anthony. I'll leave those other matters in your care." He donned his coat and headed for the stairs. The children had driven him mad demanding to know why they couldn't visit Jenny. They'd not warmed to their new nurse. Well, it was early days yet. No one could doubt Miss Green's efficiency. But her manner did seem a little unbending. It might not do the children much harm to be in the care of a disciplinarian, with Jenny there to make sure they didn't want for affection.

As he reached the northern wing where the guest bedchambers were situated, he relived the crippling anxiety of carrying her in his arms, unconscious, with the fear that he'd lost her, and the guilt sour in his mouth that he hadn't done enough to protect her.

At her bedchamber door, his breath caught in his throat as he knocked, fearing to find her unwell.

At her faint reply, he entered to a charming tableau: his children lying beside Jenny on the bed, as she read to them from a book.

William sat up. "Jenny is better, Father."

"She hasn't finished the story, yet," Barbara grumbled.

"I promise to finish it later, poppet." Her cheeks flushed, Jenny put down the book and drew the sheet up over her chest.

"Yes, later children, your nurse will be here in a moment. It's time for luncheon," he said his gaze sweeping over her to reassure himself she was well. The dark bruise on her chin was the only sign that she'd been hurt, as her lovely eyes gazed into his, full of life and unquenchable warmth. "And I must talk to Miss Harrismith."

After the children were collected by the nurse, Andrew took the brooch from his pocket and came to hand it to Jenny. "The catch will need to be mended."

"Oh, you found it!" She smiled and took it, gazing down at it fondly. "Thank you, Your Grace."

He drew up an impractical gilt framed chair beside the bed and squeezed himself into it. "How are you feeling?"

"Much better. I hoped you'd come, I must tell you what Von Bremen said. Has he been arrested?"

"No, Ivo is dead," Andrew said. "The Marquess of Strathairn joined me in the pursuit. He climbed to the top of the cliff and had no option but to shoot Von Bremen."

"I think Von Bremen knew he must die," she said thoughtfully, "But he would never have given up."

Andrew sat back and allowed himself the pleasure of just looking at her. Jenny's skin was naturally fair and there were now a sprinkling of faint but appealing freckles on her nose. Her hair was drawn back into a long braid baring the slender column of her neck which appeared tender and vulnerable. She'd forgotten the sheet. It had dropped to reveal the desirable shape of her full breasts beneath the thin lawn nightgown. He suffered a strong desire to join her in the warm bed and hold her, to kiss the soft skin of her throat. His lips twitched with faint amusement. He was hardly a rowdy schoolboy. Jenny was eminently desirable, and he suspected his relief to find her relatively unhurt had slightly unhinged him. He cleared his throat and rested his booted foot on his knee. "Please go on."

But as Jenny began to reveal how Ivo had accosted her on the stairs and how he'd threatened her, Andrew found himself edging forward in the chair, his hands gripping his knees. When she reached the point where she'd screamed, and Ivo had knocked her unconscious, it was all he could do not to go to her and hold her. Her voice had begun to tremble. "He talked quite madly about the men he knew in London. They were murdering lords and placing white lilies on their bodies. He said he hadn't been part of it, and I believe he was telling the truth, but he did plan to join them. He said they used a tavern in Seven Dials as a base."

"Seven Dials, eh? That is of great use to us, Miss Harrismith. Once I reach London, I will pass it on, but if Ivo wasn't a member of this band of murderers, I fail to understand why he wished to hurt William."

She gazed down at her hands. "Von Bremen thought you weren't going to marry the baroness. In his troubled mind he believed if you lost William, his sister would be there to comfort you with the hope of an heir. Your marriage would put an end to his troubles. He controlled her money, you see. And he'd lost most of it."

"I only wish you hadn't been dragged into it," he growled.

She rubbed her temples.

"Are you in pain? Shall I leave you to rest?"

"It's merely a slight headache. I must tell you the rest. Once his attacks on William had failed, Von Bremen decided to gain respect from his cohorts by killing you, so he planned to ambush you. There were several guns hidden among the rocks. He'd placed his rifle there the day I met him returning from Spender's Bluff, the same day he'd tried to shoot William at the river. The rest he'd brought from Oxford.

"Von Bremen admitted to the fire in the nursery, Your Grace, and leaving the cat on the tower steps to lure William to the roof." She closed her eyes. "He intended to push him over the edge."

"Thank God you stopped him." Andrew stood, fighting his feelings, drawn to say something, but it was hardly the right time. And he must hasten to London to pass this information on to Castlereagh. There was no time to lose for they might be planning another murder. The coach would have been brought around. And yet, he'd much rather remain with Jenny, which he admitted was entirely inappropriate.

Andrew urged himself to be patient and placed his hands firmly on the back of the chair. "You must rest, Miss Harrismith. Please remain here until you are completely well."

She frowned. "I should not be in this bedchamber, Your Grace, the servants will not approve."

"They have been told how you saved my son's life. They will be happy to serve you." He stood looking down at her. "You deserve that, and so much more."

She shook her head. "Who was shot? Was it Mr. Forsythe or Mr. Irvine? Are they all right?"

"My cousin, Raymond, was shot in the shoulder, but is recovering. He bravely distracted Von Bremen, by riding out in full view. It was you calling out and alerting Raymond that made him take evasive action and saved his life."

She put her hands to her cheeks. "I'm so relieved he's not badly hurt. I thought for a moment it was you, Von Bremen shot, and when

I woke, I didn't know what had happened. No one would tell me." She swallowed, and her lip trembled.

Their eyes met, and something that did not require words passed between them. "Jenny, I—" He turned at the knock on the door.

The footman entered and quaked at Andrew's glower. "Baroness Eisenberg has asked me to inform you she waits below, Your Grace."

Jenny's eyes widened.

Andrew cursed under his breath. "We will talk again when I return. My gratitude knows no bounds, Miss Harrismith."

He strode from the room.

Chapter Twenty-Four

WHAT HAD THE duke wished to tell her? Was it compassion she saw in his eyes, or something deeper? Jenny only knew that he'd left her with a dreadful yearning for something that could never be. She loved the children and wanted to be a part of their lives, but accepted that it wasn't enough for her. This foolish passion she felt for His Grace made her realize how much she needed a man's love. Coming so close to death, brought it home to her, that a governess' life would never be fulfilling. But how powerless she was to change her future! And to settle for a half-life very hard indeed.

She left the bed and slowly began to dress in the gown she'd worn when the German abducted her. Jenny shrank as cloth touched her skin, the collar and the bodice torn away, where her brooch had been. She drew in a ragged breath. In the bedchamber assigned her, she would shut herself away and try to deal with these painful emotions. It wouldn't do for the children to see her like this, not until she had gained some control of herself.

When she entered the servant's hall, a footman and several maids rose from the table. They crowded around her asking how she was, calling her a heroine, because she had saved William from a madman on the roof of the tower. The story had grown into a fantastical tale as it now seemed that she'd actually struggled with Von Bremen on the roof. How this version of events came about, was a mystery, but their concern brought tears to her eyes. And Mrs. Pollitt actually smiled at her.

Jenny was directed to a large airy room on the attic floor which occupied an entire corner with two windows. It was once the old butler's quarters. Forrester had been given a comfortable suite of rooms in the male servant's wing where the footmen were housed.

All her clothes had been neatly put away. She sank onto the bed. Mrs. Pollitt had sent her feverfew and vinegar for her temples, but her head still ached, and she discovered a bruised hip. This was undoubtedly why her emotions were so raw.

The evening was her own. She was not to see the children again until tomorrow morning. After an excellent repast she undressed and curled up in bed closing her eyes. Still exhausted, she fell asleep, and into a nightmare. Von Bremen's mad eyes stared at her, the barrel of his gun pointed at her heart. She screamed.

Loud knocking on the door brought her awake. It was morning.

"Come in." She woozily pushed herself off the bed and reached for her dressing gown.

The red-haired footman entered. "Are you all right, Miss Harrismith?" he asked. "I thought I heard you cry out."

"I am fine, thank you, Jeremy. I... knocked my leg on the iron bedpost."

He brought in her breakfast tray with a letter. "This arrived in the post yesterday, but we were unable to give it to you."

A letter from home. Just what she needed to cheer her up. "Thank you, Jeremy."

Once the door closed, she sat at the table and drank her tea, nibbling on a bit of toast. She tore the letter open and began to read Bella's neat script.

"No!" As the contents of the letter were revealed to her, she couldn't believe what she read. Bella was to marry Judd. It came home to her with a shock how wrong she'd been to leave home. She should have stayed to fight. And now, because of her, Bella would suffer.

Jenny sprang up. For a moment, she didn't know what to do. Then, having decided on the only option available to her, she pulled her bag from the top of the cupboard. She took out two dresses and laid the green wool on the bed along with her straw poke bonnet with the matching ribbons, and her cream linen spencer. She bundled up the torn gown discovering a spot of blood on the front, and left it in the bottom of the wardrobe, then after washing she dressed in her warmest dress, before pulling on the spencer. She had twenty shillings in her purse for the trip to York on the stage-coach, and just enough left over to hire a chaise to take her the rest of the journey. But as she was not on the way-bill, there might not be a seat available, even atop the coach which was something she dreaded. Several coaches stopped at the Black Lion Inn, on their way north, one as late as midnight. She tucked her purse into her reticule, then sat to remove her house slippers and pull on her half-boots. Dressed in her bonnet and pelisse, she sat at the table to pen a letter to the housekeeper, requesting her trunk be sent to Wetherby Park, and apologized for having been urgently called home. Then she wrote another, far more difficult note to the duke, unable to explain her reason for this precipitous flight. He would not understand, of course, and was unlikely to forgive her. And the children! Oh how she would miss them. Would they be all right? Her final letter to say goodbye to them was the most painful of all.

Jenny picked up her portmanteau and left by the servant's stairs. Only a housemaid saw her leave, but she merely nodded and scurried away. Jenny slipped from the house into the misty air and hurried to the stables to ask Jem for a lift in the gig. There wasn't time to walk the six miles to the Black Lion inn. The mist grew denser, curling through the trees, threatening to hold up the coach and delay her journey.

Jem scratched his head but asked no questions. While he harnessed a horse to the gig, Jenny tried not to think of what awaited her at home. Could she change her father's mind? The stage would travel all day and into the night. She would not reach York until nine o'clock at the earliest. Then she must pay for a jarvie to drive her the few miles out of town to Wetherby Park.

Finally, after some hours waiting for the weather to clear, the coach traveled away from the Black Lion, with Jenny jammed in between a stout woman and a pastor who dug a boney elbow into her side. Thinking of the duke and the children cast her into despair, especially the duke, his searching blue gaze and studied awareness of her, as he stood at her bedside. She had sensed a strong connection between them as if he might step forward and… The knock on her head must have scrambled her brains! At least now with some distance between her and Castlebridge, she could regain some perspective. He was a duke, and her employer, and she a poor baron's daughter, who was far from the gently reared young lady, a duke would seek to marry. It had been their shared concern for his children that bound them together. William and Barbara! She had promised them a story. Her throat closed, and she hurriedly swallowed. Children were resilient, and they had their loving father. In a little while, with a new governess, or a new mama… the prospect brought her low, and she fought not to cry, aware of the clergyman beside her, casting her the occasional curious glance.

She looked ahead to arriving home. How best to deal with her father? He had not listened to her before, would he now? He simply must.

As THEY TRAVELED to London, Greta glared dry-eyed at Andrew from the coach seat opposite. "I don't believe you, Harrow. You are attempting to excuse your violent behavior."

There'd been no tears for Ivo. Perhaps they weren't so close after all. "We tried to reason with Ivo, Greta. Would you have approved of him killing Miss Harrismith?"

Her face crumpled. "Miss Harrismith again! I declare you're too fond of her." She narrowed her eyes. "Have you bedded her?"

He refused to dignify that with a response. "Ivo tried to kill William. He shot Raymond. Doesn't any of that concern you?"

"You say he tried to kill William. But that was Miss Harrismith's story. Raymond should not have tried to seduce me. Ivo was only acting on my behalf."

Andrew sighed. Impossible to get through to her. She only saw what she wanted to. "Take the money I offer you, Greta. You may need it. What if you arrive back in Germany and discover your brother has lost your fortune?"

"I shall remarry. I have many eligible suitors. I don't know why I chose you." She sighed. "But it was so very different in Vienna."

"Yes, it was." She was so beautiful, many gentlemen would pursue her, and he wished her well.

Greta pouted. "I don't like England. The English are suspicious of foreigners even though your royal family hail from my country."

He had no response to that, because it was true, although his friends had always been warm and courteous toward her. But it was also true that she could not face her brother's culpability. "I shall put you up at Grillon's Hotel in Albemarle Street. It's an excellent hotel and you are welcome to remain there under my aegis until your boat sails."

She nodded, as tears filled her eyes. "I don't understand my brother at all. I must confess I never did. Ivo was always wild."

"He appeared to have lost his reason, Greta." Andrew could not tell her why Ivo wished to kill him, or about the murderous group he intended to join.

She narrowed her eyes. "If you'd treated me as you had in Vienna, dancing attendance on me instead of disappearing off to London, it would not have come to this."

"Marriage would have made both of us unhappy. I prefer country-life and you are happier in town."

She shrugged. "The country is an utter bore. And it will make you one."

They continued on in silence.

After Andrew deposited Greta at the hotel, he made his way to Whitehall. When he relayed what Jenny had told him a flurry of activity ensued.

Some hours later, as he sat with Castlereagh in White's library, news reached them that the culprits lair had been located and the three Germans shot while trying to escape. A list of their victims was found, and Andrew's name was at the top.

It had shaken both him and Castlereagh who begged him to remain in London to celebrate with him at the king's ball, but Andrew wanted only to return to Castlebridge. To his children. And Jenny. And the unfinished business between them. These dreadful events had gifted him with the knowledge, that in the end, love was all that mattered.

Chapter Twenty-Five

I T TOOK HER last penny to hire a hackney to deposit her at Wetherby Park, but Jenny was glad of it. She didn't fancy walking the five miles, not when dark clouds threatened to blot out the moon. Beyond the carriage lights acres of dark meadows and woodland surrounded them.

The jarvie pulled up at the gates and refused to go any farther. Without another penny to spend, Jenny had no option but the pay him and walk along the carriage drive through the avenue of aged limes, the air decidedly frosty. Overhead an owl hooted and flapped away on giant wings. Her half-boots crunched over the gravel, as she lugged her bag, which had become very heavy as fatigue and the effects of the last two days took their toll. At the bend in the drive, the big house appeared against the dark sky. Candlelight flickered in the downstairs windows, the upper story in darkness. As her father retired early in the country to save on candles and lamp oil, everyone had gone to bed. Papa had long since given up a footman, and the butler had retired some time ago. She was surprised to find the big oak doors unlocked. She stepped into the cold hall lit by candles in the sconces and mounted the staircase. On reaching the landing, she crept over the rug and opened a door. Arabella's room lay in darkness.

"Bella?"

No answer. Jenny crept over to the bed. "Bella?" She put out a hand and touched the cold pillow. Where was she?

Jenny's fumbling fingers alighted on a candle on the side table Next to it was the tinderbox. She struck a taper, lit the candle, and the room leapt into focus. The bed had not been slept in. Next door, Beth's bed, and the boy's the same. The familiar creaks and groans of an old house greeted her as she crossed the landing, but beyond that, silence. Where was everyone?

She put her bag down in her old bedchamber, which smelled dusty and looked sadly neglected and distinctly uninviting. Divesting herself of her bonnet and pelisse, she changed into house slippers, then ventured downstairs.

She passed the doors to the darkened drawing room and parlor and entered the library where the embers of a coal fire cast an orange glow over crimson rug. Her candlelight flickered over her father's desk piled with papers, a journal open with his careful script, his glasses, pen holder and inkwell standing ready.

Jenny was about to rouse one of the maids when the front door opened, and a chorus of voices rang through the house.

In the hall, the family trouped through the front door, and stopped, mouths agape.

"Jenny!" Bella and Beth ran to throw their arms around her.

"I'm so glad you've come home." Beth's big eyes filled with tears. "We have missed you most dreadfully." She studied her. "What happened to your poor chin?"

"I had a fall, but I'm perfectly all right. I've missed you too, Bethy." Jenny hugged her fearing she would cry too. "I've missed you all."

"We've had a turkey dinner at Mr. Judd's house," Charlie said with what have been heartless disregard for his sister's distress, but Jenny suspected was bravado. Charlie put great store by manliness.

Not so Edmond who came to kiss her cheek. "Are you here to stay, Jenny?"

"I…"

Her father edged Charlie and Edmond aside. "Jenny! Why have you come home? Did the duke let you go?"

Jenny shook her head. "I must talk to you, Papa."

"You look exhausted," Bella put an arm around Jenny's waist. "I'll pop down to the kitchen and make you a hot drink. Are you hungry? There's some bread and ham. We really should air the sheets on your bed, but a warming pan must suffice. I'm afraid the—"

"Yes, yes," her father interrupted. "Come into the library, Jenny."

Jenny sank onto a chair before her father's desk, squaring her shoulders for the battle which would surely follow. Despite it only being a little more than a year since she left, he looked older, with more white streaks in his hair, and lines painted on his brow. "Bella wrote that she is to marry Mr. Judd."

"That is correct. Is that the reason you've left your position and rushed home?"

"Papa, I told you why I refused Mr. Judd. How can you agree to him marrying Bella? To become a member of this family?"

"I have no choice. He will accept Bella without a dowry and assist in keeping the estate afloat."

"But Bella is beautiful. If you'll just give her a Season—"

"There's no money for any of that," he said with a frown. "You've no idea what bad straits we are in. I can no longer provide for my children's education. Your brother, my heir, works as a clerk. A clerk!"

She fought to keep her temper as she looked around the library crammed with Papa's books. He disappeared into the past and cared nothing for the present, and though he protested, she doubted he gave enough of his attention to the necessary changes that would assist the tenant farmers, and improve the estate's revenue. He had sold off his land to a farmer, and would do so again and again until nothing was left. But if she told him what she thought now, she would lose any chance of changing his mind.

"You cannot let Judd marry Bella, Papa. You know what I told you about him. He imbibed too much at a dance in York and manhandled me, drew me outside..." her face grew hot, "... he likes certain things... in the bedchamber. He is a violent man, Papa."

"Rubbish. He apologized for being under the weather. Judd is an exemplary man who treats women with a good deal of old fashioned courtesy. He will make an excellent husband. You display an appalling lack of sensibility, my girl. I find it extraordinary how someone of your tender upbringing has drawn such a long and most distressing bow over something you assumed he meant. You should consider the seriousness of such an unfounded accusation."

She recalled the dangerous look in Judd's eye, the rough tone of his voice. It had horrified her at the time, and did, every time she thought of it. She stared at him. "Papa, you cannot mean to make Bella his wife."

He ran a hand through his gray hair. "I do. You must accept it. Now go to bed, Jenny."

Her sisters and brothers had gathered in the parlor. The dog scurried over tail wagging while the two cats watched with apparent disinterest from the window seat. Beth's latest find, an orphaned baby otter she was raising to return to the river, observed her from its box. As Jenny curled up in an overstuffed armchair, her fingers plucking the fraying damask arms, they all began to speak at once.

"What is the duke's home like, Jenny?" Edmond asked her. "Does it have a chapel?"

"Yes, I believe so, although I didn't see it. We always went to church on Sunday."

"Is the house very big?" Beth asked.

"It's enormous, three times the size of our home, and very old."

Beth widened her eyes. "Older than this?"

"Indeed yes. Two hundred years or more."

"Was the duke in the army?" Charlie asked, elbowing his brother aside on the sofa.

Jenny pushed away the image of a pair of warm blue eyes. "No, he was a diplomat in Vienna."

"What's a diplomat? Did he fight duels?"

"Only with words, Charlie."

Charlie slumped down and crossed his arms.

Papa walked into the room. "Go to bed, children. It is long past your bedtime."

The boys grumbling, they filed out of the parlor and climbed the stairs.

Bella came into Jenny's bedchamber to see to the warming pan. "I hope these sheets aren't damp. You might suffer from rheumatism."

"I am not yet in my dotage, goose," Jenny said with a smile. She sobered. "How are you really, Bella?"

Bella shrugged. "I wish I might be more content marrying Mr. Judd. But I do want my own establishment. Papa says if I don't marry soon, I'll be too old and must remain to care for him, because you wouldn't. I'd die if I had to stay here forever."

Jenny bit her lip on a retort. "That's the last thing that would ever happen to you, dearest."

Bella perched on the bed and pushed back a golden ringlet from her brow. "Why did you come home?"

"Your letter shocked and upset me."

Bella's lovely blue eye's grew shadowed. "Papa wishes it."

"But you do not."

"Mr. Judd is all politeness. But I can't warm to him, although I do try. His mother seems kind."

"Judd is well into his thirties. He is far too old for you." She studied her pretty sister. "What about Glyn, Bella?"

Bella sighed. "Papa will never accept him."

"He considers a farmer's son to be beneath us. Do you ever see Glyn?"

"Papa says I will begin to speak like a Yorkshire farmer, so I am forbidden to speak to him now. Sometimes I see him working the land when we drive to the village. He waves to me, but we never meet."

Jenny sat down on the bed, anger bubbling up inside her. "Do you still care for him?"

Bella sighed. "I try not to think of him, but I must confess I do, at night especially. I have tried to forget him, but it doesn't help that there are no eligible men at the assembly dances either in York or Harrogate. Many are even older than Mr. Judd, or too young to marry, and none are as wealthy as Judd is."

"You asked me why I came home." Jenny picked her words carefully, aware of what an innocent her sister was. "It was because I'm determined you shall not marry him. I dislike Mr. Judd."

Bella sat beside her. "That is why you left us, wasn't it?"

"No, there was more to it than mere dislike, but I can't explain it right now, dearest. You'll have to trust me."

Bella hugged her. "Of course, I do. I'm so relieved you're here. You'll find a way, Jenny," she said with a smile. "You're so clever."

Their father's voice carried up the stairs. "Time to go to sleep. Douse the candles!"

Bella kissed her cheek. "We'll talk tomorrow. I am feeling so much more confident now that you're here."

Jenny's fears tightened her ribcage. A woman had so little power against the strictures of men. How could she save her sister from that man? Bella had never been strong, a man like Judd would destroy her. She rose and opened the window. It had begun to rain. The damp night breeze wafted in smelling of drenched foliage, banishing the stale air. Jenny rubbed her arms. Her father didn't light fires in the bed-chambers until the worst of the winter weather was upon them. They were always suffering from colds. She shivered as she undressed to change into a nightgown, then poured water from the jug to wash. Her hair quickly braided, she climbed into bed and toasted her feet near the bedwarmer. She blew out the candle and closed her eyes. There was only one thing she could do. Bella and Beth relied on her. The boys too. For that reason if none other, she was glad to be home, but she was unable to prevent her thoughts from returning to Castlebridge, to William and Barbara, and a lump formed in her throat. She pictured the duke, walking into his library with that easy grace she'd come to admire, and discovering her letter. Would he be hurt, angry, or merely disgusted to find her gone?

She must not think of him, or the children, it hurt too much. Especially now that she had made up her mind what must be done.

IT WAS LATE when Andrew arrived home. The butler had retired, and a footman opened the door to him. Tired, and looking forward to some peace at last, he went to bed, and slept deeply for the first time in months.

In the morning, his butler sought him out at the breakfast table. He looked up from sawing through a piece of ham. "What is it Forrester?"

"Miss Harrismith left yesterday, Your Grace."

He put down his knife and fork and stared at his butler, fearing his reason. "What do you mean, left? Left Castlebridge?"

"She has gone home to York. Mr. Bishop has her letter. Jem drove her to the Black Lion in the gig where she bought a ticket on the stage-coach."

Andrew sat back in his chair. What had drawn her home? Jenny would never have left in such a manner without an excellent reason. "Send Bishop to me, will you, Forrester."

Andrew was drinking coffee when his secretary came in. "You have a letter from Miss Harrismith, Anthony?"

"Yes, Your Grace, I was about to bring it. There's also a note for the children." He held them out.

Andrew took them from him and scanned her letter. Jenny wrote that she was sorry, she had been called home, on a matter of urgency. She would not be returning to Castlebridge and wished him and the children every happiness for the future.

She wasn't coming back. Andrew could hardly believe it. He pushed back his chair and rose. "What the devil? Couldn't she have waited for my return?"

"Jem has been questioned, Your Grace," Bishop said. "It appears Miss Harrismith was upset about something, but wouldn't say what it was."

"She wishes me success in finding another governess," he said, raising his eyebrows as he struggled to get his mind around it. More fool him to believe that merely caring for someone brought content-ment. He'd been proved wrong about that before.

Bitterly disappointed, he went up to the nursery, knowing how distressed the children would be. Before he entered, he took a moment to calm himself. William and Barbara were more important than anything else. Not a word against Jenny would he speak although he could not fathom how she could hurt them in this way.

He surveyed their tearful faces. William with his small shoulders stiff with sorrow, and Barbara crying in his arms. The hour he spent trying to make them understand why Jenny had abandoned them without a word, when he didn't know himself, was one of the low points of his life. Helpless to provide an answer to the cruel disappointment served on them, he finally had to leave them in Miss Green's care, after taking her aside and insisting she be gentle with them. He didn't hold with her opinion that one had to face whatever life dealt one uncomplainingly and decided on the spot that he would replace her as soon as he could. Another change to unsettle the children, he thought, despairing.

When he reached the library, his curiosity pushed away his anger. It was totally unlike Jenny to abandon his children in such a manner. She explained in her letter that it was better if he told William and Barbara rather than herself. Then they would have their loving father there to support them. Had the young woman he'd so admired, who had managed to creep through the fortifications he'd built around his heart after Catherine died, be just someone who, on a whim, left unresolved issues behind her?

Andrew grimly crumpled the letter and tossed it down. It appeared she was not the woman he thought her.

He returned to his paperwork, but he couldn't let the matter rest. Something had occurred of great significance to cause her to rush home. Perhaps her father was ill. But if so why not mention it? Her letter had been frustratingly brief and left him completely in the dark. Had the frightening business with Ivo left her more shaken than he'd supposed? Did she wish to put the whole sorry episode behind her? He thumped the desk. Then why not tell him, dammit? Was he such a tyrant that she feared to confide in him?

When he cooled down, he began to think more clearly. Retrieving Jenny's letter, he smoothed it out. The last paragraph which he'd initially skipped over, leapt out at him. *If I might ask one thing of you, Your Grace, Miss Green plans to prevent Barbara from visiting the stables. I do hope that doesn't happen. The kittens have become important to Barbara and she will be greatly upset not to be able to watch them grow.*

He shook his head. It was not the letter of someone who cared little for her charges. Jenny loved his children, he was convinced of it. Something had occurred to draw her home, and for whatever reason, she refused to tell him what it was. The least he could do would be to send a footman to inquire if she'd arrived safely. Good lord, she would have been traveling at night, alone without even a maid.

He had not given Jenny's letter to the children. And would not until he was confident the matter was at an end. He picked up his pen and thoughtfully pared the quill with a small knife, then he dashed off a letter to her, blotted it, sealed it with a wafer and went to pull the bell cord.

When a footman entered, he handed him the missive. "Deliver this in person to Miss Harrismith at Wetherby Park in York. Wait for her reply."

George bowed. "Yes, Your Grace."

Chapter Twenty-Six

AFTER BREAKFAST, JENNY walked into her father's library. He looked up from his desk. "You are indeed fortunate that I am prepared to forgive you for your disgraceful conduct, and welcome you back into the fold, and only because I have managed to keep your behavior a secret from York society."

"What did you tell Mr. Judd, Papa?"

"That you were called away to care for your aunt in London, and did not feel that, in the circumstances you could marry. Judd handled it with remarkable aplomb, which shows the character of the man. And when he posed the question of marrying Bella, I thought it extremely generous of him. A man of his wealth and breeding might choose a bride from any number of good families with generous dowries. An excellent idea it is too, as Bella still pines for the young man next door who now plows the land that was once ours, and will never be more than a farmer."

"As nothing has yet been formalized between Mr. Judd and Bella, I have decided to marry him. If he still wants me," Jenny said. "I am closer in age to him and more experienced in managing a household than Bella. You can tell him that he will be assured of a well-run house."

Surprised, Papa left his chair. "I am glad you've come to your senses, Jenny. But your objections to him were very strong why have you changed your mind?"

"I want to marry and have children, Papa. And perhaps I was

wrong about Judd. I might grow to like him when I know him better." *And I will be there to protect my sisters from a brute, she wanted to scream at him.*

There was no point in appealing to her father again concerning Judd's proclivities. He had dismissed their earlier conversation out of hand, calling it a complete nonsense. He came around the desk to rest his hands on her shoulders and gaze into her eyes. "Are you sparing Bella because of this tender she has for Glyn Millichamp?" He frowned, dropped his hands, and turned back to his desk. "Be aware I shall not change my mind about him."

"I understand that, Papa." She swallowed on a sigh, wanting to be honest with him, but what was the point? He would refuse to see it and she had to handle him carefully. "I will marry Judd if he promises to arrange for Bella to have a London Season."

"Seasons are an expensive business, and there is no one to chaperone her for her Come-out."

"Judd's mother might agree to it. Or there's Aunt Leonora. She lives in Mayfair."

"Your aunt is quite an age now, I doubt she'd agree."

"No, perhaps not, but as a married lady of almost twenty-four, there's no reason why I cannot be Bella's chaperone."

"I shall ask Judd to call on us, but I daresay he will dislike being dictated to by a young woman. And he may prefer a more malleable girl like Bella."

"Society will frown on us if your first-born daughter isn't married before the other girls." Jenny shrugged. "But if Judd refuses me I shall go to London and take another governess position."

He banged the desk with his fist. "I could take disciplinary action where you're concerned, young lady. Fathers have every right to do so."

Jenny lifted her chin. "I hope that you will see the sense of my suggestion, Papa."

He bent his head and studied his hands. "Very well. I will attempt to convince Judd of the rightfulness of marrying you."

"Thank you. May I tell Bella?"

"You may. I'm confident that Judd will agree. After all, nothing has been announced. He always seeks to do the correct thing. And as he requires an efficient wife to run his house, because his mother plans to go and live with her sister, you are certainly better suited for that than Bella, who moons about in the most annoying fashion."

Jenny left the library. She was forced to lean against the wall when her knees gave way.

Bella appeared in the hall and hurried to take her arm. "Are you all right, Jenny?"

"Yes, I was a little dizzy. I must have risen too fast. Come to my bedchamber, Bella, I have something to tell you."

Bella listened quietly as Jenny explained what she had decided to do. "You would marry Mr. Judd? Is it to spare me?"

"There's another reason."

A frown marred Bella's smooth forehead. "Won't you tell me what it is?"

"Not yet, Bella. Please, don't ask me."

Bella studied her anxiously. "I can see your mind is made up. And once that happens it would be useless for me to try to change it. But I fear for you, dearest. You are sacrificing yourself for all of us."

"No. I am twenty-three and too old to consider myself on the marriage mart. If a well-born gentleman of such excellent prospects wants me, I really should be grateful. And I will be living here in York close to the family. It is certainly preferable to working as a governess."

"There is that certainly." Bella gazed at her doubtfully. "But I wish I could believe you. If that was the case you would have married Judd when he first asked you. Isn't that so?"

"Papa and I butted heads, and I suppose I wasn't ready to marry. I wanted an adventure. Well, I've had my adventure, Bella. I'm ready now to settle down."

With a worried glance, Bella drifted over to the window. She started and pulled back the curtain, a faint flush on her cheeks. "Hearts don't really break, do they?"

"Oh, Bella!" Jenny followed her. Beyond the trees, a horseman, tall in the saddle, rode over the hill on the way to the village. Glyn Millichamp. "No, but they can be wounded, dearest."

"A farmer's son isn't a gentleman, Papa says. I shall become a Yorkshire housewife. As if I care."

Jenny hugged her around the waist. "Well at least you shall have a wonderful Season in London and meet many eligible gentlemen." She had expected Bella to be pleased, but her sister merely nodded.

JUST PAST NOON, a grand black coach pulled up in the carriageway before the house. Jenny heard the wheels crunching on the gravel and rushed to the window. The duke! Her pulse raced as she hurried downstairs, her mind in a whirl. She opened the door expecting to find His Grace, but it was the footman, George, who walked up the steps. He removed his hat. "Good day to you, Miss Harrismith."

Jenny's euphoria left her. How foolish to think His Grace would come, she was like a green girl suffering her first crush, instead of a mature woman. She fought to hide her bitter disappointment as she stepped forward with a smile of welcome. "George, how nice to see you. Please come in to the parlor."

The footman followed her inside. "I bear a letter from His Grace." He pulled it from his coat pocket and held it out to her.

Jenny took it, eager to read its contents. "May I offer you a glass of lemonade and something to eat?"

"No, thank you. I must return immediately. His Grace requires an answer."

She broke the wafer and opened it, scanning the words formed in the Duke's fine hand. While he didn't seek to berate her, the letter was short and to the point. He sought a reason for her hasty abandonment of her position. He was angry and disappointed in her. She had expected it. But it still upset her terribly. What could she tell him? Seated at the small desk beside the parlor window, she scribbled a few lines explaining that she had initially been called away due to a family emergency, but since coming home, she decided to remain close to her family and had reconsidered and accepted Mr. Walter Judd's offer of marriage. She blotted the paper, folded it, and handed it to George. "Will you tell the children..." She shook her head. "No, best not."

"They miss you sorely, Miss Harrismith," George said. "Miss Green does her best, but..." He shrugged.

"I expect my replacement will arrive soon, and once she's settled in... children do adjust in time," Jenny said faintly, failing to convince herself. George looked skeptical as well. With a deep breath, she attempted to smile. "Please give my regards to the duke and say I am sorry I left so abruptly, but it was unavoidable," she said, fighting to keep her composure. "I hope your journey home proves uneventful, George."

George looked perplexed. He cast her a sympathetic glance. "I am sorry you are no longer to care for the children, Miss Harrismith. I shall relay your message to the duke. Good day." He replaced his hat and left her.

As the coach drew away, Charlie came flying down the stairs. "I say, what a fine matched set of horses, the leader was quite splendid! And the coach! Whose was it?" He swiped his unruly curly brown hair out of his eyes. "I couldn't make out the crest on the door panel from upstairs."

"It was the Duke of Harrow's coach, Charlie. His footman brought me a letter."

"The duke doesn't want you to come back, does he, Jenny?" he asked, scowling. "You only just got here."

"No, Charlie, he doesn't." Her letter would sever her connection with His Grace and Castlebridge forever. She placed a hand on her chest where the pain in the region of her heart almost made her gasp. "Let's go down to the kitchen and help Cook and Molly prepare supper."

JENNY'S LETTER WAS handed to Andrew at dusk. He thanked George and sat in the library to mull over it. He had not expected a betrothal! Had Jenny been pining for some Yorkshire fellow? No, she had told him she'd refused the man's offer. She was even prepared to leave her home rather than marry him. Curious that she'd resolutely refused to tell him the reason.

Andrew leaned an elbow on the desk and threaded his fingers through his hair as he tried to read between the lines. What had occurred to change her mind? He found the whole business unsatisfactory. While he was prepared to believe that Jenny would prefer marriage to working as a governess, it had all happened too fast. It was far too neat. And she was too vague about the reason for her change of heart, and her rush home. While the news unsettled him, and left him suspicious, there was little he could do about it, but to wish her well.

The door opened, and Raymond strolled in, his arm in a sling. "The doctor tells me I will be able to cast this off tomorrow. I can return to London." He took a chair before the desk.

"That's good news," Andrew said automatically, his thoughts still on the letter.

"What have you there?" Raymond asked, displaying his usual lack of discretion. But somehow, Andrew welcomed the bond which still existed between them. Having discovered it was not Raymond who sought to hurt his family, he had forgiven him for falling under Greta's spell. After all, he had done so himself for a time.

"It's a letter from Miss Harrismith," he said. "She left us rather hurriedly, as you know. It appears she is about to marry. But it seems strange to me that it's all been so sudden."

Raymond eyed him thoughtfully. "You should go to York and see for yourself."

"What possible good would that do? I'm not about to invite Miss Harrismith back to take up her duties as my children's governess, rather than accept a proposal of marriage."

"No, but you might have a better suggestion," Raymond said, with a slight grin. "You have feelings for her, Andrew."

"What?" Andrew stared at him, a little annoyed by his cousin's perspicacity. He was not prepared to face these disturbing feelings which would likely lead him nowhere, or to put them into words. Was he a coward? Afraid to face further hurt? He firmed his jaw and glared at his cousin, who had stirred up these unwelcome emotions. "You are an incurable romantic, Ray."

Undeterred, Raymond chuckled. "I've seen how you look when you speak of her. It's blatantly obvious. Otherwise, why would you care if she doesn't come back? If she marries some other fellow?"

"I don't like mysteries. And the children are very upset." Andrew glanced up at the painting of Catherine over the fireplace.

"You are ready to put the past behind you and take a chance on love," Raymond said. "You considered marrying Greta, but she was not right for you. Perhaps Miss Harrismith is? The children love her. And even if you're not ready to admit that you love her too, at least go and see her."

"I don't see that such an action would serve. Not without a very good reason." Andrew turned again to the letter. "Have you ever come across a Walter Judd in York?"

"No, can't say I have, but I'll look him up if it will be of any help to you."

"I'd be grateful if you would, Ray. I want to be sure in my own mind that she's marrying a decent fellow."

"And if he is decent?"

"Then I shan't take things any further."

"Not like you to be a quitter, Andrew."

A smile lifted his lips. "Go to London, Ray. I need time to think."

Raymond headed for the door. "I'll write if I hear anything of interest."

Andrew nodded, lost in thought. When he raised his head, the door had closed on his cousin. He pushed back his chair. Best to check on the children, who had become unusually submissive and alarmingly quiet.

THE AGENCY HAD acted swiftly. Two days later, Andrew had approved a new governess' application. She was to arrive next week. He'd had success with William's tutor too. Henry, brother of Andrew's friend, Daniel Cowper, had accepted the appointment while he was studying for a doctorate at Oxford. So he expected life at Castlebridge to settle down again, which was what he wanted wasn't it? But he wished he didn't feel so hollow. Try as he might to put it behind him, Jenny's going had left him confoundedly unsettled. Raymond accused him of being in love. But he'd been rocked by the vulnerability he'd felt when he found Jenny unconscious. A deep well of fear had swept through him, a sense of loss that scared him. He didn't want to be that susceptible again. But not to take a chance on love was living a half-life. And his plan to marry a woman who hadn't claimed his heart had been cowardly. He had to admit that he'd come to care deeply for Jenny. But he was not about to turn her life upside down if she'd truly found happiness.

Chapter Twenty-Seven

NEGOTIATIONS HAD GONE on for a couple of days between her father and Mr. Judd before the marriage settlements were complete. All the while, Jenny had tried to hide her fears from the rest of the family. In the mirror, she looked pale and wan and not her best, but at least the bruise had faded. A fear that Judd would choose Bella instead, had caused her to lie awake until the mauve dawn light crept through the gap in the curtains.

Bella had stopped her on the landing as she left her room. When the men's voices rose from the hall, she paused to discern their tone. A lot of pleased chuckles rose up. Bella came to join her.

"Are you sure this is what you want, Jenny?" she asked again.

"Yes, dearest. Don't worry. It's all going to be fine."

Jenny took a deep breath and descended to the hall.

Seated on the drawing room sofa, she tucked her skirts around her. Judd straightened his shoulders and smiled, exhibiting his usual self-assurance. She'd found it surprising when he'd over imbibed that evening at the Assembly. He'd apologized the next day, and sent a flowery note along with a posy, showing the gentlemanly concern for her delicate sensibilities, that her father so approved of. He'd written that he'd been treating a cold and mixed strong medicine with wine. A very bad blend as it turned out. Judd hoped that he hadn't said anything to upset her. He would be horrified if it was so. A delicate lady should never be subjected to a man's sometimes regrettable baser instincts. She'd written back immediately to assure him he hadn't, but that she had decided never to marry.

At the time she'd thought that would be the end of it, but Papa, very angry, had insisted she apologize and go ahead with the marriage. He had issued her with an ultimatum, marry Judd or leave. Jenny knew he didn't want her to leave, he relied on her too much in the running of the house, but she decided the only way to protect her sisters, who Judd had expressed an unhealthy interest in, was to go. She had thought at the time that whatever Judd might do to her was one thing, but to allow him some control over this house was too awful to contemplate. But if he married Bella, he would have carte blanche to treat this family as he saw fit, and she had no confidence in her father preventing him.

Now Judd sat before her. He wasn't handsome, but she couldn't in all honesty call him plain. His full-lipped mouth suggested an overly indulgent nature, his brown hair already graying at the temples, a smile in his hazel eyes she'd come to mistrust. "I am pleased to see you've returned, Miss Harrismith," he said. "Has your aunt recovered?"

What was her father thinking? She would begin a marriage with a lie. It made her even more vulnerable. For a moment, she was tempted to tell him the truth, but it wouldn't do. He might refuse her and take Bella instead. "I'm afraid my aunt's complaint is due to age, Mr. Judd," Jenny said, not exactly deceitful as she was referring to Aunt Leonora. "But she is well cared for."

"I daresay your time in London was good practice for caring for someone who is infirm," he said. "Naturally, I haven't told Mother that you walked about unescorted in that immoral metropolis."

"I doubt I have suffered from the experience." Jenny saw how his implication that she was capable of behaving inappropriately was meant to weaken her.

He nodded, and she caught a dangerous flicker in his eyes. "Perhaps not."

Papa, looking pleased, stood. "Well, shall we have a glass of wine as it is all now settled? I shall place a notice of your engagement in the

Leeds Intelligencer and send it to the *London Chronicle.*"

Rising, Judd bent over Jenny's hand, his gaze probing hers so intensely she wanted to pull her hand away. "I am delighted that you have seen the sense of our marriage, Miss Harrismith."

At the swift tightening of her chest, Jenny almost gasped. She had expected Judd to be unprincipled, sly, and clever, for through his feigned interest in her father's beloved chivalric poetry, had manipulated Papa into believing Judd shared those interests, but she had not expected a deliberate campaign of cruelty. Yet there was no mistaking his vindictive expression. Did he look forward to punishing her for first rejecting him?

RESTLESS, ANDREW SPENT the next few days shut up with the bailiff in the estate room or appeasing his gamekeeper with the promise of a hunt ball in December. He visited his tenant farmers, sat drinking tea and praising the delicious cakes their wives put before him, while listening to any concerns they had. He offered Squire Grimshaw's daughter, Sally, a kitten, and she'd come to the Castlebridge stables to choose one.

Andrew had impressed on Miss Green that Barbara was to be allowed to visit the stables every day. His soft-hearted daughter became upset when the kitten that looked most like Carrot had gone to a new home. It took every bit of Andrew's diplomatic skills to smooth over the ruffled waters.

"Will Ginger have a warm bed, and lots to eat?" Barbara asked, remaining unconvinced.

"Sally promised to take good care of the kitten." He searched his mind for a helpful analogy, but nothing appropriate came to mind. Then he seized on a story he had read to Barbara a few nights previously. "Why, Carrot's baby will be like Cinderella. Remember, sweetheart? Cinderella lived in a simple hut and then went to live in a palace."

Barbara sniffed. "Cinderella was a girl not a kitten."

"Yes, that's true, but still, the kitten has gone to a far better home than our stables," he said, admitting to be failing badly.

Barbara frowned at him suspiciously. "And Sally's home is not a palace."

"The Grange is not precisely a palace, but still very comfortable," he said, burying a sigh.

Barbara's lips trembled. "We must tell Jenny."

Andrew drew his daughter into his arms. "Would you like to ride your pony before luncheon?"

"Yes, Papa."

"Papa?"

"Jenny calls her father papa."

"Does she? Then I shall be papa henceforth."

Before long, Barbara was laughing atop the piebald pony. But Andrew knew it would be short lived. He had ridden to the river with William that morning, and despite promising to fly fish for trout with him tomorrow, the boy remained subdued. Andrew held onto the faint hope that the new governess would quickly replace Jenny in their hearts.

The next day, a letter from Raymond arrived, in answer to Andrew's questions concerning Walter Judd. *He appears to be a respected member of York society, with excellent land and a tidy fortune,* Raymond wrote. *But I have discovered something of interest. Judd is known to visit a brothel when in London. Not so unusual perhaps, for a single man, except that this one caters for abnormal interests. And I've been told that one of the girls was badly beaten by him. It begs a question about Mr. Judd's inclinations. I know you will agree.*

Alarmed Andrew dropped the letter on the desk. Not the sort of man a father would wish for his daughter, surely. Should he make the baron aware of this? Or would it be perceived as unwelcome interference? But could he simply do nothing? He turned to gaze out the window at the gardens, visualizing the young lady who crossed it with his children in tow carrying the ginger kitten. He ran a hand over his jaw as his unease grew.

That evening, he sat alone at the dining table after the covers had been removed, a crystal decanter of brandy and snifter on the table before him. He replenished his glass and sipped the smooth mellow contents. While he would make her father aware of Judd's brutish nature, he accepted that he could provide little proof. His knowledge of Judd was hearsay. He could employ a Bow Street Runner to confirm what Raymond had told him, but that would take time. And if he delayed, it would prove too late. But Ray's letter had so disturbed him he was determined to act to ensure Jenny was safe. And he had to face the real reason behind all of this. He wasn't yet ready to give Jenny up, not without a fight.

He pushed away his glass before the liquor destroyed his clarity of thought. Rising from the table, he stood before the fire, staring into the flames. It had been too long since he'd faced his feelings and been honest with himself. One thing had become clear to him. He wanted Jenny, not just for his children's sake, for his, in his life, and in his bed, for as long as the good Lord chose to bless them. Trouble was, he had no idea of Jenny's feelings for him, for she'd given little sign, beyond the courtesy she afforded him as her employer. Jenny's smile, the warm spark in her lovely eyes, could have been gratitude. He was in danger of making more of it than there was.

There was nothing for it, he had to find out if Jenny wished to marry this man. If she was happy, and felt nothing for him, he would come away and attempt to move on with his life.

The next morning, after breakfast, he rang for the coach to be brought around. And as he planned to put up at a York hotel, he had his valet pack him a portmanteau and accompany him. He wouldn't leave until he was sure that Jenny wasn't hiding something from him. He knew her to be more than capable of sacrificing her own desires for those she loved.

JENNY WOKE TO gray skies. Rain threatened, which reflected her heavy mood. Papa planned to take the carriage into York today. The announcement would appear in Saturday's newspapers. Her marriage to Judd would then become a fait accompli with no chance of escape. But despite her fears, Jenny was determined to go through with it. She would match Judd's sly nature with her feminine wiles. He would not get the better of her. Unless he sought to use violence, and for a moment, that possibility made her panic, and she took several deep breaths to calm herself.

She couldn't back out now. Not after Beth crept into her room last night to tell her how much better she felt to have Jenny here.

"Nothing has happened to worry you, has it, Bethy?" she'd asked fearing her answer.

"Only Geoffrey."

"Who is Geoffrey?"

"My orphaned otter pup. Papa had ordered me to take him back to the river. He says otters bite, and they smell, but Geoffrey never bites me."

Jenny kissed her young sister's cheek. "St. Francis of Assisi would approve of you, Beth."

Beth widened her big eyes. "Why?"

"He was the patron saint of animals. He preached sermons to them and praised all creatures as brothers and sisters under God."

Beth smiled. "I would have liked him, too."

"If anything worries you, you will tell me, won't you?"

Beth pushed back a pale blonde lock and nodded. "I am taking Geoffrey back to the river this afternoon. Would you like to come with me?"

"I should like that very much. Thank you for inviting me." Jenny smiled. Beth always lifted her spirits.

Her father had loosened the purse strings, but it would hardly cover the cost of a wedding gown as other things were needed, Jenny would make her dress. She was quite good with a needle. She and Bella took the carriage into York to purchase material. They returned with a bolt of white satin, ribbons, and silk flowers to dress a straw bonnet. Jenny considered it a practical purchase. She could adapt the dress for future use. She held the material up in front of her before the mirror. Her eyes looked sad. She turned away to take out her sewing-basket, removing scissors, her silver thimble, needles, and thread.

In the afternoon, Jenny and Beth walked back from the river where Geoffrey now restored to health, gamboled, and basked in his freedom. An elegant coach stood on the sweep before the house, and a tall dark haired man had just alighted.

Jenny picked up her skirts and began to run across the damp grass.

"Jenny! Who is it?" Beth cried as she ran after her.

"Andrew George William Hale, Duke of Harrow," Jenny called back breathlessly. Her bonnet fell off and dangled by its ribbons as she leapt over the garden bed onto the gravel drive.

His Grace turned and saw her, and removed his curly beaver hat, smoothing his dark hair.

Jenny slowed her pace, her heart galloping, joy at seeing him for a mad moment blotting out every shred of common sense. But then she slowed.

She set her bonnet back on her head. Why had he come?

Breathless, she stopped and took him in, so elegant in his multi-caped greatcoat and polished hessians. "Your Grace."

His blue eyes pieced the distance between them. "Miss Harrismith. Might I have a word?"

He sounded so formal. She nodded mutely fighting to compose herself.

His Grace gestured with his hand. "Shall we walk?"

They strolled down the carriage drive beneath the avenue of trees. "I find myself curious as to why you left Castlebridge in such a hurry which you failed to address in your letter. And this somewhat rushed engagement. Did you always intend to marry Mr. Judd?"

She stared at him horrified. Did he believe she took the position to draw a reluctant proposal from Judd? Or was he here merely to condemn her for leaving his children? She sobered. "You shouldn't ask me that, Your Grace."

"But I am asking you," he said abruptly. "It's important that I know."

Jenny's throat tightened with suppressed tears. "I'm not in love with Mr. Judd, I have never been in love with him, and I did not foresee an engagement when I came to Castlebridge." She supposed she sounded bitter because he raised his eyebrows.

"I'm sure I will learn more of this later." He studied her thoughtfully, sending her pulse drumming along her veins again. "It is not why I came."

"Why then?" She waited for his criticism as she sank to her lowest ebb, yearning to run back to the house to her bedchamber, and pull the covers over her head. At the gamut of perplexed emotions, she stepped back away from him.

Two strides brought him closer. "I want you to return to Castlebridge, Jenny."

"Why?" she asked in dazed exasperation.

His eyes darkened with emotion. "Why? Because you've come to mean a lot to me, and the children."

She faltered, a refusal on her lips. Even suppose she could accept a life with him in it, loving him, while knowing she was there solely for his children, she couldn't leave Bella to her fate. She wouldn't.

He stared down at her, doubt in his eyes, which was so unlike him. He'd always been so confident, and autocratic, but that was understandable, he was a duke after all. "Dare I hope you might feel some affection for me? That you might choose me instead of Mr. Judd? And come back to Castlebridge as my wife?"

She opened her mouth in surprise. "Marry you?" Jenny feared she'd misheard him. That she'd dreamed him up again. She gazed up at him, the man she'd come to care more for than life itself. He hadn't said he loved her. For a moment she couldn't think. "I would, Your Grace, but there's Bella!"

"Your sister? What about Bella?"

She hesitated, torn by conflicting emotions. "I can't leave again. Bella was going to marry Mr. Judd, and then I said I would..." She tried to explain while he patiently listened. A shortened version of the truth. How she didn't trust Judd and would not let Bella marry him. His eyes narrowed.

He raised an eyebrow. "So you will marry him instead?"

She merely nodded. She couldn't put into words that she was better able to handle Judd.

"Will you leave that to me, Jenny?"

Could she risk Bella's future happiness? Her father was so unpredictable. Papa had so much pride, she suspected it was the reason he forbade Bella from marrying Glyn. Warmed by her love for His Grace, she gazed at the handsome man before her. She was supremely confident that he would set all to rights. Was it unreasonable of her to want his love? How she wished to hear him say those words. "You will protect Bella and Beth?"

He took her hands, his eyes filled with emotion. "Oh, Jenny love, of course I will. I give you that promise."

She was suddenly blissfully happy. "I will marry you, Your Grace. I have been miserable away from the children, and Castlebridge." She wanted to say so much more, but held back, uncertain. "It had become my home, you see."

"My name is Andrew, Jenny." He opened his arms, and she stepped into his strong embrace. Murmuring her name he raised her chin and kissed her.

"So it's my charming children that most appeal?" His amused voice rumbled against her cheek.

"I do miss William and Barbara most dreadfully, I'm so very fond of them."

He pulled back and raised her chin with a finger, his eyes searching hers. "Spare a little of that for me too, Jenny?"

She smiled up at him. "Oh, yes, Andrew."

His passionate glance sent heat rushing through her. "I like the sound of my name on your lips." He kissed her again. The lightest of caresses before he drew away with a sigh and ruefully shook his head. "This is not how it should be done. I must speak to your father. Is the Baron at home?"

"Papa's in the library." She slipped her hand in his and drew him along the driveway to the house. "I'm afraid this will be quite a shock to him. He was about to place a notice of my engagement to Mr. Judd in the newspaper."

He glanced around at the gardens taking note of the disorder. "I'm sure your Papa will come to see the sense of our union."

"My father has unusual notions," she said uneasily. "One cannot always be sure of him. I suspect Mr. Judd holds Papa in thrall due to their shared interest in Medieval poetry."

"I'll make him see sense, Jenny. Surely the safety of his children is paramount."

They strolled up to the house where her sister waited, mouth agape. "Beth, I should like to introduce you to His Grace, Duke of Harrow."

Beth sank into a curtsy. "How do you do, Your Grace." As they continued up the steps, Beth moved closer to Jenny. "Aren't you marrying Mr. Judd?" she whispered. When Jenny shook her head, Beth smiled. "I'm glad. I don't like him."

Jenny smiled mischievously at Andrew as they approached the front door. "You have just missed out on meeting Geoffrey."

He raised his eyebrows, his eyes gleaming. "Geoffrey?"

"We returned Beth's orphaned otter cub to the river this morning."

He winked at Beth. "I am sorry not to have witnessed that."

"I'm sure there will be other times, Beth rescues all sorts of animals." Jenny was floating, a little disbelieving, while fearing someone would pinch her and make her wake. But she came down with a thump at the sight of her father's face as he waited for them in the entry hall.

She hastily introduced them. Andrew, the very essence of grace and civility greeted her father warmly. Then he turned to her. "I should like to speak to your father alone, Jenny."

"You call my daughter by her given name?" Papa gestured down the corridor. "You'd best come into the library then, Your Grace."

The door shut behind them as Bella came quickly down the stairs. "Whose carriage is…"

With a whoop, Jenny ran to hug her. "Andrew has asked me to marry him, and of course I've said yes!"

Bella laughed, but raised her eyebrows in inquiry at Beth who stood by smiling. "Has Jenny lost her reason? Is Andrew who I think it is?"

"The duke." Beth nodded with a grin. "He kissed Jenny. And he's awfully handsome!"

Bella drew in a sharp breath. "My goodness, Jenny. You never led me to believe for a moment that it was a love match."

Jenny pushed away doubt. Elation made her laugh and hug her sisters. Andrew would deal with her father. And he would put a stop to Mr. Judd. He was her shining knight of old, like the ones in her father's poetry. She only hoped her father would recognize it.

"MAY I OFFER you wine, or coffee, Your Grace?" Baron Wetherby asked.

"No, thank you."

Andrew sat opposite him beside the fire. The hall had been cold, the grate in the fireplace unlit, but a hearty coal fire warmed this room. He glanced at the book shelves filled with gilt-edged tomes. More books on poetry and history were piled onto the big oak desk, along with reams of paper. He began to suspect that Baron Wetherby seldom concerned himself with much beyond this room. The estate and the house, or what Andrew had seen of it, looked to be in a bad way. He crossed his legs and met the man's questioning gaze. "As I'm sure you already suspect, I have come to ask for your daughter's hand in marriage, sir."

Wetherby took a moment to digest this. "My daughter is engaged to Mr. Walter Judd."

"But Jenny has no wish to marry him. In fact, she holds him in aversion. So much so that she, and therefore I, will block any attempt for Judd to marry Bella."

"My daughter has fanciful notions. You really shouldn't take them too seriously, Your Grace. Jenny refused Judd once, and the man has shown great generosity in renewing his suit. I greatly fear if she did so again he would make it known to society. She would be labelled a jilt. And should my daughter marry you, that too would cause a scandal, because Jenny has been living under your roof. I'm surprised that does not trouble you."

"Jenny was my children's governess." Andrew decided it would serve no purpose to tell him what had occurred at Castlebridge. It might give Judd the means to cause trouble. "Propriety was always observed."

Wetherby shrugged. "That is as may be. Her time with you will not be viewed in such generous terms by others."

Andrew leaned forward. "Surely, you don't think so poorly of your daughter to believe…"

Wetherby waved a hand. "It doesn't matter what I think. It is what society will make of it. And I anticipate that Judd will be happy to make it common knowledge."

"Then I must supply you with information about Judd that you may not be aware of."

Wetherby frowned. "Oh? And what might that be?"

Andrew told him what Raymond had discovered.

The baron paled visibly. He tugged his cravat and swallowed. "It certainly suggests… I find this hard to believe, although…"

"Although?"

"Jenny was concerned about something Judd had said to her, but I believed it to be a flight of fancy on her part."

"A flight of fancy? Surely, you know your daughter better than that? Jenny is a sensible young woman."

Wetherby nodded. "I see now that I might have been mistaken about Judd."

Andrew wasn't interested in the guilt Wetherby would now have to deal with. He wanted to remove Jenny safely to Castlebridge as soon as possible. And her sisters even if it meant crossing swords with their father. He had promised Jenny and he would not fail her. And he would ensure Judd's silence. No sense in telling Wetherby, of his plans, however. "Then you consider my suit favorable, Baron?"

"Jenny has no dowry. Judd was willing to overlook it." The baron wasn't about to give in easily.

"It is of no concern to me."

"I suppose not." He sighed. "Judd was to make a generous settlement, which would go a long way to see to the younger children's futures."

"Indeed?" Andrew seated himself at his desk and took up a pen. He wrote down an exorbitant figure and handed it to Wetherby.

The baron stared at it and then up at Andrew. "I can hardly reject such a generous sum. I shall have my solicitor draw up the papers."

"There is one further matter, my lord," Andrew said standing before him.

"Oh?"

"Jenny wishes for Bella and Beth to come with her. Bella will have her Season next year and Beth will live with us."

Lord Wetherby frowned. "I am to lose my daughters? What sort of madness is this?"

"Jenny is concerned for her sister's safety."

"Safety? In my house?"

"Should you agree, my lord, I can arrange for your eldest son, Jarred, to be accepted into Oxford."

"Oxford?" The baron held out his hand. "Welcome to the family, Your Grace."

"Thank you." Andrew shook his hand. He thought this man reprehensible in his careless disregard for his children, but he didn't consider him a bad man. Merely a weak rather naïve one, and, with little clue as to how to manage his finances and run his estate, sought distraction in his books.

Andrew left the library in search of Jenny. He didn't have to go far, she waited anxiously in the hall. She drew him into the parlor. "What did my father say?"

Andrew took her hands and smiled wanting to kiss her. "He has agreed to our marriage."

Her hands trembled in his. "Did he agree to Bella and Beth coming with me?"

"He did."

"Oh, Andrew." Jenny's eyes filled with tears and she smiled mistily up at him.

He drew her over to sit on the sofa, as a large scruffy dog ambled into the room, tail wagging.

"That's Rufus," Jenny said as the dog politely sniffed Andrew's boots then went to nudge a black and white cat stretched out on the rug. The cat rolled over and cuffed the dog's nose. With a large sigh, Rufus collapsed onto the carpet and rested his head on his paws.

"Of indeterminate breed, but a dash of pointer perhaps," Andrew said with a chuckle. He sobered, he already had a fair idea of what went on here, but he needed to hear the whole from the beginning, before he left and tackled Judd. "Tell me precisely what happened to drive you from home and what brought you back, Jenny."

She flushed and bit her lip. "It was wrong of me to leave. I should have stayed, matched my wits against Judd's." She began haltingly to describe the scene which occurred between her and Judd, which had frightened her so much she knew she could not marry him. "There was violence in his eyes," she said in a low voice. "And what he said was so disgusting, I felt sick. I couldn't allow Bella to marry Judd in my place." Her eyes grew troubled. "I had to come home straight away and put a stop to it."

He narrowed his eyes, wanting to get his hands on the man. "I'm aware of Judd's cruelty."

Unspoken pain darkened her eyes. "You are?"

"Let us talk no more of this, sweetheart. We have more pleasant matters to discuss."

"Yes. Tell me more about William and Barbara?" Jenny asked. "Is

William behaving himself and riding Lavender? Is Barbara visiting the kittens?"

"As to William, he was, and I can only hope he's behaving in my absence, although Ben and the stable staff will watch him like hawks. Barbara has become very protective of the kittens. They both miss you."

She bit her lip. "I miss them so much. I can't wait to see them."

He told her of his attempt to appease Barbara when she objected to the squire's daughter taking the ginger kitten.

Jenny giggled. "You compared a cat to Cinderella?"

"I'm afraid I lack your skill in handling my daughter," he admitted, with a shake of his head.

Jenny's eyes grew amused, and she looked so adorable, he had to kiss her.

"Now." He reluctantly drew away before he lost himself in her perfumed softness. "The wedding. Shall we be married in London?"

She flushed. "Not Westminster Abbey?"

"No. Or the chapel at Castlebridge?"

"Oh yes, that would be perfect, and then William and Barbara can attend."

"I'll acquire a special license from Doctor's Commons. We can be married in three weeks if that doesn't rush you too much. And should your father agree, I would be delighted if your family and friends were to stay at Castlebridge. Until then, you might stay with your aunt in London while you shop for your trousseau."

"My trousseau?" She frowned. She was worried about the cost. How might he tactfully suggest paying for it?

"I have accounts at several London stores, which would be expedient given we have so little time."

"O?" It just happens that I purchased a bolt of fabric this morning," she said, in her earnest manner, her gray eyes searching his. "It won't take me more than a week or two to sew a wedding gown."

He had guessed right. She doubted her father would pay for her trousseau. He didn't doubt Jenny's expertise with a needle, although he wanted to see her dressed in the finest gowns made by the best modiste in London and Paris. "I am sure my great aunt's dressmaker could fashion you a wedding gown, should you prefer it," he suggested, wanting to give her the world, while understanding how she had been forced to economize.

She bit her lip. "Do you think my dress would look too... homespun?"

"Did you make this dress?" He ran his eye over her slim figure in the straw-colored morning gown.

She nodded.

"You sew as beautifully as any dressmaker. If that is something you wish to do, then by all means make it, Jenny, I have every confidence it will be a beautiful dress. But if you'd rather spend the time gallivanting around London with your siblings, order a wedding dress from Madam De Launay as well as your other requirements."

"That is exceedingly generous of you, Andrew," she said flushing. "London would be such fun. We shall see Jarred. I hope he can get time off to come down for the wedding."

"Let me know the chambers he works for, I'm sure something can be arranged."

A smile lit her eyes. "Could you? That would be perfect."

"Would you like the navy to send Colin home for the wedding?"

She giggled. "Oh you are teasing me. I imagine Colin would be annoyed to be singled out from the rest of the sailors, and for a wedding! But Charlie would love to come to London to visit the London library where he may study Wellington's battle formations. Bella and Beth will visit the park with me and we'll see the sights. Edmond will like Castlebridge excessively too, he expressed a great interest in the chapel."

"Then I am pleased for them all," he said solemnly, while a smile flirted with his lips.

He walked with her to the door. "There is something I must do this afternoon, my love. I shall take my leave of you."

She smiled shyly. "Then we shall see you at dinner."

He kissed her hands. "I look forward to meeting the rest of your family."

The fact that his family had grown somewhat larger in the space of a few hours, appealed to him, as he ordered his coachman to take him into York where he would seek direction to the residence of Walter Judd. He found himself looking forward to their meeting with relish.

Chapter Twenty-Eight

London, two days later

"J ENNY!" BELLA GIGGLED. "Did you see that gentleman ogling us through his pince-nez? His shirt collar pushed up under his chin. He could barely turn his head!"

Jenny took her sister's arms to cross the street, with Aunt Leonora's maid and Andrew's footman in tow. They climbed into Andrew's barouche. "They are known as Bond Street beaus, Bella. Just ignore them."

Her sisters stayed with her at Aunt Leonora's townhouse in Mayfair, only a few streets from Andrew's huge stone mansion in Grosvenor Square, in order to restore some semblance of propriety. It failed to quash the gossips, however, because as soon as the announcement of Jenny's and Andrew's engagement appeared in the *Gazette*, one of the more gossip-oriented newspapers ran an effusive article about the widowed duke who'd found love again with a baron's daughter from Yorkshire. Fortunately, no mention of her being his governess had yet been discovered, but the scandal sheets followed suit, and tongues began to wag, Aunt Leonora informed her, as her card group spoke of little else.

London was thin of company, with most of the *ton* retiring to their country estates for the hunting season, and Andrew assured her that many would not return until parliament sat after Christmas; and talk would die away after they were married, especially with the royals always providing something more outrageous.

Jenny tried not to think of her father's parting words. "You are most fortunate," he said. "It appears you have become indispensable to the duke, because of your excellent care of his children. And the only way for that to continue, is for him to marry you. I hope that doesn't mean you'll become a drudge."

While she refused to believe her father was right, it did cast an element of doubt in her mind. Andrew was always attentive and affectionate. But was it just affection he felt for her rather than love? They had shared a most alarming experience as they worked to keep William safe. It had drawn them together. Was she foolish to wish for a deep passion? Andrew had been so broken-hearted after Lady Catherine died, he hadn't sought to remarry for years. How could Jenny, who was not even a beauty, replace Catherine in his heart? Or was she being unreasonable to even want to? Should she be satisfied with less? She feared it might break her heart.

"I have one more fitting for my bridesmaid dress," Beth said as the carriage rocked through the busy streets. "I can't wait to try on again. It's quite the most beautiful dress I've ever seen!"

Hours were spent at Madam De Launay's salon while the girls' dresses were made, and Jenny was fitted for a new ballgown. Andrew had insisted on a completely new wardrobe, explaining that as soon as dinner parties, routs, breakfasts, and balls began, she would have need of it. Madam was known to have created gowns for the cream of society, and her salon was very elegant. The bridesmaid's dresses of white tulle trimmed with pink ribbon sashes and five rows of silk roses at the hem and sleeves, were almost finished, in what Jenny considered to be a remarkably short time. But Madam De Launay did employ a number of seamstresses.

"Jenny is still hemming her wedding gown," Bella said with a laugh. "You'll be the first bride to marry in a half made gown, Jenny."

Jenny grinned. "I finished it last night, while you two were asleep."

"I'm relieved," Bella said. "You don't want dark shadows under your eyes on your wedding day."

Jenny's stomach tightened again with nerves. She hoped Andrew would think her pretty. It wasn't an elaborate gown, but rather simple in style, the satin good quality, and the Belgian lace had been her mother's, and was very fine. She would wear her mother's pearls and Bella was very good at arranging her hair. It was a simple affair in Castlebridge with only family and a few of Andrew's friends in attendance didn't require a lavishly adorned gown. Although the ball which was to be held in December at Castlebridge certainly would. Andrew's secretary, Mr. Bishop had already sent out four hundred gilt-edged invitations. Jenny knew that there would be much to do to arrange such a grand affair and assumed preparations were already underway. It would be required of her to oversee it. How odd to be liaising with the housekeeper. What would the staff make of her? Jenny hoped their recent benevolence would withstand the shock of her becoming their new mistress. She had managed a small staff after her mother died, but nothing of the size of Castlebridge.

She would be a duchess! The thought brought on a crippling attack of nerves, but she breathed deeply and vowed to tackle it heart and soul, determined to make Andrew proud.

Andrew had declined the few soirees and dinner parties they'd been invited to, until Jenny had her new gowns. He escorted her and her sisters to Hyde Park in the barouche which caused quite a traffic jam on the South Carriage Drive, when they were stopped by those riding and promenading, keen to speak to Andrew, and be introduced to Jenny and her sisters, while curious glances appeared at carriage windows. Beth was struck dumb by the experience and had to be told not to stare.

Jenny was quite happy to fill in the short time left before her wedding in less stressful pursuits. Her sisters accompanied her when she shopped for her trousseau, including her underwear, nightwear, shoes, gloves, and hats at the most fashionable stores. The fact that Andrew had an account there made the shop assistants eager to serve her, fussing like moths around a lantern. Boxes and packages were delivered to her aunt's townhouse hourly.

Aunt Leonora, who was in her sixty-fifth year, confessed to finding the whole affair vastly diverting, and was delighted that Andrew insisted she have a new costume made for the wedding. Surprisingly, she had expressed some eagerness to co-chaperone Bella during her Season next year.

They arrived back at the house and darted inside, laughing about a lady's outrageously tall hat they'd seen. In the bedchamber, Jenny shared with the girls, they began to open boxes and strip away paper. Bella pulled out a beaded reticule of a beautiful deep indigo blue. "This is quite lovely."

Jenny smiled at her. "Then you shall have it."

"Thank you, dearest," Bella kissed her cheek.

"Aunt Leonora and I discussed your Come-out next year," Jenny said. "And we have decided we will both be chaperones." She hoped Bella would be excited by the prospect, but her sister merely studied a royal purple velvet hat with the broad, flat brim, turning it in her hands.

Bella replaced it in its box and sighed. "That is very good of you both."

"You will be assured of an excellent Season, Bella. You're so pretty, and now with a duke for a brother-in-law…"

"Yes, I know," Bella said in a flat voice. "I am most fortunate."

Jenny put an arm around her shoulders. "But you don't want it."

"I should, Jenny. You've been so good…"

"It's because of Glyn, isn't it, dearest?"

Bella sighed again and nodded.

"Why not write to him and ask him to come to London?" Beth said.

Bella shook her head. "I couldn't do that, Bethy."

"But why not?" Beth asked.

"He may not be able to get away, or to afford such an expense."

If Glyn were to approach their papa now, might he have a better chance? Jenny wondered. "No, he may not," she said. "But you'll never know unless you ask him."

Bella shook her head. "We leave London at the end of the week, and it's pointless when Papa won't budge an inch."

"Then why don't you elope?" Beth said. "Once you are married, Papa cannot object."

Jenny laughed. "You are a minx, Beth."

"I know," Beth said with a grin. "But life is for taking chances. Look at Jenny. If she hadn't taken a position as a governess she would be married to Mr. Judd."

Jenny went cold at the thought. She hadn't asked Andrew what he and her father had discussed, but he'd told her she would never hear from Judd again. She was profoundly relieved, but still did not want her sisters to return to Yorkshire and was glad that Andrew had invited them to live with her at Castlebridge.

A rap on the knocker made them rush to the door. It opened to reveal the smiling face of their eldest brother, Jarred.

They all squealed and hugged him and dragged him into the parlor for tea.

Jenny thought he looked lanky and thin, and his hair needed cutting. He sat beside her on the sofa while the others crowded about him. "I couldn't believe it when I got your letter. I can't wait to hear how it came to pass, but not today, I cannot stay long. I must return to the Inns of Court."

Jenny told him of Andrew's promise to guarantee Jarred a place at university, beginning in the next semester, should he wish to, and that he would also ensure some time off for him to come to Castlebridge for the wedding.

Her brother was speechless for several minutes. He cleared his throat. "I should like it above anything, Jenny."

"Then you will come to the wedding?"

Jarred grinned. "Just try to stop me."

ANDREW SAT IN White's library with Castlereagh. He wasn't completely confident when he'd decided to ask him to stand up as his best man. But when Andrew saw him, he decided against it. Castlereagh seemed forgetful and distracted. He was severely overworked and suffering great criticism, which seemed to have impaired his fine mind.

"The congress system is teetering on the edge of collapse," Castlereagh said, tapping a finger on the leather arm of his chair. "There's sure to be more trouble, the dissidents might be better organized next time. I give it another year."

Andrew nodded, filled with compassion for his friend. "I am in agreement with you. What shall you do, Robert? You need to rest."

Castlereagh nodded. "My doctor has advised it. I am about to retire to Cray for a time, perhaps Loring Hall will perform its magic and heal me."

"I'm sure it will," Andrew said forcing enthusiasm into his voice.

Castlereagh rubbed his forehead. "You had something to tell me."

Andrew smiled. "I am about to be married."

"Then I must congratulate you, my friend," Castlereagh said. "I hope you have chosen wisely. The Baroness, isn't it?"

"No, the lady's name is Jenny Harrismith. She is the daughter of Baron Wetherby from York."

Castlereagh stared at him. Then a grin flittered across his face. "By Jupiter, that is good news, Harrow!" He reached across to thump Andrew on the arm. "I thought it would be the German lady."

Andrew wondered how he would think it possible after the business with Ivo, but he merely nodded.

"Rather quick, I must say. Fallen head over heels, one might hope."

"You will like her, Robert, she is a wonderful young lady, brave, resourceful, kind, compassionate…"

"And comely?"

Andrew smiled. "Very."

Castlereagh nodded wisely. "Head over heels."

Andrew left White's saddened by the state of his friend's health. Carrying his valise, he strolled to Lady Naughton's house. A smile from Jenny would raise his spirits.

After greeting Lady Naughton, he requested a quiet moment with his bride to be. Jenny came into the parlor soon after. Dressed in a primrose colored gown, her hair done in a new and flattering style with curls framing her face, she came forward holding out her hands to him. "I am so glad to see you! I have so much to tell you."

He pressed a kiss to each hand. "You are not tiring yourself, sweetheart? Do your preparations go well?"

"Very well indeed." She invited him to sit. "What a pity you have missed Jarred. He has just returned to the Inns of Court. When he learned he could attend Oxford, he was speechless! He wishes me to thank you although he shall himself at the wedding."

Andrew sat beside her on the sofa. "No need for that, it is my pleasure to do it. I'm pleased that your father has agreed to it. It can't have been easy for him to admit to a failing."

"No, it would not be, but Papa has seen the sense of it, and his own time spent at Oxford meant a lot to him."

Andrew still struggled with her father's shabby treatment of his children, but he pushed the thought away, and opened the valise he carried. He withdrew the jewel boxes from Rundell, Bridge & Rundell jewelers, and those from his bank that he'd visited earlier. He placed them beside him on an occasional table. "I have something for you, your sisters and your aunt."

Jenny put her hands to her cheeks. "Oh my goodness."

"I intend to spoil you, Jenny." He smiled enjoying her delight. The first time in her life that anyone had spoiled her, perhaps. "I can have the size adjusted, if need be." He flipped open a small box to reveal a diamond ring set in gold.

He took her hand and slipped it onto her slim finger. "This was the duchess'."

She held the diamond ring up to the light causing it to flash. "Oh, it's exquisite, Andrew. And fits perfectly."

Andrew had chosen one of the daintier diamond necklaces and earrings from the Harrow jewels kept at his bank. The Harrow diamond tiara was at Castlebridge, should she wish to wear it to the wedding. "I trust this will go with your gown?"

She gasped. "How beautiful! They would dress any gown. Now I shall perfectly look the part."

At the hint of something in her voice, he took the box from her hand, and put it to one side. He smiled into her lovely eyes. "You will make a fine duchess, Jenny. Of that I have no doubt." He slid his arms around her waist and took her mouth in a kiss. She reached up a hand to his nape.

The door opened, and Lady Naughton appeared. She paused, and cleared her throat, while Bella and Beth, lacking the same delicacy of mind, pushed past her.

"What have you there, Your Grace?" Beth asked.

Jenny shook her head. "Bethy, you really should learn patience."

Andrew stood. "A gift." He handed both her sisters a small box.

"Oh! How divine!" Thrilled, Beth put it on and held up her arm to admire the dainty diamond bracelet.

"Thank you, Your Grace," Bella said with a shy smile.

"And this for Lady Naughton." Andrew handed her the larger box.

Her cheeks flushed, their aunt took out the sparkling diamond and ruby brooch. "It is magnificent, thank you, Your Grace. May I offer you refreshment?"

"No, thank you, Lady Naughton. I must go. I shall see you all at the wedding. And what a bevy of beauty there will be to decorate my chapel!" He held his arm out to Jenny. "Walk with me to the door, Jenny?"

At the front door, Andrew lifted her chin with his finger and scanned her face. He dropped a light kiss on her lips. "You are content? Nothing worries you?"

With a smile, she reached up to touch his cheek. "Goodness no, why should there be? I would be most ungrateful."

After leaving her, Andrew walked toward Grosvenor Square. Was Jenny perfectly happy? Had he caught something in her eyes, a slight shadow of doubt? Or was he searching for something that didn't exist? It was just that he knew her. While the ring and the diamonds delighted her, she was not one to be bowled over by presents, even jewels. Her family was more important to her, the comfort and security of far too many souls, in fact, seemed to rest on her slim shoulders. He couldn't help but admire her selflessness and generosity. She had claimed his heart and given his life meaning.

Chapter Twenty-Nine

IT OCCURRED TO Jenny that Bella was acting oddly. Her sister seemed preoccupied and had disappeared for nearly half an hour while shopping with Aunt Leonora. Jenny was so busy, she pushed it to the back of her mind, intending to broach it with her. But now they were about to depart for Castlebridge, and it was hardly the right time for confidences. Her aunt's maid traveled with their trunks and bandboxes in the chaise while Andrew's coach waited in the street to take them to Oxfordshire, drawing attention from passersby.

When Beth had one foot on the coach step, she suddenly squealed and dashed onto the road. A passing hackney driver yelled at her. A small shaggy dog had just passed beneath its wheels. Beth scooped it up, and hugging it to her chest, returned to the coach.

"The poor animal," she cried, climbing inside with the thin dog in her arms. "He was almost run over! He is all skin and bone."

"Dear heaven," their aunt cried. "We shall be covered in fleas, and goodness knows what else!"

Jenny laughed as the dog burrowed in between her and Beth and rested its head on its paws, for all the world as if it traveled in a fine coach every day of the week.

"I don't know what His Grace will say," Aunt Leonora said mournfully. "He will not be allowed to join the duke's hounds."

"With a bath and some good food, I daresay he will shape up well enough," Jenny said with a giggle. She didn't think Andrew would object.

With six horses and two postilions, they reached the estate in the early afternoon. Her sisters were astounded by the size and grandeur of Castlebridge, even Beth fell silent when two footmen in livery came to put down the steps and usher them through the tall front doors to the waiting butler.

Jenny was surprised that Andrew was not here to meet them. Forrester bowed before her. He was momentarily fazed by the animal in Beth's arms, as she introduced him. "Ladies. Welcome home, Miss Harrismith." His expression remained as impassive as ever, but she caught a twinkle in his eye. "Perhaps the footman can take the dog to the stables for now?"

"Yes, Beth. Until Horace is bathed he must remain there," Jenny said.

"You will give him a good meal of meat first?" Beth asked, clutching the dog to her breast.

"Rest assured it will be done, Miss Beth."

Forrester snapped his fingers, and the footman took the dog from Beth's reluctant arms. "We shall take good care of him, miss," George said.

Forrester cleared his throat. "Miss Harrismith, an upstairs maid, Susan, will attend you and awaits you in your bedchamber. Mrs. Pollitt has placed you all in the guests' wing. I trust you'll find it satisfactory." He signaled to the footman. "Take the ladies up, Jeremy."

"We will go to the schoolroom, Forrester," Jenny said, pulling off her gloves and handing her coat and bonnet to a footman. "Are the children there?"

"With the new governess, my lady."

"I shall go directly to my room," her aunt said. "I need to wash off the travel dust." She cast a frown at Beth. "And I trust it is only dust."

"Certainly, Lady Naughton," Forrester said smoothly. "Your maid has been sent to the servant's quarters. She will join you directly."

When Jenny and her sisters entered the schoolroom, a small, neatly dressed, red-haired woman leaned over the table as the children wrote in their books. William and Barbara looked up and saw her.

Barbara squealed.

William pushed back his chair and greeted Jenny with a formal bow. The young heir had adopted an air of consequence, which she suspected hid the hurt he suffered at what he must feel was her betrayal. Her heart went out to him, but aware of his pride, she must deal gently with him.

"Jenny!" With a sob in her voice, Barbara cast herself onto Jenny's breast.

Jenny kissed the little girl's cheek streaked with tears. "Now, is that the way to behave, Barbara? You must introduce me to your new governess."

"I should like you to meet Miss Wagstaff, Miss Harrismith," William said stiffly.

The governess' smooth round face bore a pleasant expression. She came forward to greet them. "How do you do, Miss Harrismith?"

"I am sorry to interrupt your lessons, Miss Wagstaff. We shan't stay above a few minutes. Please meet my sisters, Miss Arabella Harrismith and Miss Elizabeth Harrismith."

After the introductions, Beth bent and whispered to Barbara something that made the little girl giggle. William overheard her and edged closer. "You brought a dog with you, Miss Beth?"

"Yes, Horace is a new member of the family. I shall introduce you to him when he has had his bath."

"And has your hedgehog left home?" William had begun to look more like the young William, Jenny knew, as his stiff formality dropped away.

"Yes, Heggie has returned to the woods. But I must tell you about Geoffrey when we meet again. Geoffrey is my otter cub."

"An otter? Oh yes, I should like that," William said, grinning.

"If Miss Wagstaff will please bring you to the yellow salon at four o'clock, we shall have tea and a lovely long chat," Jenny said. "I must speak to your father."

"Will you come and visit the kittens, Jenny?" Barbara asked. "They've missed you."

"Have they, poppet? I am sorry. Shall we go to the stables after tea and you can meet Horace?" She hoped the dog would not upset the kittens.

"You and the duke must not meet, Jenny," Bella said as they were shown to their bedchambers. "It's bad luck when the wedding is tomorrow."

Jenny laughed. "I don't hold with superstition, Bella."

"Oh? Then why did you sew a blue ribbon onto your best petticoat and borrow my pearl hair comb?"

"Oh, very well." Jenny laughed and tucked her hand into her sister's arm. "I don't see how we can avoid Andrew at dinner. Must we eat in the kitchen?"

"I hadn't considered that," Bella said.

"And I need to discuss the wedding guests with him. He must accompany me when I meet the staff."

"But haven't you met them?" Beth asked in surprise.

"Not as their new mistress." The prospect unnerved her. She needed Andrew at her side before she faced them. Where was he?

The question was answered as she was directing Susan with the unpacking of her trunk. Andrew knocked and strode in. One gesture sent the maid scurrying from the room. "Jenny, I didn't expect you for another hour."

"You can thank your coachman, fine horses and postilions for a swift journey," she said with an impish smile. She gazed up into his beloved face. "Bella will disapprove, I am not supposed to see you until tomorrow."

"Did she? Then we shan't tell her." He drew her into his embrace and nuzzled her neck. "My best man, John Strathairn, and Lady Sibella arrive today, as does my cousin, Raymond, and his mother, my Aunt Augusta who wishes to meet Lady Naughton. With your pretty sisters, we shall enjoy a lively pre-wedding dinner party."

"Beth is only thirteen," she said sternly. "And Bella is not yet out."

He planted small kisses across her cheek and took her mouth in a passionate kiss, leaving her breathless. "We have no such rules at

Castlebridge," he murmured huskily.

She laughed and drew away from him while attempting to ignore her desire to draw him close. "You are in my bedchamber, sir. I believe it shall be required of me to set a few rules."

A smile tugged his lips. "And here I am thinking I'm marrying an angel, when it appears I'll get a strict schoolmarm instead."

She placed her hands on his waistcoat and gazed up into his smiling eyes. "We shall see, Your Grace."

He raised his eyebrows. "Will we? I find I can hardly wait." He cast a brief glimpse at the bed. "A few steps and we might find out now."

"Andrew!" She grinned and pushed at his chest.

He sighed heavily. "Very well. I am a patient man. Or will have to be at any rate."

"Yes. Especially with my Aunt Leonora in the next room."

He held up a hand. "I am leaving. But first tell me, have you seen the children?"

"Yes." She sighed. "It might take William a while to forgive me."

He smiled. "An hour or two, perhaps."

"I do hope so. He was beginning to thaw a little," she admitted. "And I like what I've seen of the new governess."

"Yes, she isn't you, but the next best thing, perhaps. And William's tutor begins in a few days."

"And Nurse Green?"

"She has mellowed, a little nervous at first, I suspect. The children will grow accustomed to her, and of course, they have a mother's love to protect them."

And she would be checking on Miss Green to make sure the children were happy and contented with their nurse. In fact, she would be there so often, Miss Green would undoubtedly lose patience with her.

"You have yet to introduce me to your staff, Andrew."

"You shall meet them all tomorrow, after the wedding. As my Duchess."

Her throat tightened, and she swallowed. "Yes, of course."

"You shall make a very lovely and regal duchess." He lowered his head for another brief kiss, then stepped back away from her. "I am leaving, Jenny." He pulled open the door, threw her a kiss, and was gone.

Jenny sank down onto the bed as warmth flooded through her. She dwelt for several pleasurable minutes on her betrothed before Susan returned. If he'd stayed much longer, her defenses would have weakened, and then where would they be? Such a devastatingly attractive man she was marrying, could she hope to be everything he wanted in a wife?

She shook her head, annoyed with herself for woolgathering, and rose when Susan knocked. There was much to do, her father and the boys would be arriving this afternoon. She must ensure their needs were well taken care of although she had little doubt they would be.

After tea, Beth, Bell, and the children walked to the stables. When they entered they were met with a surprise. Horace was lying on the straw with a kitten clinging to his neck and another playing with his shaggy tail. "It seems he's being made welcome," Bella said with a laugh.

As Andrew made his way down the great staircase, through the long window, a carriage drew up at the door. Two young lads, and the eldest boy, Jarred, alighted with their father. The Baron gazed around as he unbuttoned his coat. Andrew continued his descent determined to make him welcome.

He was greeted first by Charlie. "I'd like to visit the stables, Your Grace," he said without preamble. "I bet you've got some prime bloods."

"Indeed I do, Charlie." He held out his hand to Baron Wetherby. "Welcome to Castlebridge, Baron. I trust you had a pleasant journey?"

The baron shoved his gloves in his pocket and shook Andrew's hand. "Good day, Your Grace. Carriage journeys are never what one might call pleasant, but here we are without mishap."

"Your daughters arrived an hour ago. They will be taking tea in the yellow salon at four. But a footman will direct you to them should you wish to see them now."

Wetherby shrugged out of his greatcoat and handed it and his hat to a footman. "Might we first have a word in private, Duke?"

"Certainly." Andrew turned. "George, take Master Charles and Master Edmond to the stables. I believe William is there and I know he's eager to meet them."

"I'll go with you," Jarred said, revealing a shared interest in horse-flesh.

"Please come this way, Baron."

In the library, Andrew poured them both a glass of claret, and directed the baron to an armchair. It appeared the man had something to say.

Wetherby accepted the glass of wine with a nod of thanks. "I took my sons to London for a treat before we came here," he said. "Put up at Kirkham's Hotel, in Brook Street for a couple of nights, quite enjoyed it, as did the boys. I visited Bow Street Magistrate's Court and made a few inquiries."

"Learn anything?"

"Indeed I did. I discovered the truth of your claim concerning Judd." He took a long swig of his wine and his pale face warmed a little. "I was appalled, and must apologize to you, for doubting you. I simply had no idea, Judd was always so obliging, I'd never seen any evidence there was violence in the man."

"No need to apologize to me, Baron, but you might wish to do so, to Jenny," Andrew said.

"Yes, I will, of course. After the wedding. Such discussions have no place here."

He took another deep sip. "It's relieved my mind that my heir will attend Oxford. In fact, I've changed my opinion on a number of matters." He drank the last dregs in his wine glass and put it down. "Now, if you'll excuse me, I will freshen up and then seek out my daughters. They are all at the stables?"

"Yes, meeting the new acquisition?"

"A horse?"

"No, a dog. Rather a ramshackle animal, apparently. Beth saved it from being run over and brought it down from London."

"Oh, good heavens!" The baron threw back his head and laughed. "I do apologize for my daughter, Your Grace!"

Andrew grinned. "No need." He rose with a half bow. "I will see you at dinner. We have quite a party."

"Oh?" Wetherby nodded with a pleased smile. "I shall look forward to it."

Chapter Thirty

A S SHE ARRANGED the shawl collar on her new morning gown of white muslin with pale blue dots, and tied the frilled cuffs, Jenny gazed out the window of her bedchamber. Her view took in the stables, and part of the carriageway where it emerged from the park, bordered by the fringe of home wood. She gasped when Bella hurried into sight. Carrying a portmanteau, she ran across the lawn and crossed the carriageway. A moment later, she disappeared into the trees.

Jenny's heart sank. She quickly finished dressing and left her bed-chamber. Ten minutes later, she hurried across the lawns after her sister. Where was Bella off to? Had she left them without a word? Jenny refused to believe her sister would do such a thing. They had always been close; why keep this from her?

She reached the trees, and holding up her skirts, dashed along the bridle path. Voices reached her. When Jenny emerged into a small glade, Bella stood with Glyn, their handsome brown-eyed neighbor from Yorkshire, his arms around her.

Over Bella's head, Glyn met Jenny's angry gaze with a look of dismay.

Bella swung around.

"You are eloping," Jenny cried. "You would leave the day before my wedding? Without a word? Don't you trust me, Bella?"

Bella left Glyn and ran to her. "No, that's not how it is, Jenny! We plan to go tomorrow after the wedding. I didn't want to upset you before then. I'm just here to give Glyn my bag."

"Are you sure this is the right thing to do, Bella?" Jenny asked, fearing for her sister.

"Yes, we…"

Loud voices erupted from the direction of the carriageway. Bella turned to Glyn. "You must go!"

His face set, Glyn shook his head. "I won't leave you, my love."

Moments later, Charlie, Edmond and William appeared.

Charlie hurried up to them. "What has happened? We saw you from the stable yard."

"It's not important, Charlie," Bella said impatiently, "I just wanted to talk to Glyn."

"But you have a portmanteau with you," Edmond observed. "Are you going away with Glyn, Bella?"

"She is not," came an angry voice. They all spun around as Papa emerged into a shaft of sunlight.

"Papa…" Bella took two steps toward him. "It's not Glyn's fault. I had to see him."

Glyn gently moved her aside. "Milord, we wish to marry, and because you refuse, we plan to elope."

"Arabella has not come of age. I could have you thrown into jail."

"Oh, Papa, you wouldn't," Jenny said. "You must understand their feelings. You were in love once."

He blinked at her. "*Once? Once?* I will always love your mother, girl, and don't you forget it! But we did things in the proper manner."

While he stood scowling at them, Bella returned to stand by Glyn. She held his arm. "You won't stop us, Papa."

He shook his head. "I certainly could if I chose to, Bella. Come to the house, Glyn. We need to talk."

Astonished, Jenny gazed at her sister, then they followed their father through the trees, the boys running ahead.

An hour later, when Andrew joined them in the salon for tea, the matter had been settled. Bella and Glyn would marry next year, on her eighteenth birthday. Glyn was to stay at Castlebridge for the wedding and then return home to tell his parents the news. Bella was floating on air.

Jenny couldn't wait to tell Andrew. It seemed as if Castlebridge had wrought some magic. Something of great importance had happened to her family. But it was ultimately Andrew who brought it about. The miraculous change in her father could only be put down to his improved finances, and the heavy burden removed from his shoulders. Papa accepted that Bella would soon be gone, and Beth would remain here with her. He also gave them details of his plan to employ more staff and improve the lot of his tenants, so the estate would be in a sound position when it came time for Jarred to inherit. In the meantime, Jarred would return home during the long university holidays to learn the many things he would need to know.

That evening, Bella preferred to dine with Glyn, Jarred, Beth, and the boys, while the guests ate in the dining room, an elegant room with walls painted pale green with scrolling vines, and the floor covered in a patterned Axminster carpet. A chandelier sent down dancing lights from the high ceiling, the long table covered in starched white linen and laid with sparkling crystal, porcelain, and silverware and flowers. A merry fire crackled in the marble fireplace, footmen and the butler standing ready to serve them.

Jenny's father appeared to enjoy the company of the amusing guests, which he had long denied himself. Jenny finally met the Marquess of Strathairn and his beautiful dark-haired wife, Sibella, who had the most beautiful emerald green eyes Jenny had ever seen. What a delightful couple they were. The big, fair-haired man exuded a calm strength. Jenny was so grateful to him for saving her life, but he swept away her attempts to thank him. Aunt Leonora and Lady Augusta seemed to get on famously. The French Baron was warm and charming, his wife, Hetty, a vivacious red-head, had invited Jenny to one of her poetry readings in London. The Montsimon's quite obviously still very much in love.

Then the covers were brought in, bringing delicious aromas to blend with the scents of beeswax and the floral arrangements placed about the room, and Andrew caught and held her gaze from where he sat at the head of the table, flanked by the two older ladies. Jenny had worn her new evening gown of light green silk with alternating bands of satin and taffeta, cut in a low square at the neck with a tight bodice, and her diamonds. When Andrew's eyes conveyed his impatience to be with her, Jenny lost the thread of her conversation with the vicar who expressed how delighted he was to be marrying them in the Castlebridge chapel, which had always been a wish of his.

"And I look forward to many baptisms," he said, slightly flushed from the wine and champagne, and earning a frown from his wife.

THE MORNING OF the wedding dawned cool and fine. Beyond Jenny's window, the sky was a wide expanse of gray-blue. The rattle of another guest's carriage arriving at the stable block, sent excitement, and a quiver of nerves down her spine.

Surprisingly, she had slept well. She sat at her dressing table and drank her chocolate and nibbled on a warm roll, her mind on the wedding. The preparations for the ceremony and the wedding breakfast were swiftly accomplished as if by invisible elves, the servants slipping out of sight into the many passages in the old house. Susan described the delicious food Cook had prepared for the wedding breakfast as she laid out Jenny's wedding gown. "Your dress is very pretty, Miss Harrismith, it will suit you."

Jenny certainly hoped so. She ran a critical eye over the soft satin folds. The bodice was cut square round the bust, and ornamented with white satin roses, a narrow satin sash beneath the bustline. More lace and roses decorated the short full sleeves, and the bottom of the skirt. Bella thought it lovely: the trimming tasteful, and the general effect understated and elegant. Jenny agreed, especially because it was sewn with love.

At the thought of Andrew's passionate glances, another frisson of excitement raced through her. After she left this room, her clothes would be taken to the duchess's apartments. She had viewed the rooms yesterday. The walls of the bedchamber were papered in a floral pattern of rose and green with matching bed hangings and curtains, the overall effect delightfully feminine, a dressing room adjoined, and through another door, there was a sitting room which led to Andrew's apartments. She stood quietly in the bedchamber, nerves fluttering in her stomach at the thought of sharing his bed. This is where their lives really began. Her love for him was so deeply passionate, he could never disappoint her, she only hoped she would please him.

Bella and Beth came into the room. "Is it time to dress, Jenny?" Beth said breathlessly.

Jenny laughed, "No, Bethy. Be patient. Not for a couple of hours yet."

ANDREW STOOD BEFORE the altar in the Castlebridge chapel with its long arched stained glass windows, barrel ceiling, and dark oak pews, where many of his ancestors had married. It seemed right for them to marry here at Castlebridge, where they had first met and where they would spend a good deal of their lives. He turned to smile at his children, who sat beaming from the front pew beside Aunt Augusta and Raymond. Opposite, were Jenny's three brothers. Behind them were Andrew's friends who had made the trip from Ireland, Flynn, and Althea with their blond baby son in her arms. Beside them sat Guy Fortescue and Hetty who had left their brood behind at Rosecroft Hall.

Castlereagh had remained at his country estate, but sent his best wishes.

"Nervous, Duke?" Strathairn asked, standing beside him.

Andrew chuckled. "Rather more eager than nervous."

"As it should be. Sibella and I approve of your bride. In fact, Sibella was very taken with her, found her delightfully unaffected."

The organist struck up the Wedding March and Andrew turned as two pretty young ladies in white gowns decorated with rows of pink roses, a circlet of roses in their hair, and bouquets from the Castle-bridge hothouses, advanced slowly single file down the aisle. Then behind them, the bride. Jenny, a vision in white walking serenely down the aisle with a hand on her father's arm. He caught his breath. She had never looked more beautiful, in the slim-fitting gown of white satin embellished with white and silver roses and froths of lace. A small veil floating from the Harrow tiara, diamonds at the ears and her throat.

The music swelled and soared up to the arched ceiling as they advanced down the aisle toward him, the guests turning to view the bride from their pews decorated in white flowers and silver ribbon.

Jenny stood beside him with that special smile she reserved just for him.

The sadness he'd always carried in his heart eased away, and he looked forward with joy to the future.

Chapter Thirty-One

AFTER JENNY DISMISSED Susan, she perched on the stool before the mirror in her negligee, a little nervous, as she waited for Andrew. She was a duchess! Did she look different? More confident, perhaps. It had been a small, intimate, and perfect wedding. The ceremony passed in a blur. Andrew, smiling down at her, so handsome and imposing in his superbly cut black and white clothes, a diamond winking from his crisp white cravat. His best man, Strathairn, beside him. The vicar looked nervous and cleared his throat several times before reading from the Book of Common Prayer. Her father, smiling his approval of her at last, gave her away, then the exchange of vows and the wedding ring, and Andrew's too brief kiss. After signing the register they joined hands to leave the chapel for the wedding breakfast. Her sisters, so lovely in their pink and white dresses, Bella smiling at Glyn, and little Beth flushed with pleasure. Jenny couldn't wish for more.

She had warmed to Andrew's friends. The handsome French-born baron, Guy Fortescue, and his poetess wife, Hetty; the Irish diplomat, Viscount Flynn Montsimon, and the lovely Althea. The guests gathered in the double drawing room where the furniture had been removed to create a dance floor. A trio played Bach until Forrester announced that the breakfast was served. How elegant it all was, and how perfect. The delicious food, and the amusing and uplifting speeches, Andrew's friends made, toasting them with champagne. The cutting of the cake, a huge white marzipan covered cake rich with brandy. And later, in Andrew's arms dancing the bridal waltz as he murmured teasing and sensual things in her ear, which made her laugh and yearn for him.

Jenny smiled into the mirror. Afterward, Andrew had taken her below stairs and introduced her as his duchess to the staff who were enjoying their own party. He thanked them all, and especially Cook for the elegant repast. The servants then toasted them with glasses of champagne. But best of all was when William had allowed Jenny to hug him, and Barbara had called her Mama.

The door opened, and Jenny's heart began its wild beating. Andrew walked in dressed in a midnight blue silk dressing gown with gold tassels. She caught her breath. She refused to believe her father's warning that Andrew had married her for his children's sake. And she'd dealt with whether he could love her after he'd mourned Catherine so long. It no longer concerned her. She trusted her future to the fine man she had married.

Jenny rose as he crossed the carpet, trembling a little, to meet him. Her gaze roamed his face from his firm, freshly shaved jaw to his slow smile. She was caught by the passionate fire in his eyes.

"I am the most fortunate of fellows." He took hold of her hands. "Such a beautiful bride walking down the aisle on your father's arm." The touch of his lips on her palms sent an erotic thrill through her. "It all went well, didn't it?"

Filled with an almost painful longing, she smiled, wanting to kiss him. "It was quite perfect," she murmured.

"The children are so happy to have you back again."

"As am I. I love them dearly."

"Yes, I know you do." One arm slid around her waist. He lifted her chin and lowered his mouth to hers in a long passionate kiss, which left her breathless. "While I am happy for my children's sake, Jenny," he said after he'd drawn away, "Please know that I married you for my own selfish reasons." He tucked a long curly brown lock back over her shoulder and untied the bow at the neck of her negligee. The garment slipped from her shoulders, and he drew it away and tossed it onto a chair.

She yearned to declare her love for him, the words trembled on her tongue. Might she embarrass him? What if he didn't wish to hear it?

"I want you so much, darling," he said as her nightgown joined her dressing gown on the chair. She stood naked before him. He stroked her arm with the lightest of caresses and just looked at her. "You are very lovely, Jenny," he said in a husky voice. The raw passion in his eyes made her shiver in anticipation.

He stripped off his dressing gown and stood naked before her, proud and erect. Rendered breathless by the sight of his strong, muscular body, and the evidence of his desire for her, her senses reeled. Slowly, he drew her against him, a bare touch of skin against skin, and took her mouth in another long, demanding kiss. She breathed in his masculine smell and the beguiling hint of his citrus cologne, the frisson of needy desire making her murmur.

Beneath her hands, his smooth skin stretched over the taut muscles of his back, tapering to a slender waist and powerful buttocks.

"Jenny!" He stroked down over her waist and hip to cup her buttocks and pull her hard against his erection and she gasped.

He pressed kiss after kiss on her lips, and with a soft moan, moved down over her throat. When his mouth covered a nipple, a rush of excitement shot through her and shortened her breath. Her knees weakened and threatened to give way, and she melted, mindless, clutching onto him.

Andrew swept her up and carried her to the bed, laying her gently down. He leaned over her. "I've wanted you from the first moment I saw you, Jenny. I admit to suffering a measure of guilt. A man doesn't like to admit he fancies his children's governess."

She grinned. "You did?"

"Unforgivable lust, Jenny. But it's not like that now."

She gazed at him, surprised. "You don't feel that way anymore?"

A devilish look came into his eyes. "Of course I want you. *Ah,* Jenny. I want your love. I've fallen head over heels in love with you."

Jenny bit her lip to stop the sob rising in her throat. Her hand at his nape, she drew him down for her to kiss. "I love you, Andrew. So very much."

He lay over her on the bed, pulling her closer. His hand cupped her head as he kissed her, easing her lips apart to stroke the inside of her mouth. The taste of him flowed through her, champagne and brandy and something essentially him. At so intimate an act she lost herself, her tongue dancing with his.

With a soft moan, he explored her with his hands and lips, pressing kisses down over her throat to take a nipple in his mouth. Jenny moaned and wriggled in ecstasy. Blushing furiously she stilled as he turned his attention to the thatch of brown curls at the base of her stomach. She whimpered and gasped while his mouth and skillful fingers aroused her in a way that was beyond her imagining.

He edged her thighs apart and moved between them. "Jenny, love," he murmured and entered her.

With a deep moan, Jenny gave in to the exquisite sensation of being joined with him in this most intimate of acts as she hugged him to her.

ANDREW WOKE TO the sound of knocking. He glanced over at his lovely bride, sleeping soundly beside him. He grinned. They'd had very little sleep. She stirred and opened her eyes. Her gaze settled on him and she smiled. "Good morning."

"Someone has knocked at the door. I must say I'm surprised. Anyone who dares disturb us must desire a period spent in the dungeon."

Her eyes widened. "I should get up." She moved to leave the bed, then recalled she was naked beneath the blankets.

"Pass me my dressing gown, my love."

He picked it up and held it out smiling at her. "Here it is."

She frowned. "Andrew!"

Another knock, this time the latch rattled.

"Good thing we locked the door, isn't it?" He grinned and walked over to her. "I believe I've seen every inch of you, darling, and I have a strong urge to do it again."

She giggled.

He handed the lacy garment to her then pulled on his dressing gown. Tying the sash, he unlocked the door.

The children scampered in. Barbara lifted her arms to him. "Why are you here, Barbara?" He scooped her up and dangled her squealing over his shoulder, before setting her on the bed, where she immediately crawled over to Jenny.

"Where is your governess?" he asked William.

William grinned. "We lost Miss Wagstaff on the stairs, Father."

"You lost her? Perhaps we require a governess who is more fleet of foot," he said to Jenny. Jenny smiled and shook her head.

"Oh, no, Father, we like her," William said.

"Then this will not happen again," Andrew said, attempting to sound stern.

"No, sir." William smiled over at the bed. "But we wanted to make sure Jenny was still here."

"She is here, as you see." Andrew glanced over to his wife who was cuddling his daughter. "And she has promised to stay."

THE END

Printed in Great Britain
by Amazon

24654363R00148